Dear [handwritten],

[handwritten] ... wishes!

ABOUT THE AUTHOR

John Charles Hall is a Business Consultant in the Horticulture Industry, helping small, medium and corporate organisations to grow their businesses; especially in the areas of business planning and development.

Having lived all his life in and around the villages of the South Downs and the West Sussex Coastal Plain, John has a great love and understanding of these rural communities. He has often wondered what might have happened had they been invaded and occupied during the Second World War.

John lives with his wife Anne in Felpham, West Sussex. They have three grown up children and Under the Yew Tree is his first novel.

Best wishes,

John. 1/8/18

Under the Yew Tree

JOHN CHARLES HALL

Copyright © 2017 John Charles Hall
John Charles Hall has asserted his right under the Copyright, Designs and Patents Act, 1988 to be identified as the author of this work.

This book is sold subject to the condition that it shall not, by way of trade or otherwise, be lent, resold, hired out, or otherwise circulated without the publisher's prior consent in any form of binding, cover other than that in which it is published and without similar condition including this condition being imposed on the subject purchaser.

All the characters in this publication are fictional and any resemblance to real persons, living or dead is purely coincidental.

ISBN 978-1548505592
Book design by The Art of Communication www.artofcomms.co.uk
First published in the UK 2017

DEDICATION

In loving memory of my Mum & Dad:
Poppy and Charlie Hall.

ACKNOWLEDGEMENTS

I have received a great deal of encouragement from my family whilst writing Under the Yew Tree. Much love and thanks to my wife Anne, our grown-up children and their partners: Laurie and Alicia, Rebecca and Alex, James and Lisa, and our grandchildren: Ruby, Elias, Henry, Soraya, Jeremiah, Freddie, Thomas, Oliver and Magdalena.

I am also very grateful for the professional support that I have received along the way. My special thanks go to: Christine Unitt, Sally Orson-Jones, Edward Couzens-Lake, Louise Hopkins, Christine Hammacott at Art of Communication, Christopher Joyce and friends at Chindi Authors and Alan Mahar at The Literary Consultancy.

UNDER THE YEW TREE

FOREWORD

by Edward Couzens-Lake
Author and Broadcaster

The events of World War Two are now, for much of the population, a part of our history that was experienced by other people.

To have a personal memory of any event that took place within those terrible years, means that person will now be in their late seventies, whilst the youngest surviving combatants of that war will almost certainly be in their nineties.

It's a sobering thought but, nevertheless, also a very real fact that it will now not be long before there is no-one left who can look back on the war and be able to say, "I was there".

Yet the course of events that took place from 1939 to 1945 still grips the minds and imagination of those whose only experiences of World War Two come from the stories we were told by parents and grandparents.

Why did it happen, we ask them; how was it ever allowed to happen and what could we have done to have prevented it from ever happening in the first place?

The optimism of youth to think we have all the solutions to yesterdays' problems when we cannot even begin to offer any for those that haunt us today, some of which could lead us into another terrible conflict that might be so cataclysmic in its nature that there will be nobody left on the earth to write about it when the fires are sated and the smoke clears.

Better to try and understand why the last war occurred so, rather than look back in anger, we apply what we learn from the errors of the past and use them to build a better future.

Fervent nationalism in Nazi Germany; expansionist policies; premature acceptance and appeasement of same; the slaughter of millions of innocents and a Europe left so scarred by the experience, it's nations have since done everything they can to draw themselves together in peace in the hope that such unity can help ensure such a dread conflict never rips Europe and its people apart again.

So far, we have been successful in achieving that aim. Which begs the other question that contemporary historians are now asking themselves.

What if the ultimate victors in World War Two had been Nazi Germany and her allies and Adolf Hitler's vision of a Third Reich that would endure for a thousand years looked as if it was going to become a reality?

What would our lives be like now?

What would they have been like at the time?

In Under the Yew Tree, John Charles Hall envisages how a Nazi controlled Europe would have impacted on the day to day lives of a small rural farming community. Not London, Manchester, Birmingham or Glasgow. And no visions of Nazi motorcades streaming down Pall Mall or vivid descriptions of how the great and the good of our Cities fell.

He looks much, much deeper than that, telling the story of enemy occupation as it affected the lives of ordinary people living ordinary, decent lives in a small West Sussex village; one that is more used to living in the benign shadow of the South Downs rather the sound of the jackboot.

People whose lives were utterly turned upside down. And who knew that those lives would never be the same again.

This is a story about how they met their fate, how they

coped, how they tried to carry on with the day to day.

And, slowly but inevitably and against odds that far exceeded the impossible, began to fight back.

The story is compelling because it is about people who had no right to anything other than to accept their fate, to lie back and think of an England that they once knew but which had now changed forever.

Yet fight back they did. And this is their story.

John would, I am sure, have fought alongside them. And with great gusto and a sense that what he was doing was the right thing.

Like his characters, John is a countryman. His love and appreciation of the Sussex countryside shines throughout this book. He'll take you there; you'll share the same sights, sounds and smells as his characters; you'll feel their pain, their fear and their hope. This is a book you won't just read, this is a book you will feel.

You'll walk in Joseph's footsteps. Every inch of the way. And you won't want to put the book down until you see where, ultimately, they take him.

So, turn the page and start your journey with him now.

Chapter One

THE DEER SEAT

At the age of twelve, Joseph's father Charles gave him a shotgun for his birthday, which was more or less a rite of passage for boys of a certain age in the countryside. It wasn't a new shotgun; it was ten years old, a single barrel, bolt action, 4.10 bore.

Joseph couldn't have been more pleased. He had been out hunting with his father and uncle many times since he was nine years old, and although he had been allowed to fire his dad's double-barrelled twelve bore on the odd occasion, he had never had a shotgun of his own. Like most of his friends, he was used to shooting with air rifles; but owning a 4.10 put him in a completely different league. Air rifles were great for target shooting, and every now and then, if you got lucky, you might get a shot at a rabbit; but even Joseph, who was renowned by all the other boys as the best shot in the district, rarely managed to get one. He felt that on his twelfth birthday, the odds against getting a few rabbits now swung firmly in his favour.

From the age of ten, Joseph had been allowed to go with his father and his uncle to cull deer. This didn't happen very often, maybe three times during the winter time, usually in January. Joseph understood that there were strict rules about deer hunting. Charles had said to him many times, "You can't just wander around the woods with a rifle, hoping for a shot; that way, people get shot by accident and deer aren't killed cleanly. They stumble off deep into the woods, badly injured, and take days to die from their wounds, terrified and in pain, not understanding what has happened to them, and all alone. We can't have that, can we?"

"No;" Joseph replied solemnly, "That wouldn't be right: that wouldn't be fair." Although Joseph was becoming a hunter, the thought of an animal suffering, in pain, filled him with horror. The first time that he was allowed to fire his father's bolt-action Parker Hale .22 rifle was in January 1937.

By now he was fourteen and a half years old. He had held the gun before, carrying it on his shoulder for his dad when they walked up through the beech woods on the south facing slopes of the South Downs above their farm.

When he first looked through the telescopic sights and lined up the crosshairs on the great trunks of the beech trees, he was amazed. Even in the weak light of that January day, he could clearly see the individual lines on the bark; black on one side where the tree trunk was wet; and silvery grey on the dry side, with all the detail crystal clear. When he trained the sights on the bright red berries of the old yew trees that still grew in the beech woods, it was more difficult. It was hard trying to hold the rifle steady enough to focus. He adjusted the sights; but no matter how hard he tried, he couldn't hold the line. One moment a particular berry was in focus and lined up through the crosshairs; the next it had gone. After a while he realised that it wasn't the sight that was wrong; it was him.

He stopped trying for a while, lowered the rifle and

looked straight ahead at the great tree about thirty yards in front of him. He remembered that his father had told him that some of the yews in these woods were hundreds of years old. He wondered how old this one was, and found himself thinking about what it might have witnessed over its long life. He knew that the beech woods had only been here for about forty years – what had been here before? Several times, Joseph had been to the huge yew forest about ten miles to the west at Kingley Vale. He wondered if these woods used to look like those at Kingley. He thought that they probably did; and then he wondered if there was a yew forest here when the Romans were farming in this area. His mind was wandering now. What about further back? He knew quite a bit about local history, from what his family had told him and from what he had learnt at school, and as he thought more, it dawned on him that the yew forest might well have been here before modern man. He felt calm now. He always did when his mind was lost in the trees.

He looked down at the rifle again. Then, breathing slowly and deeply, he thought about his heart. As he felt its beat slowing, he leaned against the trunk of the nearest beech, raised the rifle, and looked again through the telescopic sights at the yew tree. This time, the berry that he lined up in his sights held still in the cross hairs in perfect focus. He held his aim for ten seconds: and not for one moment did he lose concentration, whilst the cross hairs and the bright red yew berry seemed to be one. He slowly lowered the rifle, hitched the strap over his shoulder, turned and walked back through the woods to the farm.

They walked for about an hour along the ancient flint drovers' track. It took them uphill and in a north-easterly direction, dropped down on a forest track for a few hundred yards, and eventually reached the furthest boundary of the beech woods. Here the conifer forest began, and stretched out for miles to the east. They turned downhill again, following the track that divided the two forests, until they reached a clearing, a hundred yards long and thirty or forty yards wide. Although it was mid-winter, extra light poured into the clearing, revealing a far wider range of broad-leafed plants, grasses and brambles than those that grew under the canopy of the beech woods and even darker canopy of the fir trees.

The two large woods were quite different to each other, and this green space was a different world again. He could pick out many of the different species of plants growing here, even though none were in flower. A large area of short brambles covered the full length of the opening along and under the edge of the beech woods; mainly blackberries, but with a few old brown canes of wild raspberries sticking up here and there. Well-trodden tracks were worn through the brambles, every ten yards or so apart, where the deer would break from the cover and safety of the forests when they came to the clearing to browse.

Firmly fixed to the trunks of the fir trees, about ten paces apart and facing south west, were three deer seats. That's where the hunters sat, high above the clearing; although in reality, they stood as often as they sat when they were shooting deer. The seats were made from the soft wood of the fir trees. Built just like a wooden ladder but about three times the normal width, they had deep heavy timber steps and two sturdy timber poles planted firmly into the ground about one yard out from the base of the tree, narrowing in at the top and leaning in where they were roped tightly to the trunks of the firs. The hunters would climb up and, seated on a high rung, wait in total silence for the deer to emerge from the forest into the clearing. From their lofted positions the hunters could look down on the deer. Having carefully selected their targets, they could fire safely, knowing that if the bullet travelled through the body of the animal, or if the shot was to miss its target altogether, it would bury itself harmlessly in the ground, and not travel on, risking injury to other deer in the herd or even to someone walking in the woods.

That morning, Charles had said, "After we've finished culling the deer this afternoon, you can have a few shots with the rifle if you'd like?" Joseph hadn't expected that. "Thanks Dad! That would be great!" Now he sat in his usual place, right on the top rung, leaning on the trunk of the fir tree and holding firmly to a small branch that conveniently grew out at right angles to his position. Charles sat on the next rung with his feet on the third one down. Off to his left Joseph could see his Uncle George, set up and waiting in a similar position, and to his right, Harry Taylor, their forester friend, was sitting and waiting on the third seat.

They had arrived and got themselves in position about an hour ago, and since then they had kept as still and as quiet as they could. The men had smoked their last cigarettes before starting their walk up through the beech woods from the farm; they didn't want the smell of smoke scaring the deer away. It was late in the afternoon; the January light was fading fast and dusk wasn't far off. They didn't have to wait much longer.

Off to their right, three roe deer came into view, walking slowly and cautiously in single file down the track towards the clearing. Joseph knew that this particular young buck and the two young does with him would be safe today because as the hunters had walked up through the beech woods, he had heard Harry say, "No roe today boys. They've been culled enough in these woods. Concentrate on the fallows; the old ones that is."

After a while, the three animals relaxed and started to browse on the blackberry brambles, occasionally stopping, looking around and sniffing the air. Joseph loved to watch them like this; it was like being let in on a private world. Immediately ahead of him, coming out from under the gloom of the beech woods and along one of the bramble tracks towards the clearing, was a very dark skinned fallow doe. She stopped when she got to the centre of the clearing, looked across at the roe deer, looked up and down the clearing, sniffed the air and having decided that all was well, she also started to browse on the blackberry brambles. The roe deer stood and watched her for a while, and then realising that she posed no threat, went back to work on the brambles themselves.

Thirty seconds later, five more joined her in the middle of the clearing. For the next two or three minutes, Joseph and the men watched in amazement as large numbers arrived; until thirty-two deer stood spread out in the clearing; the roe deer retreating slightly further back towards the track as each fallow arrived and the herd grew. Joseph had seen big herds of fallow before, but nothing as big as this. He noticed that some of the does had last year's youngsters with them. It was easy to pick them out as they were only half grown and stuck close to their mothers. It was difficult to say from this distance which of the youngsters were does and which were bucks, but certainly none of the adults were male. Joseph knew that at this time of the year, it was quite normal for the does to run in herds and for the bucks to run on their own or sometimes in small herds with other bucks.

Charles, George and Harry studied the herd, deciding which of the older fallow they would take. For many years, these three had worked out a good system when culling. Knowing that they would each only get the chance of one shot, it was very important that they all knew what they were doing. Harry was the lead gun. As usual they had already agreed that he would shoot first and that Charles and George would get their shots away as quickly as possible after his. Joseph could feel his heart-beat quicken as he scanned the herd. He knew from past experience that it wouldn't be long now before the deer would be shot. He took in several deep controlled breaths and almost immediately felt his heart calming. He looked across at Harry, just as he identified his target, and then looked towards the others for their signals that they were ready. Both Charles and George slowly nodded and then each gently raised his rifle and lined up the selected target in his sights. Joseph held his breath and started to count. On the count of seven – Harry fired. Within a split second of Harry's shot, Charles and George followed, their shots going off so close together that it was impossible to separate the sounds.

Three fallow deer lay dead in the clearing; each one killed outright with a shot to the heart. The fallow herd and the roes took off in all directions. They were so shocked, so frightened by the cracking, air splitting noise of the shots breaking the silence of the late afternoon, that instead of turning in one direction as a herd, they exploded from the clearing like uncontrolled sparks from a fire. Within less than a minute the sound of the deer charging away through the woods had ceased and all fell quiet again.

Harry waved his right arm in the air and shouted, "Good work boys!" Joseph pressed a hand on Charles' shoulder and whispered "Good shooting Dad." Charles looked up at Joseph and smiled. They climbed down from their deer seats and Harry walked over to inspect each of the fallen fallow deer. "Right," said Harry, "That's good work. Now let's get these three sorted before the light goes."

The men dragged the deer away from the clearing and under the edge of the first row of fir trees. Joseph watched from a short distance as they set about preparing the animals for their last walk in the woods. Quickly and efficiently, one at a time, using a strong rope slung over a low branch, they hoisted each deer up by its hind legs until its nose was only just off the ground. Harry; using his hunting knife, slit through the skin of the belly with ease and reached inside with both hands to remove the steaming mess from within. As he pulled at the guts, they plopped in a pile onto the pine needles that formed the forest floor. Charles and George lowered the carcass back to the ground, where they cut off its head and lower limbs. The three men then repeated the operation with the other two deer, and spread the waste out on the ground. They knew that the foxes would make short work of this free meal during the night, and that if there was anything left over, the buzzards, crows and magpies would soon clean it up in the morning. The men then took large canvas bags from their back packs and lifted the carcasses into them. Helping each other, they hoisted the bags onto their backs, tying the straps off across their chests. They were ready to go.

Joseph moved towards Charles. "Dad, don't forget, you said that I could…" his voice trailed off. "Yes; so I did!" Charles replied, smiling. "Wait lads! I forgot, I promised young Joseph here that he could have a few shots with my rifle. You go on; we'll see you back at the farm."

"Right," they grinned, and set off at a steady pace back through the beech woods.

Charles pointed to the middle deer seat. "Up you go then. We'd better be quick; the light's going fast now. It'll be dark soon."

Joseph moved quickly to stand at exactly the same position as his father had some twenty minutes before. Charles, on the first rung of the ladder, handed up his rifle, then stepped to the next rung and handed him six bullets. "Don't load yet," he said; "let me set you up some targets in the clearing."

Charles disappeared into the woods for a minute, quickly emerging carrying six fir cones. He waved them so that Joseph could see what he had, and walked into the clearing until he was about fifty yards from his son. He sat two on top of some blackberry bushes, two he jammed into the forked branches of some young hazel trees, one he left on top of a mole hill to the side of the clearing and the last one he balanced on the top of a rotten old fence post that was sticking out at an angle from the big patch of brambles where they had watched the roe deer browsing. Then he moved back towards where Joseph was sitting and leaned against the deer seat. "Right," he said. "Load up, and see what you can do with those cones."

Whilst watching his father set up the targets, Joseph had already started his breathing exercises, and by the time he pulled back the bolt to load the first shell, his heart rate was already low. As he raised the rifle and took aim at the first target sitting on top of a bramble bush, he was completely calm; his whole body was as still as the late afternoon air.

He squeezed the trigger and fired.

The crack of the shot echoed between the two forests as the cone flew to pieces. After reloading, he chose the cone on top of the fence post, sending it flying across the clearing as the shot again echoed around the woods. Charles watched in disbelief as Joseph moved his aim from cone to cone until all six had been dispatched. When he had finished, the boy left the bolt of the rifle open and stepped back down the ladder. His father took the gun from him as he stepped down onto the mulchy ground and clapped him on the shoulder. "Great shooting lad!" Joseph looked up and smiled before ducking behind the ladder to retrieve his ejected brass shell cases. Cupping the precious treasure in his hand, he lifted them to smell the strange intoxicating mixture of hot metal, sulphur and cordite, and then slipped them safely into his pocket. Then, taking the rifle from Charles, he hitched it back over his shoulder. His father adjusted the canvas bag on his back and they set off through the woods for home.

The light had almost completely gone now. The air was cold, and a few snowflakes were beginning to fall in the silence of the beech woods. It would be another hour before they reached the warmth of the farmhouse.

Chapter Two

THE PLOUGHING MATCH

Joseph loved ploughing. One of his earliest memories; from when he was about five years old, was being allowed to sit up on the back of one of the great Suffolk Punch carthorses that his grandfather Harold used to plough the fields.

For most of his childhood, horses were the main source of power all around the farm. It was only in the years just before the war that tractors began to become more commonplace and to take over many of the everyday jobs. For many years, there had been steam ploughs, drawn across the fields by stationary steam-driven traction engines, and threshing machines, usually parked up in the main farm yard after harvest – but it was only when the first petrol engine tractors arrived that they took over the day-to-day work of the horse.

When he was ten years old, he was allowed to walk along behind the plough with his father, grandfather or one of the farm workers, as their two main Shire horses, Napoleon and

Wellington, clumped along up front providing the power. Sometimes he was allowed to hold on to the plough handles for a while. But, like all other ten year olds, no matter how big and strong he was, he was never tall enough or strong enough to guide the plough properly through the soil or for any length of time. But he loved to be in the fields when there was ploughing going on. There was the rhythmic clinking that the leathers and chains made as the horses pulled at a steady pace, and the sound of the plough shears themselves as they cut through the earth. There was the murmur of the ploughmen, gently talking to their horses as they worked, and every now and then the animals would answer back with their muffled snorting. There was the call of the seagulls whirling overhead as they looked out for the brown and pink worms that suddenly appeared wriggling on the smooth shiny soil as the plough shears magically turned the earth over. There was that strange feeling for a young boy of walking behind the plough in a freshly turned furrow, and sensing the warmth of last summer releasing from its hold as if the long-trapped air couldn't wait to escape and mix with the refreshing air of autumn.

The smell of this turned soil was intoxicating, always subtly different, depending on which crops had been growing there, which part of the farm they were on and what the weather conditions were. Sometimes conditions were wet, and the soil smelt of cold mud; sometimes it was too dry and smelt of nothing but dust. At other times, when the conditions were right, the soil smelt like ripe apples. On sunny days, the moist, freshly turned clods shone like a mirror reflecting the light back up to the sky, and on cold mornings, steam would rise from the still warm earth as it was turned over, and from the backs of the great horses and the men as they laboured in the fields.

Joseph had been allowed to sit up with his father or grandfather many times, on their laps, or more dangerously, on the mudguards of the tractor; holding on tight and sometimes having to grab an arm to keep balanced. But on his twelfth birthday, he was given his first proper tractor lesson by Charles, when for the first time he was allowed to drive it, on his own, across a field of stubble. It was almost impossible to change gear as his legs weren't quite long enough to reach the clutch: he could only do it by sliding off the hard seat and using all the force he could to get it down with his left foot whilst shifting the heavy stick over. Turning the steering wheel was another problem. He just wasn't strong enough. Well before the tractor reached the end of the field, Charles would clamber back onto the footplate, and whilst Joseph pulled himself up onto the mudguard, he would take control, turn the tractor, line it up and jump off again so that his son could have another go. It wasn't until he was fourteen that Joseph was strong enough to turn the steering wheel and dip the clutch without having to slide off the seat.

Once he was safe enough to drive the tractor, he started to learn how to hitch up the various implements, how to set them up properly and how to use them in the fields. He enjoyed using all the equipment, but his favourite job was ploughing. When he first started to plough, he enjoyed it so much that he just thought of it as a fun thing to do.

As he improved practically and technically, he thought of ploughing as a skill, and took pride in his work, until, eventually, he stopped thinking of it as work altogether; he thought of it as an art.

Just after his 17th birthday, the same September that war broke out, his father entered him into a local ploughing match at Newlands Farm on the other side of the village. There were twenty teams entered in the horse-drawn ploughing competition, and nine or ten tractors each entered in the two separate categories of tractor-drawn ploughs; one for the larger tractors and one for the smaller ones. Joseph was entered in the smaller tractor category, and Harold had entered Napoleon, Wellington and himself in the horse drawn category. Charles, was there with them, and helped make sure that everything was in order before they made their way to their allotted places, ready for the start. When the judge rang his bell, all of the horse-drawn ploughs set off immediately, but none of the tractors moved, although all of them had their engines running.

None of the drivers were in their seats; they were all standing down behind their tractors. All of them had tape measures and spanners in their hands, and they were all making final adjustments to the set-up of their ploughs before starting off. The last words that his dad had said to Joseph before he strode off to watch the horses, were: "Don't forget – it's all in the set-up son: it's all in the set-up." There were plenty of adjustments to make. The height settings had to be adjusted for the main cutting wheels, the linkage arms had to be set level so that the plough sat evenly on the ground, crossways and from front to back. After a few minutes, several drivers sat back on their seats, opened up their throttles and started to cut the first furrows. One after the other, the tractors pulled their ploughs across the field. There were no baffle plates inside the exhaust pipes and so the noise was deafening, the echo from their engines bouncing back from the hill on the other side of the farm.

Joseph was the last to start ploughing, confident that he would be able to complete his work within the hour that they were allowed. Charles watched them all from a distance, casting his expert eye over the competitors' work.

After forty minutes, two of the larger tractors finished, and over the next ten, one by one the others came to the end of their work, until Joseph was the only one left. With three minutes remaining, he closed the last furrow and parked his tractor and plough in its allotted place.

Charles smiled as he walked across the far end of the field; even from such a distance, he could tell whose ploughing was best. He watched as the judges walked in pairs up and down the field, stopping every now and then to point something out and to discuss some technical point in detail. The even depth of the furrow was important; as was the clean cut of the soil and the level of the folded earth; and, probably most important, the clean finish of the closing furrow. As Charles, had said, "It's all about the set-up. If you don't get the set-up right and if you don't get the measurements right, you won't start right, you won't do a good job and you won't finish right."

The judges knew a good job when they saw it. After twenty minutes of deliberation they made their way back to the front of the field where the competitors were waiting, collected their marker sticks and then pushed them into the ground at the head of each plot to indicate first, second and third places. There were three sets of markers; one for the horse drawn ploughs, one for the larger tractors and one for the smaller ones. The two bright red rosettes, indicating first place, stood out from the blue and green for second and third on the marker sticks, and quivered gently in the mid-afternoon breeze that now blew across the field. Harold walked up to his red rosette and turned and waved at Joseph who stood by his. Charles chuckled to himself as he walked towards them, as the other men gathered around, happy and smiling and keen to shake the hands of the oldest and youngest ploughmen in the field.

As the men stood chatting, they were distracted by the sounds of engines in the distance. They all turned to see a small convoy of British Army trucks travelling west along the road that led away from the village. Each vehicle was towing a field gun or an ammunition trailer. The men watched in silence as the convoy made its way down the road and eventually disappeared out of sight. Joseph turned to his father. "Where do you think they're going then?"

Charles replied, "Portsmouth, I'd say. Most likely off to

join a ship to France."

The men discussed what they had seen for some time and then the conversation turned to what they thought this war was all about and how it might play out. It was the same conversation that they had all had over and over again with their friends and families. A minority thought that it was a storm in a tea cup and that it would all be over by Christmas, but most weren't so sure. The news sounded more alarming with every day that went by.

After a while, the men started to say their farewells and make their way back to their horses and tractors. Some of them had a fair bit of work ahead of them: unhitching the horses and getting the ploughs onto the low trailers so that they could be taken back to their farms. The horses were kept harnessed together as the men walked them home along the roads or, wherever possible, across the fields.

Chapter Three

PRELUDE TO THE RESISTANCE

Joseph's parents, Charles and Mary, had moved in to the old farm house at Hill Farm with his grandparents when they were married in 1920. Since then, they had gradually taken over more of the day to day decisions from Charles' father, and now, Charles was the farmer and Harold, at 65, was pretty much retired. He still did odd jobs around the farm, and during harvest time he worked as hard as the rest of the family, often being the first down to breakfast and amongst the last back from the fields at supper time.

His wife of 41 years, Catharine, had been ill with a serious heart condition for the last few years and now spent much of her time in bed or sitting in her favourite chair in the kitchen. She couldn't do much these days, but made it her business to make sure that the kitchen range was kept fed with wood and that a kettle was always on the boil. Harold was grateful that his son and daughter-in-law had taken over the farm, and that he was still able to make a contribution. He took great pleasure in seeing Charles and Mary's hard work come to fruition with each crop and harvest safely gathered in, and with each animal sent to market. There were hard times of course, but most years turned out well, and nowadays he particularly enjoyed the company of his grandchildren; Joseph and his little sister, Lily.

Joseph, having lived and worked on the farm all his life, knew almost as much about the day to day jobs as his grandfather, and Harold was at his happiest when they were working side by side. It gave them the chance to talk. Harold liked nothing better than to hear Joseph's stories about some prank that he and his young pals had got up to in the village. It reminded him of his youth, and of course, he always promised not to tell Charles or Mary. Joseph on the other hand loved to hear about the old days from his grandfather, and Harold had plenty of stories to tell. Lily was now 13, and although starting to grow into a young lady, she was still very much a country girl, and loved talking to her granddad about when he and Catharine were young.

Often, on her return home from school, unless it was harvest time, Granddad would be the first person that Lily would bump into; and so, Harold was usually the only person in the household to have all the facts of a story or a new piece of gossip. Lily had a list of daily chores to do when she got home from school, and often, Harold would walk with her, chatting away, holding a basket for her as she collected the eggs, helping her to carry feed down to the pigs, or pushing a cart full of hay down to the stables to their two great shire horses, Napoleon and Wellington.

Although for the last few years they had owned a small tractor and a flatbed truck that did much of the work, the shire horses still did a lot of important jobs around the farm, and everyone thought the world of them. Napoleon and Wellington were Lily's favourites, and when she was on her own with them, she would often tell them long stories that she didn't even share with her grandfather. Most of her stories recently seemed to involve what the boys at school got up to; especially one called Richard.

The Carter family were close. Because they lived on a farm, they were never short of food, and although they couldn't afford many luxuries, they had a good standard of living. Recent generations had enjoyed a reasonable education at the village school, and Joseph had stayed on at the secondary school until he was fifteen; the first one in his family ever to have stayed so long. Charles and Mary were hoping that Lily would also stay to the same age, but since the war had broken out, it was difficult to know what the future would hold for her. It was difficult to know what the future held for anyone.

When the Czechoslovakian crisis of 1938 occurred, most British people, especially those living in rural areas, thought that it was just more sabre rattling by Hitler and a few hot-headed Nazis. Germany had already taken over Austria and was now laying claim to the Sudetenland, the Czechoslovakian region that bordered Germany with its mainly German population.

Most people didn't know or care much about the Sudetenland, and had little idea about its complicated history. They felt that this was probably unfinished business from the First World War, and that although it might not suit the Czechs, a negotiated agreement would probably soon be reached. At the Munich Agreement in September 1938, held between Britain, France, Italy and Germany – but without the Czechs approval – the Sudetenland was handed over to Germany, and on 1st October 1938 her troops took up occupation. Over the next few weeks, Poland claimed and occupied parts of Czechoslovakia where there were large numbers of Polish people, and Hungary did the same to an area of Czechoslovakia where many Hungarians lived. After that, as predicted by most people, everything seemed to calm down again. Then suddenly, in March 1939 German troops marched into the remaining regions of Czechoslovakia until the whole country was occupied and on 1st September 1939 Germany invaded Poland.

For a while it seemed that there might be a solution, and that Hitler would withdraw his troops from Poland. Neville Chamberlain, the British Prime Minister, finally issued an ultimatum to Germany, stating that if Hitler did not withdraw, Britain would honour her agreement with Poland and declare war on Germany. Hitler did not respond to the ultimatum, and on the 3rd September 1939 both Britain and France declared war on Germany. It suddenly dawned on people all over the world that soon, the whole of Europe might be in turmoil once more.

The Carters listened to the news from the BBC on the radio as often as they could, and if they missed a broadcast; the postman or some other delivery man would soon update them as to the latest developments. Whilst they went about their work on the farm, Joseph often talked to his father and grandfather about the war. They especially talked about what they had heard on the radio over breakfast that morning.

When the news finally came that Britain and France had declared war on Germany, their conversations became far more serious and concerned. There were many unanswered questions. How strong were the Germans? Would they attack France? Were the French defences good enough to stop them? Would British forces soon be arriving in France? What about the Russians? Would the Americans be drawn in? Charles and Harold did their best to answer Joseph's and their own questions, but it was difficult to come up with clear answers. There was so much that they didn't know. Hitler was obviously set on making Germany a great power again. He had already occupied Austria, Czechoslovakia and now Poland. Was that enough for him, or was his appetite even bigger? Surely his ambition couldn't extend to the occupation of the whole of Europe... could it?

Neither Charles nor his father had fought in the trenches during the Great War; but they knew plenty of men who had. Many families in the area had lost fathers, sons, brothers, uncles and cousins: there was a memorial to them in the village with the names of fourteen men carved into the cold, grey granite stone. Joseph and Lily knew their names off by heart, having stood next to the memorial many times with their separate classes and teachers from the village school when they had history lessons. One of the names carved there was that of Eric George Atkins, a cousin of Joseph's mother, Mary. He had been killed at Ypres in 1916.

When Charles and Mary were alone together, usually as they were preparing for bed, they would share their thoughts and express the fears that they kept to themselves during the day. The sort of thoughts and fears that everyone, especially parents, were now feeling across much of Europe. They knew that although Charles himself was probably too old to be called up for active service, and both Joseph and Lily were currently too young to be involved, next September Joseph would be eighteen. This was just one of their fears. They talked about their friends and their friends' sons; young men who they knew well. They talked about the farm, their farming friends, the local markets and their village. They were becoming more concerned with every day that went by.

During the winter of 1939/1940 nothing much seemed to change, and many British people wondered if the worst was already over. Life continued much the same for the Carter family and for the other farming families in the area, although noticeably, from time to time, particular goods would become more difficult to get hold of. Usually it was something fairly unimportant, such as bananas or washing soda, but at other times it was more serious, especially when there was a shortage of paraffin for their lamps, or spare parts for the tractor. Without warning, on 9th April 1940, German troops invaded Denmark and Norway.

At about that time, Joseph had started to go with some of his friends to meetings in the village, but more often to outlying farms and sometimes on a Sunday to special meetings deep in the forest. This was the start of Joseph's association with the Resistance.

Since September 1939, small groups of men had started to organise themselves into resistance groups throughout Britain. Some were well led, well organised and professional in their operations; others were the complete opposite, with little leadership and even less proficiency. As the months went by, more and more groups made contact with each other, and gradually a network of Resistance units grew. By March 1940, there was even a central organisation with many of its leaders meeting regularly in London.

On 10th May 1940, Germany invaded Belgium, Holland and Luxembourg. Fear spread amongst the French people, but the French authorities reassured them that their defences were strong, and with the help of the British Expeditionary Forces that were now in northwest France, they would hold the line. Charles Carter wasn't so sure. He had read about the horrendous German bombing that had taken place in Poland and how quickly the German war machine had moved through that country. He knew how fast the Germans had occupied Austria, Czechoslovakia and Denmark, and how they had attacked Norway. Now that they were in the Low Countries, why stop there?

On the radio, they heard that Neville Chamberlain had resigned, and a new Prime Minister, Winston Churchill had replaced him. Although Charles and his family didn't know much about politics, they had heard a fair bit about Churchill, both on the radio and in the newspapers, and knew that he had spoken out strongly many times about the dangers of appeasing Hitler. "Well," said Charles at the supper table, "at least we've got a strong leader now. I wonder if the rest of our politicians have the guts to stand up to that bloody madman Hitler."

The news over the next few weeks was dreadful. Almost every day there was more worrying news from Europe, including the worst news of all – the Germans were on French soil. On the 15th May 1940, Holland surrendered to the Germans, and on the 26th May 1940, the British Expeditionary Force, along with a large retreating French force, was evacuated at Dunkirk. On 27th May 1940, Belgium also surrendered.

The British Expeditionary Force had been a disaster. During the spring of 1940, Britain had sent a large army to northern France to reinforce the French forces defending its northern borders. For a number of years, the French had concentrated its main defences along a fortified line known as the Maginot Line. The French Generals were convinced that their defences were well planned and strong enough to repel a German attack from the north. During May 1940, the Germans pushed through the Ardennes and cut off the British and Allied forces that were advancing through Belgium. 400,000 British and French soldiers were forced back towards the English Channel and were pinned down there for weeks, until eventually they were evacuated from the beaches at Dunkirk by the Royal Navy and a huge flotilla of merchant ships and private boats of every shape and size that ferried the soldiers back to the British coast.

Churchill had flown to Paris on 16th May 1940 to meet with the French government, and when he asked General Gamelin, "Where are your reserve forces?" he was told that, "There are none." Later, Churchill claimed that Gamelin's statement was the greatest shock that he received during the entire war. Following that meeting, Churchill knew that France would not be able to hold out for long. Throughout the rest of May 1940, Allied forces, including those commanded by Colonel Charles De Gaulle, attempted to hold the German advance into northern France, but without success.

On 5th June 1940, the Germans simply by-passed the Maginot Line and advanced into the main body of France. The news that the British and some French forces had been evacuated from Dunkirk was received badly by most French people and when the news came through that the Maginot Line had failed, they feared the worst.

The French government left Paris and set up its new base in Bordeaux. On 10th June 1940, Italy declared war on France and on 14th June Paris was occupied by the Germans. Between 15th and 25th June 1940, a further 200,000 Allied troops were evacuated from Saint-Valery-en-Caux; an area near Cherbourg and Le Havre. On 25th June 1940, an armistice came into effect between France and Germany, and France found herself divided into three; the Germans now occupied the north and the west, a small area in the southeast was occupied by the Italians and for the moment, the south was governed by the collaborating government, under the leadership of Marshall Philippe Petain at Vichy.

During late May and early June 1940, many French political and armed forces leaders, including Charles De Gaulle, managed to escape from France and set up new command structures in London. In a radio appeal broadcast on 18th June 1940, De Gaulle refused to recognise the Vichy government and began to organise the Free French forces from London. For the remaining days of June 1940, the British people feared the worst.

Following the emergency evacuation from the beaches of Dunkirk, the British Army was in a mess, with all initiatives gone. Churchill, his Cabinet, and the leaders of the Armed Forces were in almost permanent emergency session. Although much of the Royal Air Force remained fully operational and the British Navy continued operations around the British Isles, most of the British Army fell back to regroup at its bases north and west of London, the Midlands, northern England, Scotland and Wales.

As British Forces withdrew from the South of England; the only ones left to defend the country were the men and women who belonged to the Resistance.

The Germans had long had plans, through operation Sea Lion, to invade Britain, but Hitler and the heads of the German Luftwaffe knew that the destruction of the Royal Air Force was essential if an invasion of Britain was to be successful. In early July 1940, the Luftwaffe began to test Britain's defences by attacking cities and towns along the southeast coast of England. Time after time, squadrons of RAF Hurricane and Spitfire fighter planes flew out from their bases across southern England to meet and engage with the enemy. By early August; Britain was losing aircraft faster than she could build new ones. The Luftwaffe was also losing aircraft at an unprecedented rate, but for the moment, she was managing to produce at a slightly better rate than she was losing them. By mid-August, Germany was beginning to win the battle of attrition. The Battle of Britain was in full swing.

Whilst Joseph worked on the farm that summer, he would often stop and look up at the sky which seemed to be constantly filled with the spectacle of aircraft on the move. Mostly, the images were of distant black dots and streaky white lines against a powder blue sky. It was often impossible to tell one fighter aircraft from another from a distance, let alone which one was chasing and which one fleeing.

Sometimes, he could see a sudden change in the patterns, as the white streaks turned to long dark descending clouds as the black dots fell from the sky. On the few times that he had witnessed such a thing, it left him feeling cold and lost, standing alone in the middle of a field gawping at the sky. On one occasion Harold, alarmed at seeing Joseph standing there staring with his mouth wide open, called out "Joe! Joe, close your mouth boy, or you'll be catching flies soon!"

There was no response.

"Joe! Joe - Joe can you hear me? Joe, what's up?" Even more alarmed now, Harold dropped his hoe and walked over to Joseph; gently placing his hand on the lad's shoulder and looking straight into his eyes. Slowly, Joseph closed his mouth and dropped his gaze to his grandfather's face. Harold smiled and patted Joseph's cheek gently with his other hand.

"Are you alright Joe?" Harold's voice was quavering. There was a long pause before Joseph finally replied.

"Grandad – What if we lose? What happens then?"

Harold patted Joseph's face again. "Don't be silly Joe. That's the RAF up there, and they don't even know the meaning of the words 'to lose'." He walked back to where he had been working, picked up his hoe and returned to where Joseph was still standing. Taking him by the arm he led him towards where they had left their lunch bags hanging on one of the old fence posts that lined the headland of the field. "I think it's time for a cup of tea and a sit down."

Two nights later, Joseph awoke at two o'clock in the morning to muffled sounds coming from somewhere in the distance. He sat up in bed for some time trying to make sense of the noise. He had never heard anything like it in his life before, but whatever it was, it was coming from just one direction. He climbed out of bed, and, without lighting a candle, made his way out of his bedroom, onto the landing and towards the window that faced southwest across their farmland, on over the coastal plain of Sussex, above the great spire of Chichester Cathedral and eventually to the Isle of Wight in the far distance.

As he reached the window, he realised that his parents were already there. They stood and watched together as orange flashes lit up the western sky in the distance, and the boom of explosions reverberated through the house. Twenty-five miles away, Portsmouth was being bombed. They stood watching and listening for half an hour; and not for one moment did the ferocity of the sounds or the intensity of the flashes ease off. Eventually, Mary said, "I'm going to make some tea," and with that, she turned and headed off down the stairs. As she did so, Lily walked slowly across the landing to where Joseph and her father still stood.

"What's going on?" she asked.

"They're bombing Portsmouth," her dad and brother replied in unison. Five minutes later they were all sitting around the kitchen table, staring at the table top in total silence, listening to the awful noises of war in the distance. As the kettle came to the boil on the kitchen range, Harold joined them at the table and spoke quietly to Charles:

"Portsmouth?"

"Yes, I'm afraid so" his son replied.

Mary poured the steaming water from the kettle into the big old brown teapot. After a while, Harold poured a cup of tea and took it back to Catharine who was now sitting up in their bed, listening to the distant rumblings.

"Is it Portsmouth?" she asked, as Harold handed her the tea.

"Yes," Harold confirmed. "It's been going on for about two hours now."

"My God," Catharine murmured; "those poor people."

Harold took the cup from her and placed it on her bedside table, then sat down carefully beside her, and kissed her gently on her forehead. "Don't worry my old love," he whispered, "You're safe with me." Catharine looked up at him; tears running down her soft face. Harold squeezed her hands, reached over for the cup of tea and handed it back to her.

News the next day was grim. Stories started to filter through to the rural communities of Sussex about the devastation and loss of life in Portsmouth and the surrounding Hampshire towns and villages. The Dockyard had been hit hard. There were unconfirmed reports of major damage to some of the British warships at anchor in the supposed safe haven of Portsmouth Harbour. Reports were coming in from anti-aircraft positions along the South Downs about the massive numbers of German bombers that had passed over during the night, too high for most of the shells from the anti-aircraft guns to reach, although plenty had tried. During the day, RAF fighters were more prevalent than ever, constantly on patrol in the skies above the South Coast. When they flew low enough, the locals could clearly make out the markings on their fuselages, and were able to identify them as squadrons from the nearby airfields of Tangmere, Ford, Merston, Bognor, Westhampnett and Thorney Island.

The children were particularly good at this, and when they weren't at their school desks or busy with chores at home, they would watch the planes hurtling across the skies for hours, and soon became experts at identifying the British and German fighters and bombers. During the daytime, they often witnessed dog fights, as RAF Spitfires and Hurricanes tangled with Luftwaffe Messerschmitt 109s and Stukas. At night, it was very difficult to identify the planes, especially if there were large numbers of them and if they were flying high. If single planes flew over at night, most people could identify them by the sounds of their engines; the easiest being that of the Spitfire and Hurricane, with their distinctive and comforting deep double rumbling sounds. Harold told Lily that they were Rolls Royce Merlin engines. "You can't get better than Rolls Royce" he said.

Twice more that week, during the night, the Luftwaffe bombers returned to Portsmouth – and twice more the Carter family sat grim faced in the kitchen until the ordeal was over. Other cities in the South of England, including Southampton and Plymouth, were also being bombed regularly, but surprisingly many smaller towns were now also being targeted in Kent and Sussex; especially the port towns of Dover,

Folkestone, Eastbourne and Shoreham. Civilian losses were rising rapidly, with an estimated five thousand people killed in Portsmouth in one week alone. The Battle of Britain was becoming more intense with every day that passed, so that by late August 1940, it was estimated that both the RAF and the Luftwaffe had both lost about two hundred fighter planes. Since the disaster of the British Expeditionary Force and the extraordinary events at Dunkirk; Winston Churchill and his War Cabinet had been receiving regular intelligence reports from French Agents concerning the build-up of German forces along the northwest coast of France.

Now that coastal towns in Kent and Sussex were regularly being attacked, Churchill was convinced that the Germans were preparing to invade England. Orders were issued to the RAF to move its men and planes away from the South East to airfields that were more difficult for the Luftwaffe to reach, but still in a strong position to attack the enemy if an invasion came.

The Royal Navy dispatched all able-bodied ships from Portsmouth to other ports around the British coast, followed across land by line upon line of trucks full of men, equipment, munitions, fuel and stores to support their ships in their new ports.

On the morning of 25th August 1940, a squadron of Messerschmitts flew high over the English Channel, and were surprised to find no RAF planes coming out to engage with them. They were even more surprised to reach the Kent coast without seeing a single enemy aircraft. They dropped down to a lower altitude, turned westward and flew about five miles inland following the Kent and Sussex coastline. After twenty minutes, they had not seen a single enemy aircraft and had only encountered light anti-aircraft fire from a position on the top of the South Downs to the northwest of Eastbourne. As they turned south over Brighton and then immediately east over the Channel to head back to their base just beyond Calais, the Senior Pilot, Captain Ernst Roff, was on the radio, calling his control centre back at the airfield.

"Orange two seven four calling base. Orange two seven four calling base. Are you receiving?"

For some minutes, there was nothing but a crackling in his earphones. In his excitement, Captain Roff had forgotten that he was a long way outside normal radio range. Once he guessed that his group were about half way across the Channel, he tried again.

"Orange two seven four calling base. Orange two seven four calling base. Are you receiving?"

After a few seconds, he heard a faint and still crackly reply. "This is Blue Bird calling Orange two seven four. This is Blue Bird calling Orange two seven four. We are receiving you on level one."

Captain Roff spoke again: "Orange two seven four calling Blue Bird. Urgent message to Major Weiner. No RAF in the skies today. Repeat. No RAF in the skies today." Blue Bird replied immediately. "Message received and understood."

Before Captain Roff and his squadron landed at Blue Bird airfield, just inland from Calais, the urgent message had been relayed to Major Weiner at his headquarters near Lille. Without delay, the Major called an urgent meeting with his fellow senior officers based in and around his headquarters at Lille and at the same time, sent an order to Blue Bird airfield for Captain Roff to be driven to his headquarters as soon as he landed.

As Captain Roff climbed down from his aircraft, he could see a Mercedes staff car coming towards him. As he started to walk towards the temporary wooden buildings that were the control centre for Blue Bird airfield, the car turned and pulled up beside him. The driver stayed at the wheel, the engine still running, and a sergeant opened the front passenger door, jumped out, straightened himself up and saluted. "Captain Roff?"

"That's me sergeant."

The sergeant handed a folded piece of paper to the Captain. "Urgent orders Sir. I'm to take you straight to headquarters in Lille."

Captain Roff read the orders, nodded to the sergeant and spoke to one of his fellow pilots who had walked up to join him. "File the flight report for me Jan. I've been ordered to headquarters."

"Yes; of course", Jan nodded, and with that, Captain Roff handed him his flying gear and followed the sergeant to the car.

Within an hour, they arrived at headquarters in Lille. Captain Roff was escorted directly to the large conference room where Major Weiner was waiting with twenty of his fellow officers.

"Welcome Captain Roff", said the Major. "Now I'm sorry to rush you, but we understand from your earlier report that you have had a very interesting flight over the south of England this morning and we would like you to tell us what you found".

"Thank you Major", Captain Roff replied. "I would be pleased to."

Major Weiner gestured towards a chair at the head of the table; "Then the floor is yours. Coffee?"

Captain Roff moved towards the chair and sat down. "Thank you Major, coffee would be very welcome. It's been a long morning."

He looked around the table, not recognising any of the officers, all of whom were now looking straight at him. The Captain cleared his throat and began to speak. "Good morning gentlemen. I will do my best to give you a full account of our sortie over the south Coast of England this morning. Please do not hesitate to interrupt me if anything isn't clear."

Major Weiner placed a steaming cup of coffee on the

table next to the Captain and sat in the vacant chair next to him.

"I took off with my squadron from near Calais early this morning and flew directly towards the English coast. We did not encounter any enemy aircraft as we crossed the Channel – which was unusual. We crossed the English coast about twenty kilometres east of Dover at 06:30 hours".

Captain Roff stopped to sip his coffee and then continued to describe in every detail that he could remember exactly the route that his squadron had taken, at what altitude it had flown, the time that they had taken to fly over parts of Kent and Sussex and what they had seen or not seen on the ground and in the skies. He stopped several more times to take a sip of his coffee, but none of the officers interrupted his report. After about twenty minutes, the Captain stopped speaking and invited the officers to ask him questions.

For about ten seconds there was no response. There was absolute silence in the room and only the faint sounds of vehicle movements drifted in through the half open window that looked out across the beautifully manicured gardens of the country house. Eventually, one of the Officers spoke. "Your report is quite remarkable Captain Roff. What do you think that this means? Do you think that the RAF has disappeared; or perhaps they were just a little late getting up this morning?"

This was clearly not a clever thing to say. None of the other officers sniggered or showed any signs of support for such a sarcastic question. There was silence again. Captain Roff shifted uneasily in his chair, not knowing quite how or whether to attempt a response. Major Weiner glowered at the officer who had just spoken and was about to tell him to keep his clever remarks to himself, when the door opened and a uniformed young lady entered the room carrying a sheet of paper. She walked quietly up to the major and placed the paper on the table in front of him. She bent down and whispered, "I'm sorry to disturb you Major" she said, "but this urgent message has just come in and Intelligence thinks that it's important".

The room fell quiet again whilst the Major read the paper.

"Well, well," he said. "Here's another report from a Squadron Leader Ballack. His squadron flew a similar route to you this morning Captain Roff, but about an hour later. His report is almost identical to yours". Major Weiner looked at Captain Roff, smiled, placed his elbows on the table and leaned slightly forward. "Gentlemen," he said, "I have no doubt that we will receive similar reports throughout the day. I will pass this information up the line without delay, but in the meantime, we need to test things further afield. We need to fly sorties further north and west to establish just how far back the RAF have withdrawn, for trust me, that's what they've done: the RAF have pulled back from the south of England." All at once, most of the officers raised their hands and asked for permission to speak.

The Major waved his arms in the air and shouted, "So, you've all got something to say now have you!"

Once more the room fell silent and Major Weiner turned to Captain Roff and said, "Captain Roff. The intelligence that you have brought to us this morning is invaluable. This could be the turning point. I will contact your commander immediately and have you transferred over here to headquarters. I need you here to interpret the fresh information that I'm sure will be pouring in over the next few days. I'll leave you to make your own arrangements for transporting your personal belongings over here."

Captain Roff stood, straightened his jacket, picked his papers up from the table, bowed slightly towards Major Weiner, and walked briskly towards the door. As he left the building and made his way to his waiting car, he stopped and glanced up at the sky for a few seconds. He looked down at the gravel drive and took in three deep breaths. He felt inside his jacket pocket and took out a pack of cigarettes, tapped it on the back of his hand, pulled out a cigarette and lit it.

He took a deep drag and looked at the lighter in the palm of his hand, remembering that his wife had given it to him on his last birthday. He wondered how Cristina was today and when he might next get home to see her and his family.

Chapter Four

IN THE VILLAGE

Autumn 1940

Joseph Carter leaned on a flint stone wall, his rifle pointing towards a bend half way down the street. He was listening to the changing sounds that he knew belonged to the engines of the army vehicles; just out of sight, hidden around the corner. He had never felt such fear, but at the same time, with adrenalin pumping through his veins, he had never felt so alert. His heart was beating so strongly now, and so loud, that it was beginning to drown out all other sounds. He knew that he needed to regain control. Concentrating hard, he took long, deep breaths, and as he did so, as his heart-rate dropped, he felt his whole body relaxing. He was calm. After all, this was why he was here; this was why the Commander had chosen him. Although he was not quite eighteen years old, he was, by some distance, the best shot in the local Resistance.

During the hastily arranged training camps organised during the winter of 1939 and throughout 1940 – held deep in the woods that covered the South Downs, North of the village – Joseph had quickly emerged as a first class shot. It was uncanny. It was as if he had been born to fire a rifle: to be a sniper. His ability was a total mystery to everyone, but as his Commander Henry Clay repeatedly said, "Stop worrying about why he's so good; start thinking how best to use his talents, and thank God that he's on our side." Joseph knew, though, that his skill was no accident. It was through years of hard work and application that he had arrived at this point, so well prepared for what lay ahead.

Joseph's first memory of being able to control his body was from the summer when he was ten. It was at his Uncle's farm in the neighbouring village of Slindover. It was a hot day. He and some of his cousins and friends were running wild outside, playing in the old orchards a little way up the gently sloping hill behind the farmhouse.

They'd played cowboys and Indians, cops and robbers, war games. Most games seemed to involve pretending to ride a horse, or drive a get-away car at break-neck speed around the old trees in the orchard. By mid-afternoon they were all very hot and out of breath, their patchy faces the same colour as the red geraniums growing in the tubs that stood on the rough timbered floor of the veranda that ran along the side of the old farm house. One of the younger girls suggested that it was about time that they all slowed down a bit and played her favourite game: hide and seek. Although this was not the first choice of most of the boys, whose instinctive reaction was always to vote for the most violent game that they could think of, they were also tired, and secretly quite pleased to have an excuse to slow down for a bit.

Quickly it was decided who was to be the first seeker; Julia, the little girl whose suggestion it was to play in the first place. The others all ran off to hide whilst Julia counted to one hundred. She soon found the first child, her best friend Alice. Julia had little trouble tracking her down: she was squatting behind a large apple tree, still gasping for breath from her earlier exertions. Joseph watched from his vantage point from behind a stone water-trough that had long been abandoned, as, one by one, Julia rooted out her friends. Most of them, he noted, gave themselves away by moving too much as Julia cast her eyes around the orchard like a searchlight. Joseph knew from long experience that it was usually sudden movement that gave away a position: just like the deer in the woods. He had often sat motionless in the beech woods near home, watching for movement. You never knew where the deer were, or how many there were in the herd, until they moved. If they stood stock still, they were almost impossible to spot. It was the same with children, and if it wasn't sudden movement that gave them away, it was sound: a cough, a whisper that was too loud or the cracking of a dry twig under a small shoe.

Julia was especially pleased when she found Joseph. She loved him as if he was her big brother. The world always felt like a better place when she was close to him; warm and safe. As he was the last to be found, he had to be the next to play the role of seeker. The children all ran off again as he started to count. He counted slowly and purposefully, and at the same time, he tried to calm himself down. Just like the others, he was still hot and bothered, but he wondered; if he could control his breathing, maybe he could improve control of his body and his senses? As he slowly counted, he realised to his amazement, that his breathing was starting to fall in line with the rate of his counting. By the time that he had reached one hundred, he felt much calmer.

He looked around and stepped forward a few paces, and with his breathing more under control and his heart rate falling, he realised that his senses were far more tuned in than they were only a few moments before. He could hear much better now, as the mysterious and confusing internal noises of his heart and lungs were no longer competing with his external senses. Strangely, his vision also seemed to be improved. He couldn't think quite why this should be, but wondered if it was something to do with being still. He felt very alert and very calm and quickly found the hiding places of the others. For the rest of the day, through the heat of the afternoon, the hide and seek went on. The countryside was quiet with just the occasional buzzing of bumble bees busy collecting pollen from the purple and white clover flowers in the old orchard, the screeching of swifts as they flew high overhead in the summer sky and the mewing call of a single buzzard somewhere in the distance. It was a perfect afternoon. Although none of the other children noticed what he was doing, Joseph carried on with his experiments. He was learning, by concentrating and controlling his breathing, to regulate his heart-beat.

The noises of the oncoming engines were louder now, and somewhere in the midst of the muffled sounds that reached him, there was the distinct noise of a motorbike engine. Although Joseph had never been on active duty before, he had seen German convoys many times over the last few weeks. Since the German invasion during June, he had seen countless numbers of them on the main roads not far from Watersham, but this was the first time that they had come into the village. He stiffened, readjusted his feet, and lined up his rifle sites at a point just above a low brick wall that ran along the edge of the pavement on the far side of the road, near the bend. He knew the spot well. He had walked past it countless times as a child. The entrance to his old primary school was about one hundred yards further down the road on the right-hand side. His mind wandered for a while as he thought back to his school days, and for a few seconds, he remembered holding his mother's hand as they walked to school for the first time.

His concentration returned in a flash as a German motorbike and side-car showed itself for the first time in the middle of the road. It was travelling at no more than walking speed, its rider advancing with extreme caution through a village that he knew nothing about and was treating with the utmost suspicion. In the side-car sat a soldier with both hands firmly gripping a machine gun mounted in front of him. Joseph was not surprised by what he saw; he knew what to expect.

Nevertheless, his heart skipped a beat. He took two steady breaths which immediately relaxed him, slightly adjusted his feet once more, moved his site line from just above the wall to the chest of the motorbike rider, and gently squeezed the trigger. Although he had fired his rifle many times in practice, this was the first time that he had fired it in anger. He had never thought that one day he would be firing down the main street of his own village. The loud retort of the gun, enhanced by the hard surroundings of buildings, walls and the road, startled him. In the forests, where he had practiced for hour upon hour, the soft trees muffled noises and seemed to wrap all sounds in cotton wool.

This was different. This was very real and very loud. Everyone in the village must have heard the shot, unmistakeable in both its loudness and its tone; like a firecracker exploding on a clear and frosty night. This was certainly the sound of war.

The bullet hit the motor cyclist in the middle of his chest, killing him instantly and knocking him out from his seat, so that he completed a full backward somersault before landing spread-eagled on the pavement. The motorbike continued, oblivious on its journey, gently mounted the kerb, and came to rest as the front wheel met the brick wall, its engine momentarily racing and then spluttering until it stalled and died. The machine gunner desperately tried to sit himself up straight in his seat and to swing his weapon to point in the direction from where he guessed the rifle shot had come; but before he had a chance to pick a likely target, Joseph had him in his sights, and with another squeeze of the trigger, the second shot rang out, sending the gunner hard back into his seat, dead. The front of an army truck was now just visible, but it came to a stop as the shots rang out. Joseph could still clearly make out the rumbling of more engines further back down the road. The sounds of the shots echoed against the red brick and flint walls of the surrounding houses and unseen villagers drew back from their windows and headed for cover. Further away, men looked up from their labours, straightened their backs and stared at each other and towards the village. They stood in silence, straining their ears, listening hard for a clue as to what was happening – although many guessed immediately.

Earlier that morning, Joseph had been riding his bike from the family farm down towards Watersham, on his way to join some of the other men in the village for their latest training exercise in the local woods. As he approached the village, he was met by one of his unit, Alexander Miller, riding a motorbike at full speed towards him. On spotting Joseph, Alexander jammed on his brakes and skidded to a broadside stop across the road. Joseph braked hard too, and just managed to avoid running in to him.

"What the hell's up with you?" Joseph yelled.

"There isn't time to explain now!" Alexander panted, "Get yourself down to the back of the old sports pavilion as quick as you can! There's big trouble! Go on, quick, I've got to round up as many of the others as I can. I'll see you there."

Joseph and Alexander knew each other well. They had been to school together and were now both working on their family farms. There was no doubt in Joseph's mind that there must be big trouble coming as he had never seen Alexander so animated. As the young man sped off in search of more help, Joseph pedalled as hard as he could towards the pavilion. He arrived at the same time as three others, and without delay, they joined the small group already gathered behind the building. Their Commander, Henry Clay, looked worried. He was talking earnestly to some of the older men in the group, whilst the others remained quiet, awaiting orders. Clearly, there was going to be no training today.

After a few minutes and the arrival of four or five more men, the Commander waved to them to come closer. "Listen up men. I don't have time to give you all the details; but what you need to know immediately is that we are going into action." Henry paused for a few seconds to allow time for his words to sink in. The men glanced at each other. No one spoke; there was no need to. There was a whole bag full of questions, but they knew that now wasn't the time to ask them. The Commander started up again. "I've received information from HQ that the Germans will be sending a convoy through the village to secure the bridge at St. Michael's".

The locals knew exactly how strategically important the bridge was. If it couldn't be used, as had happened ten years earlier when it was out of action for repairs for three months, it added over twenty miles and more than an extra hour to any journey to the larger towns and main roads along the coast. The Germans had obviously just become aware of the strategic importance of the crossing, and were intent on making sure that it was secure under their control.

The Commander gave out clear instructions to his men. "The main aim is to blow the bridge. Alan Benton and his team have already set off to get the explosives and to make their way down to the bridge as quickly as they can." Commander Clay was confident that they had enough explosives to do the job and the skills to set them properly, but they needed to buy some time. He gave out more orders. "Malcolm and Jim; take the heavy machine gun and set yourselves up behind the trees at Blacksmith's Corner."

Commander Clay's instructions continued, until each group and each individual had been allocated a role, except for one man – Joseph. He waited until the Commander had given out his last instructions. His final words were, "Good luck men and remember: you're not to get yourselves killed. Your jobs are to hold the Germans up for as long as possible, cause some damage and then fall back and eventually get out and away as best you can. I'll get a message to you as soon as possible as to when and where we will next meet. Now go!"

As the men ran off to get their weapons and explosives; hidden in various places around the village, he turned to Joseph and said quietly and calmly, "Joseph, where's your rifle hidden. Is it far away?"

"No," Joseph replied "it's just down the street".

"Right", said the Commander, "I'll follow you. Quick, let's go".

Joseph, with the Commander following, ran at a steady pace down the street until they reached a gate that opened on to a path running down the side of a small cottage.

Joseph ran quickly down the garden path, heading towards some outbuildings to the rear. The Commander paced up and down in the road. He knew that if he got this wrong, it wasn't just his life on the line, but the lives of his men, and who knew how many other lives after that. He stared at the cottage in front of him. A curtain twitched as Joseph came running back down the path with his rifle.

"Good," said the Commander. "Follow me".

Two hundred yards further down the street, the Commander stopped and walked up a gently sloping grass verge towards a low flint wall that surrounded a garden that belonged to the house where he knew Miss Estelle lived.

"Right," he said, "Now get yourself over this wall and set yourself up here. You've got a good view of the road from here, and pretty good cover. They have to come this way. There's no other way for them to get to the bridge than to come through the middle of the village. Joseph, this is where I need you. This is where you can do most damage. It's a lot to ask, I know, but you're the best man for the job and I know that you won't let us down".

His voice cracked slightly. Here he was, asking his youngest unit member to stop a German convoy in the middle of the village. What was the world coming to? He hesitated for a moment, but quickly regained his composure. He had to get on. There wasn't time for emotion now. "Joseph," he said "Just do what I know you can do. Hold them up, pin them down for as long as you can, and then for God's sake get out. Don't you dare get yourself hurt!"

He patted him firmly on the shoulder several times and turned to go. Joseph reached out and grabbed the Commander's arm.

"I won't let you down Sir."

"I know you won't son."

And with that, Joseph let go of his arm and Henry started back down the street to check on the rest of his men. He jogged back to the pavilion, picked up his own rifle and kit bag – full of tools and wires – from inside a coal bunker to the side of the building, pulled his bike from the hedge where he had hidden it, and pedalled off towards Blacksmiths Corner.

As he rode along, his thoughts turned back to Joseph. It was a lot to ask of a boy to do such a job. He would never forgive himself if he was injured or killed. How could he possibly face his parents? What would he say? How could he explain his decision to put his youngest unit member in such a dangerous position? But as he approached Blacksmith's Corner, his mind returned to the job in hand. Were Malcolm and Jim there? Had they got the heavy machine gun set up yet? He skidded to a halt by the huge lime trees that lined both sides of the road for about fifty yards, and, still holding on to his bike, he walked towards the grassy bank. There they were – perfect – set up in exactly the right spot, with good visibility, looking back down the main street, in a slightly raised position on top of a low bank, with the giant trunks of the lime trees for cover.

"Good boys!" he shouted, "Do you have everything you

need? Are you clear what you have to do?"

Malcolm shouted back. "No problems Commander; we're ready!"

"Don't forget…" the Commander began.

"Yes, we know!" they called in unison; "Don't get killed!"

The Commander smiled for the first time that day, waved at his men, remounted his bike and started off again towards the bridge at St. Michael's. Riding towards the bridge made him more aware than ever of the time and distance involved in what they were trying to do. It was clear that if the Germans could not be held up at the village, they would have a free run down River Road and be at the bridge in no time. He resolved then that if he found preparations to be going well with the explosives at the bridge, he would order as many men as he could spare to line the road down which he was now riding; to cause even more damage to the convoy, and hopefully gain enough time for his men to finish the job on the bridge.

He was hoping that none of that would be necessary, and that by the time the Germans got through the village, it would be too late – that the bridge would have been blown and all his men would have melted safely back into the countryside. Fifty yards in front of the bridge, two men were busy digging in by the side of the road. Piles of steel munitions boxes were scattered around, some as yet unopened, others tipped over spilling what remained of their contents on to the road. Several drums of cable had been left leaning against the first main upright pier that supported the bridge on the left side. Henry dismounted, leaned his bike against the railings, walked back a few paces, steadied himself by putting his hand on the main pier, swung around sharply and then slowly slipped and slid down the first part of the bank so that he could see under the bridge. Immediately, he could make out several figures clambering over the girders that supported the bridge.

"Alan!" he called. "Alan; Alan are you there?"

Alan Benton was in his early fifties, originally from Portsmouth, where he had worked for thirty years as an engineer for a small civil engineering company. He had started in the workshop, learning most of the trades by working as first mate to the older highly skilled craftsmen.

He could form, cut, bend, weld and join just about every type of metal known to man, and by the time he was thirty, he in turn had become one of the most skilled men, not only with his firm, but within the wider engineering community in and around the city. He spent much of his time teaching apprentices, often in the yard, on the shop floor or on construction sites. He and his wife, Gail, had moved to Watersham some three years before. She worked part time at the Post Office and Alan ran a small engineering workshop in the old farm buildings just off Church Lane. Most of the local farmers used his services to fix their machinery.

Most days he could be found welding ploughs, cultivators and other implements back together. The other villagers used his services almost as much, bringing in for his attention a constant stream of smaller machines and implements; cars that needed a bit of work underneath, lawn mowers that needed new or sharpened blades and there was a never-ending supply of bicycles that needed his attention. He helped local farmers to build and install new bull pens, cattle crushes, grain stores, irrigation tanks and just about anything else made out of metal that a farmer might need. Only last year he had designed and manufactured a steel bridge for a local land owner who wanted to gain access to one of his fields by bridging a stream only about four miles from where he was now. And here he was today, about to blow up a bridge some twenty times the size of the one that he had so painstakingly designed and built, so that they couldn't access the land on the other side.

Alan was trying hard not to dwell on this too much. He

was working as quickly as he could, carefully placing the explosives in key places on the steel girders, and running cables between the charges and back to a single point on the road some twenty yards on the far side of the bridge. Alan heard Henry call for him and immediately shouted back so that he knew which of the men he was.

"Over here Henry!"

Henry shouted again. "How's it going Alan? How much more time will you need?"

Alan had been making mental calculations ever since he and his men had arrived on the bridge. He reckoned that they were about a third of the way through the job already, so with him and the four others who had some training in setting explosives, they were making good progress.

"At least another hour!" he shouted back.

"What about more men?" Henry suggested.

"No. They're not trained and they might slow us down!"

Just as Alan finished speaking, the sound of two rifle shots rang out in the distance from the direction of the centre of the village. Everyone around the bridge stopped and looked towards their Commander. Several seconds clicked by before Henry responded. He was pretty sure that it was Joseph's rifle shots that rang out, and to reassure himself and his men he called out again.

"Don't worry lads – that's one of ours. Keep up the good work men! Alan; whatever happens, don't wait for further instructions. As soon as you are ready, blow the bridge and get out of here. You will be on the other side of the river, so just get away as fast as you can and we will all meet up safe and sound in a few days' time. Good luck." The men returned to their work, as Henry called out to his friend Alan one more time. "Alan, I'm going to leave you the two men guarding the far side of the bridge, in case anyone approaches from that side, and the two men who have dug in in front of the bridge – the others I'm taking with me back down the road."

"Good idea!" Alan shouted back, and with a half-hearted attempt at some humour to cut through the tension, he added, "See you in the pub for a game of cards on Thursday?" Henry didn't answer. He just smiled and put his thumbs up.

As quickly as he could, Henry scrambled back to the road, called out to the group still standing on the bridge to follow him, and picked up his kit bag and rifle. Grabbing his bike, he then started to walk at a steady and purposeful pace back towards the village. Soon the others caught up with him, keen to at last do something more useful than carry munitions and guard a bridge. Two had their bikes with them, but the other three were on foot, as they had ridden on the back of the truck carrying the explosives, which was now safely parked about one hundred yards on the far side of the bridge. The Commander gave his instructions as they continued to walk quickly back down the road.

"In about another two hundred yards, I want the three of you on foot to set yourselves up down one side of the road about thirty yards apart. That way, if the Germans get this far, you can let them have it with all that you've got. It could make all the difference. It could just give Alan and his men enough time to finish the job. But don't forget, we need you all to fight for another day, so as soon as it starts to get tricky, get yourselves out of there! And as soon as it's safe to do so, get yourselves home."

When they reached a line of old elm trees, Henry gave them some more instructions, pointed to the best positions for them to set themselves up, and with the two remaining men, they said their farewells, mounted their bikes and set off again towards the village.

Chapter Five

ST MICHAELS BRIDGE

Joseph took aim at the tyre on the front right side of the truck. He fired, and it instantly deflated, as a German soldier carrying a rifle ran out from behind the far side of the vehicle, jumped the low wall and dived to the ground. Joseph studied the wall for a moment and then decided to finish the job that he had just started. In rapid succession, he fired a shot into the other front tyre, three shots equally spaced low through the windscreen and for good measure, three shots in a triangle through the middle of the radiator. A cloud of steam issued immediately, and the engine spluttered and died. No doubt, the bullets that had passed through the soft leaves of copper that made up the greater part of the radiator had done further unseen damage to some vital parts of the engine before coming to a stop.

Throughout this rapid firing, Joseph kept part of his attention on the low wall behind which the German soldier was now hiding, and another part on the front far side of the truck from where the soldier had emerged. Would another soldier be brave enough to try the same trick? After firing, he left his rifle lined up with a point about one yard above the ground and one yard in front of the truck's front right wheel. The last of the steam hissed from the burst radiator, and for the first-time Joseph could hear German voices. He could also hear the sound of more unseen engines from around the corner.

Suddenly, a second soldier burst out from behind the truck towards the low wall. Joseph hadn't lost his concentration, and, without having to aim, he pulled the trigger again, hitting the young soldier as he took his second stride. Although the man dropped immediately to the ground, the momentum that his run had built up carried him forward until his helmeted head came into contact with the base of the wall, and there he finally stopped: his face hard down on the pavement, and his legs splayed out behind him with his feet hanging out over the curb stones – his rifle laying in the gutter.

Where was the other soldier? How far could he crawl behind the wall without having to show himself? Would he suddenly jump up and take a shot at Joseph? Had he spotted where he was hiding? Was he a trained sniper too? Would another soldier be brave enough to try to get over the wall having seen what had just happened to his friend? What was going on behind the truck where Joseph couldn't see?

Joseph trained his rifle to a point on top of the low brick wall about ten yards nearer to him. Having searched his memories of his days as a child, and having thought about the numerous times that he had walked along the top of that wall on his way to or on his way home from school, he was almost certain that at about that point in the wall there was another low wall that adjoined at right angles and ran back to the terraced houses that were set back no more than ten paces from the pavement.

He hoped that it was still there. The soldier would have

to show himself somewhere between where he dived over the wall and that point. Joseph made a bet with himself that the man would appear right where he was aiming.

Although he felt reasonably calm, Joseph was starting to get concerned about what was happening behind the stranded truck. He had no idea how many troops were there, neither did he know what sort of vehicles they had in the convoy – for all he knew they might have light tanks. One thing that he was pretty sure of was that they would not want to be pinned down where they were for long, and that they would be thinking of ways of both clearing the stricken truck out of their way and of finding another route around the houses to get at him. Of course, they didn't know that he was on his own. For all they knew, there was a whole platoon guarding the road ahead. Joseph knew that if foot soldiers made their way back and up the short lane that led to the primary school, they could then cut across the recreation field to its side behind the houses and come out into another lane that led down to the other side of the garden in which he was now standing.

If they went the other way, they would have to go a long way around the church, across some open fields and fair sized ditches before cutting back towards the main street through the back gardens of the terraced houses that were a little further down the road and off to his left.

How long could he wait? If he stayed where he was, he could probably hold them up for some time yet, even if they managed to clear the truck out of their way. But the longer that he waited, the more certain it was that some of the soldiers would find their way around the backs of the houses, and he would be stuck. Whatever happened, the vehicles would have to come through the centre of the village; there was no other way through for them.

The Commander and his two men arrived at Blacksmiths Corner, pushed their bikes through an open farm gate that led to the fields behind one of the stands of lime trees, and hid them in thick brambles that were growing over a small dilapidated tin shed that used to house an irrigation wind pump. They joined Malcolm and Jim, who were even better dug in and camouflaged now that they had had a bit more time to prepare.

"Did you hear all the shooting?" Jim asked.

"Yes," Commander Clay nodded. "Don't worry: Joseph knows how to look after himself." As soon as he said it, he realised, as did his men, that that wasn't strictly true. Joseph might well be the best shot in the unit, but they all knew that this was the first time that he had faced the enemy. In fact, it was the first time for all of them.

"Right," the Commander continued, briskly. "I've brought you reinforcements; me and the two Jacks".

The two Jacks were both in their late twenties and of similar build and colouring. Those that didn't know them so well were always getting them mixed up, and the Commander often had difficulty knowing which one was which himself. They were in fact quite different.

Jack Saint was a self-employed carpenter who earned his living from doing a wide range of jobs, both for local small builders and also for his own customers in the village. He had only last week finished putting in new wooden floors in the cottage just back down the road from Blacksmiths Corner. He and his wife, Lucy, and their two young children lived in a small terraced house, at the other end of the village.

Jack Miles was a school teacher. He lived in rooms at the independent school where he had taught for the last four years. The school was for teenage boys who had been sent there by their relatively well-off parents to get an education of some sort; any sort, as most of the boys had not done well academically in their previous schools. Park House, situated in parkland to the north of the village, was an old country manor house that had been converted to a school at the turn of the century. Jack Miles was a fairly quiet, studious type, but he rubbed along well enough with the others, and they with him.

Commander Clay was very happy with the way that Malcolm and Jim had set themselves up. He looked up and down the side of the field behind the lime trees, across the road at the trees on the other side, to the corner where the old blacksmiths building stood, and back down the street towards the centre of the village.

"We'll set ourselves up to your right" said the Commander "behind the trees on the bank."

Jim and Malcolm nodded and the three men moved off. The Commander and the two Jacks soon found a good spot behind the last lime tree. It had suffered some damage when it was young, probably losing its original growing point, causing two main trunks to grow rather than one. A perfect 'V' shape had been formed about four feet from the ground where the two trunks separated, and as luck would have it, standing behind the tree and looking through the V gave a perfect view straight down the main street.

The Commander placed his kit bag down and lent his rifle against the tree. "That's my spot," he said. "Now let's find the best positions for you two."

He walked back down on to the road and studied North Lane. "I need both of you just back up here a little way. If they turn here and start heading down the road towards the bridge, you can fire at the rear of their vehicles. And if they make a mistake and turn up North Lane, then you will have them right under your noses; alright?"

"Right," the two Jacks agreed in unison.

Joseph watched as the damaged truck was dragged slowly backwards. Clearly the Germans had managed to attach a tow rope to the stricken vehicle and they were going to haul it back far enough for the rest of the convoy to get by. He imagined that the next vehicle to come around the corner would be the toughest that they had. He hoped to God that it wasn't a tank.

As he suspected, hidden from his view, two groups of soldiers were receiving instructions from a very frustrated Captain. He waved the soldiers off – one group setting off to the south and one to the north, just as Joseph had predicted. Staring at the corner where the truck had been, he spotted a slight movement out of the corner of his eye.

The soldier behind the wall had finally showed his position. Just the very top of his helmet, no more than a couple of inches, poked up above the wall. Joseph adjusted his aim slightly to line up with the top of the helmet, and then he waited. He knew that eventually the man would want to lift his head just a little higher so that he could get a clear view over the wall. It was just a matter of time. But Joseph knew that he didn't have much more time. He couldn't wait much longer, or he might never get out in one piece. Just as he was thinking that enough was enough, the sound of a new engine reached him. Whatever it was, it was much louder than anything that he had been listening to for the last ten minutes, and he had a horrible feeling that it was going to be the next vehicle coming around the bend. The young man behind the wall decided that now was the time to have a quick look down the road and started to lift his head, but before he could see much more than the top of the wall, Joseph squeezed the trigger and the young soldier saw no more.

It was time to go. Joseph moved back from the wall, and keeping low, he picked up his backpack and slowly made his way across the garden towards a gate that he knew to be on the other side.

As he stole past some apple trees, his thoughts flashed back to an autumn evening seven or eight years before.

He and some of his school friends had been messing about in the village for most of that Sunday afternoon, when they found themselves leaning against Miss Estelle's garden wall. The apples and pears in her garden were there for everyone to see, and to the boys, they looked like they were ready for picking. In single file, they made their way along to the gate just a bit further along the wall and one by one they slipped into the garden and started picking the fruit as quickly as they could. Once they each had as much as they could carry in their pulled-up shirt fronts, they started back towards the gate. As the first boy reached it, the side door of the house flew open and Miss Estelle came rushing towards them, waving a broom and cursing them with words that they had never heard before.

They were so shocked, that most of their pickings fell straight to the ground as they ran as fast as they could through the gate and down the lane. They looked back over their shoulders to see Miss Estelle in the middle of the road, still waving her broom at them. They ran on until they reached an old hay barn on the edge of White House Farm where they collapsed onto the hay bales, out of breath and half crying with excitement as they related to each other how close they had come to being caught by the screaming, mad old broom-waving woman. From that day on, all the boys of the village referred to Miss Estelle as 'the mad old witch'.

From the back of her kitchen, Miss Estelle watched Joseph leave her garden; in fact, she had been watching him from the moment that he had climbed over her wall. "Stay safe," she whispered to herself "and may God be with you". She certainly wouldn't be chasing him today.

Having stepped out into the lane, Joseph stopped and took several long deep breaths to calm him down. The noises coming from the various vehicles in the convoy were as clear as they had been earlier. A slight breeze had got up that made the leaves at the tops of the small stand of whitebeam trees, on the other side of the lane, give off a slight clicking noise as they rubbed together. There were no animal noises, not even a dog barking in the distance. There was, though, a clear smell of diesel fumes in the air; no doubt coming from the convoy.

He started to walk slowly down the lane, all the time listening for something different, something unusual, something out of the ordinary. He knew that if his earlier hunch was right, that by now, soldiers would be working their way around the back of the village; possibly on both sides. After a hundred and fifty yards, he came to the last house that stood on the left side of the lane. Moving in closer to the hedge that ran along the side of the garden, he came to the corner where a chestnut-rail fence surrounded a large meadow.

The semi-metalled part of the lane ran out here as it became the gravelled drive that some three hundred yards further on led to White House Farm. Every ten yards or so, hard against the fence, a row of poplar trees stood. He peered around the corner of the hedge and, seeing no signs of movement across the other side of the meadow, walked quickly to the first tree and then peered out again to get a better view. Almost immediately, he spotted movement.

At the rear of one of the houses, just beyond the far side of the meadow, three soldiers were emerging from behind a garden shed.

As he watched, three more appeared from the side of the next garden. Using the tree as cover, Joseph started to walk very slowly backwards, making sure to keep the tree between him and the soldiers. He was now walking through a piece of rough ground that hadn't had much work done to it for a long time. Walking backwards was tricky; there were large tufts of grass, brambles, and, every now and then, a discarded brick or piece of barbed wire to contend with. He was half way across the field now, and right out in the open. If he was spotted, he would be in big trouble. When he got to within twenty yards of the small copse that lay on the edge of the field; realising that a single poplar tree would not be able to protect him from view any longer, he hoisted his rifle onto his back, turned around, dropped to his knees and then, keeping as straight a line as possible, crawled on all fours to the safety of the trees.

Once he was sure that he was far enough into the copse and out of sight, he stood up, unhitched the shoulder strap of his rifle and looked out from behind the low branches of a willow tree. The six soldiers had made good progress and were easier to see now that they were about half way across the meadow, but still hugging the fence on the south side. Joseph wondered what he should do next. He could just slip away and try to get back to join his comrades down by the bridge, or he could stay where he was and wait until the soldiers had turned to go up the lane.

He thought back to what the Commander had said to him before they parted: "...Hold them up, and keep them pinned down for as long as you can..." He thought about it again, and then moved a few paces further under cover until he found a large oak tree. He put his back pack down, and checked his spare ammunition. Then, snapping off a few twigs that were in his way, he looked out to check on what progress the Germans were making.

They were only about thirty yards from the corner of the field now, and he could see quite clearly what weapons they were carrying. Four of them had standard issue rifles, and two were holding sub-machine guns. Joseph braced himself behind the oak tree, resting the barrel of his rifle on the stub of an old branch that stuck out from the side. He lined his sights up on the nearest soldier, held himself steady... and squeezed the trigger. The man fell backwards into one of his comrades – his rifle flew up into the air, twirling as if in slow motion. Two soldiers fell to the ground, the second waving his arms and shouting as he tried to get out from under the dead weight of his colleague. As soon as the shot had rung out, three of the others had dropped to the ground and the one furthest back had dived between the fence railings and slithered away behind a patch of stinging nettles.

None of them had spotted where the shot had come from. The second soldier managed to extricate himself from under his fallen colleague, and was now lying on his back, his tunic soaked in blood, breathing heavily, shivering and in a complete state of shock. The last man had now managed to crawl further off to the side, and was lying behind a row of cabbages in the garden of one of the cottages that bordered the field. Now that they were all on the ground, Joseph no longer had a clear view of any of them. He was particularly worried about the one who had managed to get through the fence. The only way that he could get a better view of the soldiers lying in the field would be to move his position further forward. He quickly decided that that would not be a wise thing to do.

Slowly, moving back behind the trunk of the oak tree, he hitched the rifle strap over his shoulder, picked up his bag, dropped down onto all fours again and started to work his way deeper into the copse.

After a few minutes, he looked back over his shoulder and satisfied himself that it was safe to stand up. As he did so, a cock blackbird, standing on a branch just ahead of him, started up with its alarm call, warning every living thing in the woods that there was an intruder on his patch. Joseph dropped straight back to the ground again, thinking that even if the German soldiers were city boys, with little knowledge of the countryside, they would almost certainly have their attention drawn to the alarm song of the blackbird and would suspect that their assailant was nearby. He continued on all fours for what seemed like an age, and eventually the blackbird stopped singing, satisfied that his good work had driven the predator off. Joseph imagined that the soldiers would probably stay where they were for some time, fearful of moving, in case the sniper opened up on them again.

Once through to the other side of the copse; he stood up again and rubbed his knees. Then, heading south, he followed the line of the copse until he reached a hedgerow that went east towards the top end of North Lane. He pushed through the hedge and walked quickly, occasionally stopping and listening for the sounds of soldiers following him.

As he stopped for the third time, about half way along the hedgerow, he realised that engines in the distance were getting louder. There was a lot of noise and he could now make out the unmistakeable sound of two, possibly three heavy vehicles; if they weren't light tanks, they were certainly armoured carriers of some description. The convoy was obviously on the move again through the village. As he broke into a slow run, he wondered if he had enough time to get down to Blacksmiths Corner before they did.

Commander Clay, the two Jacks, Malcolm and Jim had heard Joseph's latest shot and realised that it had come from a position further to the North of the earlier shots. What did that mean? They could now hear the sound of the convoy much more clearly as it moved towards them. Malcolm cocked the bolt on the heavy machine gun and Jim made sure that there was nothing obstructing the magazine of bullets that trailed from the metal case by his feet. For the tenth time in the last few minutes, he looked around at the other cases that he had stacked up ready for action, and imagined going through the motions of reloading that he and Malcolm had practised in the woods so many times before. It was a warm day and sweat trickled down Jim's forehead into his eyes. He brushed it away and stared down the road. He knew that the convoy would soon be in sight.

Alan Benton and his men were making good progress. Most of the explosives were in place, and Alan was standing on the bridge, opening boxes of detonators, rechecking his calculations, and shouting out instructions to the men who were still running out cables under the bridge. They too had noticed that the noise of the convoy had become much louder in the last few minutes. The guards on each side of the bridge were pacing up and down.

Further back along the road, between the bridge and Blacksmiths Corner, the other men, having done all that they could to dig in and camouflage their positions, tried to calm their nerves by one moment sitting, the next standing and the next, checking and re-checking their weapons, before sitting back down and starting the process all over again. Absolutely no one had passed by during the time that they had been at the bridge. Word had obviously gone around the village area very quickly that this was not a good place to be.

Joseph was now standing under trees on the edge of North Lane. He looked both ways, and immediately spotted a small group coming towards him from the northern end of the lane. He dropped down on one knee, rested his rifle on the other and waited.

Since meeting Joseph earlier that morning, Alexander Miller had spent a further hour on his motorbike, rounding up a few more men from the surrounding hamlets and farms. Not knowing where the Commander and his men now were, he had sent three or four of the men that he had managed to find the long way around the village to approach the church from the south. He didn't have authority to give them orders, but suggested that they approach the village with absolute caution from the south, whilst he would do the same from the north. Hopefully, both groups would eventually meet up before the convoy arrived. Alexander realised, by the sounds coming from the middle of the village, that they might be too late.

Recognising Alexander, Joseph waved and stepped out cautiously into the middle of the lane. Alexander and his little team ran on to meet him. Joseph explained that the convoy had now managed to break through and was headed towards Blacksmiths Corner, where he thought that the Commander and the rest of the men were dug in. "Anyway," he concluded, as he began to run with the others falling in behind him, "All we can do is get down there, and see what we can do".

The four men that Alexander had sent the long way around had just entered the church yard by the small kissing gate on the south side, and were now walking slowly along the stone paved path towards the church. At the same time the second group of German soldiers came into the church yard through the wide lytch gate on the north side, and were slowly walking towards its main doors. Sergeant Matteus Weiss was leading the group.

He was a professional soldier who had been in the army since 1935. He had recently seen action in Poland, Belgium and northern France. As they reached the church doors, he slowed slightly and looked back down the path as his men rounded the corner of the church just ahead of him.

Both groups of men were equally surprised to see each other, but at least two from each side instinctively opened up with their machine guns, firing at each other with no more than ten or twelve paces between them.

Alarmed by the sudden noise, a great flock of pigeons clattered their way out and away from the ivy-covered elm trees that ran down the West side of the church yard. Peter Smith, Harold Turner and his cousin David Searle were hit by a swarm of bullets that killed them instantly and they fell to the path, where pools of their blood ran together and collected in shiny dark puddles in the dimples of the sandstone paving. Henrich Smidt and Tobias Groen, two of the German soldiers, were also killed instantly and fell sideways onto the grass between two large gravestones. Two other German soldiers had been hit in their legs and had fallen on grass behind some smaller gravestones on the other side of the path. They were both lying on their fronts, moaning quietly.

Sergeant Weiss had hit the ground as soon as the first shot had been fired and had managed to avoid injury. He was now on his stomach, gazing straight ahead towards where the bodies of the English fighters lay.

Frank Daltrey, walking a few paces behind the others, had also dropped to the ground as soon as the shooting had started and for good measure had rolled three or four times to his right, so that he was now hiding behind a large stone tomb. Slowly straightening up; he peered over the top. There was no movement ahead, and he had no idea of what the damage might be. He looked to his left and saw, with horror, his three mates lying on the path. He stared at them for a long time. There was no movement.

He then became aware of the moaning coming from the injured German soldiers and turned to look towards the corner of the church. As he did so, he just caught sight of Sergeant Weiss crawling across the path to the other side and then disappearing behind some more grave stones. Frank knew that there was only one of him left on his side: he wondered how many there were on their side. As quietly as he could, and using the gravestones as cover, he started to make his way across the churchyard towards a thick clump of rhododendrons on the east side. He crawled under a fence, through a pile of old grass cuttings and the remains of a burned-out bonfire, before reaching the safety of the trees.

Matteus looked out from behind a gravestone just in time to see Frank disappearing into the darkness of the undergrowth on the far side of the church yard. He waited for another minute and then very cautiously stood up. Nothing happened. He spoke quietly to the two injured soldiers next to him, checked his comrades for any signs of life, and finding none, walked slowly down the path, all the time looking along behind the rows of headstones, until he reached the three fallen Englishmen. One by one he felt their pulses and found none. He looked around again, and, now satisfied that the immediate danger had passed, returned to his injured men. Propping his machine gun against the back of a gravestone, he took off his back pack and started looking through its contents for bandages.

Inside the church, the Vicar, the Reverend Timothy Simms, the organist, Stanley Simpson, and a regular helper, Mrs Elizabeth Turner, knelt, partly in prayer and partly taking cover behind the pews. They had taken up their present positions when Joseph had fired the first shots some thirty minutes before.

The horrendous noise of machine gun fire from the church yard outside had frightened them half to death. Stanley Simpson clasped his hands so tightly together in fear and prayer that his knuckles were pure white. Mrs Turner stared at the church floor and quietly sobbed. The Vicar clenched his teeth and stared straight ahead towards the silver cross that stood on the alter table; his body shaking gently with equal amounts of anger and fear.

Everyone in the village heard the shooting. The Commander wondered why on earth the sound of machine gun fire should have come from the direction of the church. Alexander Miller feared the worst, but there was no time to dwell on that now, as the convoy was fast approaching Blacksmiths Corner.

Malcolm saw the first of the armoured personnel carriers come into view. He waited a few seconds, leaned forward slightly to be certain that everything lined up and opened fire with the heavy machine gun. The first burst of bullets fell slightly short; ricocheting off and up from the metalled road, up under the oncoming carrier, but nevertheless blowing great holes in both of the reinforced tyres on its right side. The carrier instantly careered off to the left, mounted the pavement and scraped along a low flint wall which eventually gave way, causing the carrier to shudder to a stop as the falling flint stones became too much of an obstacle for the carrier to push aside.

Inside the house immediately behind the wall, Carole Hammond grabbed her children and pushed them under the kitchen table, quickly dropping to her knees and crawling in with them. Nine years old Susan and six years old Michael were terrified and clung on tight to their mother. Betty quite expected at any moment for the kitchen wall to come crashing down on them and for their lives to be over.

The carrier's engine eventually stalled, and Malcolm opened up with a second burst; this time spraying the carrier down its side and across its top. One of the soldiers pushed open the rear door and staggered out; his comrades close behind him, all ensuring that they kept low and protected behind the stranded vehicle. Malcolm was now concentrating his fire on the second carrier, and as he fired, so the machine gunner on board, having now seen where the oncoming gun fire was coming from, opened up on Malcolm's position. Jim was hit several times in his chest from the first burst of fire and fell backwards, spread-eagled in the field. The gunner, still sitting inside the first carrier, had now regained his senses, and also opened up on Malcolm's position. Malcolm managed one more burst of fire at the second carrier, making a direct hit through the slit through which the driver looked out. The driver was instantly killed, but the carrier kept going straight ahead towards Malcolm's position. He realised that the vehicle was heading straight at him and as he stood up in readiness to run, the gunner from the first carrier fired again, hitting him in the head and sending him spinning backwards to lie next to Jim.

The second carrier crashed head-on into the earth bank in front of the lime trees, leaving its occupants in a pile of stunned and tangled bodies, munitions, and equipment. Commander Henry Clay trained his machine gun on the carrier, firing in withering bursts as he edged his way along the bank, behind the lime trees and towards the heavy machine gun.

Joseph, Alexander and the others arrived at Blacksmiths Corner just in time to see Malcolm cut down and the carrier crash into the bank. They too trained their guns on the crashed carrier and watched the Commander as he reached the heavy machine gun. The third carrier had stopped some way back down the street, and its occupants were pouring out and moving to the side of the road. Behind the third carrier, two canvas covered trucks had also stopped and about twenty soldiers were clambering down from each.

Further back, there was a staff car with a driver and three German Officers, four motorbikes, two more trucks full of troops, a fourth armoured personnel carrier and two motorbikes with sidecars taking up the rear.

As Commander Clay broke cover and ran from behind one lime tree to the next, the gunner inside the first carrier sprayed the bank and the trunks of the trees with a long burst of fire, and other German soldiers opened up with fire from their positions behind the carrier.

Joseph and Alexander were now also trying to move along the bank behind the lime trees so that they could see the enemy in the main street. The two Jacks held their positions just inside North Lane, their rifles trained on the rear of the second carrier. The third carrier, having finished unloading most of its men, now accelerated towards the bank, its gunner firing continuously as it advanced. The gunner from the first carrier was still firing in short bursts, as were many of the German soldiers advancing on foot on both sides of the road from behind the first carrier. As soon as Joseph and Alexander started to work their way along the bank, two of the men from Alexander's group, Albert Rose and Philip Greenfield, slipped through the side gate that led to the yard behind the old Blacksmith's shop, and prepared to throw grenades over the low roof into the main street on the other side.

The third carrier swerved hard to the right and headed south at a good speed with the two Jacks firing after it. The rear door of the second carrier was now slightly open and a dazed soldier was peering out and surveying the scene. The first two hand grenades landed unseen in the middle of the street and exploded simultaneously. Shrapnel flew in all directions, shattering glass as metal fragments flew through windows, embedding themselves in timber posts and frames, digging into stone walls and ricocheting off of the armour of the first carrier.

Several of the soldiers hiding behind the carrier were hit, and fell to the ground. The rear door of the second carrier opened further. The noises from the exchange of fire and the hand grenades were deafening.

Albert and Philip lobbed the next two grenades over the roof, this time about twenty yards further to their left. As the German soldier pushed open the door wide enough to climb out, the next two grenades exploded on the road only five yards away. The soldier, who had only managed to reach a crouching position as he prepared to step out from the carrier, was thrown straight back, limp and dead, into the men waiting behind him. The two Jacks fired into the back of the carrier and two more grenades exploded in the open doorway.

The third carrier had stopped about eighty yards down the road and had turned slightly to the left. The machine gunner, who now, looking back, had a clear view of the two Jacks' position, sent a long burst of fire straight at them. Jack Miles took several shots to his body and fell sideways into the road where he lay motionless. Jack Saint, hit twice in his right arm, fell into the bank and instinctively started to pull himself up towards the relative safety of the trees and the field beyond.

Due to the deluge of gun fire, neither the Commander nor Joseph and Alexander had been able to make any further progress. The trunks of the lime trees were peppered with bullet holes and great pieces of bark; splintered wood and broken branches were hanging from the sides of the trees or lying in the field behind the trees. The Commander, realising that they couldn't hold out for much longer, waved his arms at Joseph and Alexander and shouted as loudly as he could, "Pull back!!, Pull back!" Albert and Philip were still throwing grenades over the roof, causing huge confusion in the street, and, for the moment, stopping the foot soldiers from advancing.

Carole Hammond and her children huddled closer under the kitchen table as shards of glass and splinters of wood flew across the room from the shattered windows. Dust filled the air and the sounds of the raging battle in the street outside reverberated through the cold stone floor. Carole turned her head slightly to look towards the back door that led to the garden.

Slowly, Commander Clay, Joseph and Alexander crawled their way to the last lime tree where they found Jack Saint, leaning against the tree with blood dripping from his lifeless arm.

"I'll get the others!" Alexander shouted; and without delay, he ran headlong down the bank, across North Lane, through the gate and into the yard at the back of the Blacksmiths. The gunner in the third carrier fired as Alexander ran across North Lane, but his shots hit the road harmlessly behind his steps.

"We've got to get out!" Alexander yelled. "Let's go!!"

On hearing this, Albert and Philip pulled the pins from two more grenades, threw them over the roof, picked up their rifles and back packs and ran after Alexander back through the gate. As they crossed North Lane, they each fired blindly in the direction of the third carrier, ran up the grass bank and into the field. The Commander, Joseph and the injured Jack Saint had already started to make their way north alongside the hedgerow that separated them from North Lane. The other three were soon hard on their heels, and every few seconds, another burst of machine gun fire rattled up North Lane, through the hedgerow and against the resilient lime trees; but with each step that they made and with every second that passed by, they were another few paces away from the madness. Eventually the gunner in the third carrier stopped firing, and for the first time in what seemed like a lifetime, the air fell silent.

Carole Hammond released her grip on her children, listened for a while, and deciding now was the time to move, started on all fours across the kitchen floor, with Susan and Michael crawling after her. They kept going through the house, out through the back door; and still crawling, made their way down the garden path. They continued underneath the white cotton sheets and pillow cases that gently swayed on the washing line, until they reached the old shed where Carole's husband, Bill, kept his gardening tools. As Carole reached up to lift the catch on the shed door, the chickens in the run next to the shed cackled and ran forwards to see if she was bringing them any food. Quickly she pulled open the shed door, waved the children inside and pushing them gently but firmly, followed them in, and pulled the door closed behind them.

Carefully, she stood up, brushing her knees with her hands as she did so. She leaned down and whispered to her children, "Stand up now, but keep quiet." Susan and Michael stood up and copied their mother by brushing their knees. They didn't speak. They were too frightened to say a word, and too frightened to cry. Carole peered out through a narrow gap between the door and the door post. The line of white washing moved gently in the afternoon breeze, and to the side of the shed she could hear one of the chickens still clucking. Suddenly, the sound of heavy engines starting up filled the air again. She stepped back and felt some of the garden tools behind her. The shed was comfortingly warm and dark and for the moment she felt safe. There was a faint smell of creosote left over from where Bill had painted the inside of the shed some years ago, mixed with the scent of grass cuttings and of the earth floor. She wondered where Bill was. She reached out and touched Susan and Michael on their heads. "Don't worry" she whispered, "we're safe here. Daddy will be home soon." Susan and Michael leaned into their mother's legs and pressed their heads against her dress. Carole patted her children gently and they all stood in silence. Tears trickled down Carole's cheeks, but she bit her bottom lip so that the children couldn't hear her crying. Out in the street, on the other side of the house, she could hear the sound of men shouting.

When the Commander and his men reached the top corner of the meadow, they ran headlong into the old hazel coppice on the northern side of the village where they came to a track that took them up towards the fir trees. The woods stretched over thousands of acres on the gently sloping hills that sheltered the village on its north side and were well known to the men and to the locals, but strangers to the area were always getting lost in them: one pathway looked very much like another.

For the moment, the Commander knew that they were safe.

They stopped.

He pulled his hunting knife from its sheath and expertly cut into Jack's jacket sleeve, high up near to his armpit. He cut right round the material so that he could gently pull the whole sleeve down and away and then repeated the action with Jack's blood-soaked shirt sleeve. By the time the Commander had finished, Alexander had dug out some field dressings from his back-pack, and quickly wrapped a length of bandage around Jack's arm, pulling it as tight as he could. Joseph stepped in closer and placed a finger on the bandage as Alexander tied two knots. The tourniquet did its job almost instantly and the blood running from the two gaping wounds on his arm slowed to a trickle. Commander Clay picked up the discarded jacket and shirt sleeves and stuffed them into his backpack, and then, looking straight into Jack's eyes, he said "Good man – you'll live." Without another word, they walked off deeper into the woods.

The German officers jumped out of the staff car, looked around at the havoc, quickly assessed the situation and stood together for a minute talking and deciding on a course of action. The senior officer, Captain Jan Muller, walked over to the third carrier and spoke to the sergeant, who, having pushed the top hatch of his carrier up, was now standing and looking down from his vehicle. The other officers were giving out orders to the various sergeants, corporals and drivers who had gathered around.

Most of the convoy was to continue, leaving one of the officers, Lieutenant Helmut Stein at Blacksmiths Corner with one truck, twenty foot soldiers and one of the dispatch riders. They would secure their position and do what they could for the wounded, before attending to the damaged vehicles. Four soldiers walked over to where the fallen Englishmen were lying, and checked for signs of life. Finding nothing, they collected up their weapons and laid them out, including the heavy machine gun and the spare ammunition, on the side of the road. As the German soldiers picked up their dead and tended to the wounded, the convoy set off again, heading down the road towards the bridge.

Alan Benton and his men were nearly finished down at St. Michael's Bridge. They had heard the sound of every bullet that was fired, every burst of machine gun fire, each exploding hand grenade, the noise of the engines and then, worst of all; they had heard the sound of silence. Each of Alan's men had their own worst thoughts racing through their heads throughout, but they had continued undeterred with their work, knowing that whatever had happened back in the village, it would all be in vain if they didn't blow the bridge.

When Alan heard the sound of the convoy coming their way again, he knew that time was running out. As the vehicles moved off down the road, Sergeant Matteus Weiss strode along the street with five soldiers whom he had met up with near the village centre; the same men that Joseph had tangled with in the field. Seeing Lieutenant Stein, Sergeant Weiss saluted and gave a brief report as to what had happened back at the church, and from what he had just been told, what had happened to the other group.

At the same time, Frank Daltrey, having taken a circuitous route across the fields after getting away from the church yard, had finally reached River Road; where, to his surprise, David Miller called out to him from his position behind a large elm tree on the other side of the road. Frank checked the road both ways and then ran across, noticing as he did so the distinctive sounds of the convoy on the move again. He started to blurt out what had happened in the church yard, but David held his hand up.

"Frank, tell me later, we don't have time. That bloody convoy's going to be on us in a minute, and we've got to do our best to slow it down before it gets to the bridge. Alan and his boys are down there now, wiring it up." Frank got the message and moved off quickly to take up a position behind an ash tree about twenty yards back towards the village. David shouted after him, "George is about thirty yards to my left and Morris another thirty yards further along!" Frank waved back, put his thumbs up, checked the magazine on his sub machine gun, dropped his back-pack in front of him and pulled out his spare magazines. They had trained many times for this sort of situation, and Frank ran over what they had been taught to do. He knew that he would have to hold his fire until the guys furthest down the line opened up on the first vehicle; that way they would know that they had most of the vehicles covered between them. If he opened up too soon, the convoy might stop and the others would not be able to engage.

The first armoured personnel carrier, followed by a truck carrying troops, some motorbikes and another carrier, roared past his position. Head down, Frank waited. The convoy drove on past David, past George, and as it drew level with Morris, he opened up with his sub-machine gun from behind an old concrete block covered in thick ivy, once the corner stone of a long ago dismantled farm building. Within a split second of Morris opening fire on the carrier, the other three followed suit. They were in good positions, and they had caught the convoy by complete surprise: the Germans really hadn't expected a second assault.

The first carrier drove straight on, bullets ricocheting in all directions from its armoured plate, but then thirty yards or so past Morris, it began to slow as both rear tyres suddenly deflated as he changed the angle of his attack, aiming low, as the last of the bullets in his first magazine ran out. George emptied his first magazine through the canvas side of the first truck carrying about twenty soldiers, the driver accelerating and swerving as he realised what was happening. David stayed low and sprayed his fire left to right and then right to left, first hitting a motorbike rider, who cartwheeled across the road and into the ditch on the far side. His motorbike slid on its side for some distance, throwing up sparks, eventually coming to rest some thirty yards further on. His shots also ripped into the side of the staff car as it passed, miraculously only striking one of the Officers through his hand and failing to do any serious damage to the vehicle.

The driver accelerated, braked and swerved to miss the motorbike that was lying in his path, accelerated again, and had caught up with the still slowing first carrier by the time the ambushers had reloaded. Frank aimed short sharp bursts of fire into the canvas side of the second troop-carrying truck, and into its rear as it passed. His last burst was aimed at the side of the second carrier, but his bullets, like Morris's, ricocheted off the armoured plating and the carrier drove on with no serious damage.

By the time the men, had dropped their empty magazines and jammed fresh ones back into their machine guns, most of the convoy had passed by, except for the last motorbike and sidecar. The soldier in the sidecar did not have a fixed machine gun mounted on the front but was carrying a large machine gun cradled in his arms. The moment that the firing had started, he raised it as best he could and started to fire into the hedge immediately to his left in a continuous steady burst as his partner accelerated down the road. Bullets flew over Frank's head and he ducked down without being able to return fire. More bullets ripped into the elm tree next to David, and he too dived for cover.

George managed to fire one more burst of fire after the main convoy, before seeing the motorbike and sidecar approaching out of the corner of his eye, and with a split second to spare, he threw himself down and the bullets passed harmlessly over his head. Morris didn't see the motorbike and sidecar coming and although he heard the machine gun, he turned too late, the massive blast from the machine gun killing him outright and knocking him sideways into a hawthorn bush. With the motorbike and sidecar and the deadly machine gunner now safely gone by, Frank, David and George jumped to their feet and fired again after the convoy.

Some of the German soldiers were dismounting from the trucks and a growing number were starting to return fire. If the three of them waited much longer, the machine guns from the armoured carriers would open up, and then they would be finished. George desperately wanted to check on Morris, but he knew that it would be too dangerous – and he knew in his heart that there was nothing anyone could do for him. He picked up his things and, ducking down, moved as quickly as he could behind the hedge and towards David. As soon as David saw George coming towards him, he too, grabbed his bag and headed off in the same fashion towards Frank.

When they reached him, Frank hissed, "Where's Morris?"

"He's bloody dead!" George shouted.

George carried on running, bent half double, along the edge of the field. David and Frank followed him. The firing from the Germans was easing off now and most of their bullets flew high, harmlessly across the field.

George, Frank and David ran as fast as they could over the last fifty yards of the field and jumped into a partially overgrown ditch that adjoined River Road at right angles and ran along the north side of the field. There was only a trickle of water in the ditch. Tall, yellow irises and bull-rushes grew in great clumps, and on top of the bank, young blackberry bushes were in full flower. Everywhere, there were thick, lush patches of stinging nettles. The three men pushed on quickly along the ditch, and were nearly at its end by the time that the last shots rang out from River Road.

Several German soldiers searched along the bank and behind the trees, but could only find Morris's body and empty magazine cases. The Germans had lost seven more men with a further eight injured, and had sustained more damage to their vehicles. Captain Muller was angry and was wondering how he was going to explain today's events to his superiors. He couldn't afford any more surprises, and he certainly couldn't afford any more losses in securing the bridge. He spoke directly to those that he needed to, again giving out clear orders, and got back into the staff car. A small group stayed behind to take care of the wounded and the convoy set off towards the bridge.

Alan Benton and most of his men were now working in the road on the far side of the bridge, running out the last of the wires. They had heard very clearly the sounds of the shooting in River Road, and knew that the Germans were now approaching fast. Alan had sent one of his men, Ted Riggs, back across the bridge to fetch the two others who were still dug in and guarding the bridge on the village side. As Ted told the men to get themselves back over the other side of the bridge, the sound of the oncoming convoy reached them. Glancing back down the road, Ted urged the men to hurry, and started back across the bridge. Alan and his men were now thirty yards on the other side, cutting and joining wires together. Alan stood and shouted, "Get back to the truck! Get back to the truck, get loaded up and get ready to move out!"

The men snatched up their guns and equipment, and hurried off towards the waiting truck, leaving empty boxes and wire drums on the bridge and on the road. Alan waved Ted past and waited for his last two men to get to him. It seemed to take forever for them to reach him and to run on towards the truck. As they went, he heard the reassuring sound of the truck engine start up behind him. He looked back down the road, and as he did so, the first of the armoured carriers came into view. Crouching down on his knees, he checked that the wires were firm under the brass terminals, wound the small handle on the side of the detonator box six times and lifted the plunger. He hesitated for a few seconds. If he waited until the vehicles were on the bridge, he could blow them up at the same time. The thought didn't stay with him for long. Shouting ... "What a fucking stupid idea!" he pushed the plunger down with both hands.

The force of the explosion was enormous; so much so that the shock-wave knocked Alan backwards, banging the back of his head on the road. He sat straight back up, mouth wide open, staring at the great cloud of dust rising up from where the bridge had been, as pieces of debris rained down around him. He had no idea if any part of the bridge still stood; the cloud of dust now surrounding him was so thick that he couldn't see more than a few feet in any direction. He picked himself up, loosened the terminals on the detonator box, pulled the wires out, hoisted it up under his arm, and started running towards where he guessed the truck to be. His ears were ringing so loudly that he couldn't make out much, but as he stumbled on, he could just make out the sound of the truck starting to move off. As he caught up with it, he threw the detonator box over the tail board, grabbed hold of the rungs of the short steel ladder that hung over the back, and with the help of several pairs of hands reaching down to him, pulled himself up and over and onto the floor. The truck accelerated away, hidden from view by the dust and the steep banks and trees that lined the narrow road.

The German convoy came to a stop about twenty yards from where the bridge once stood. Captain Muller stepped out from his staff car and, accompanied by the other officers and some of his men, walked slowly towards the great cloud of dust. There was debris all over the road. Bricks, pieces of wood, sections of railings, part of an iron girder and branches from trees that had overhung the road were strewn everywhere. They picked their way around the obstacles until they reached the jagged edge of the road. As the dust began to settle, they could see a great yawning gap where the bridge had once stood, and as the dust settled further, the torn and broken edge of the road could be seen on the other side. They stood in silence for some time, small pieces of debris still falling around them. No one dared to say anything. Eventually, Captain Muller could contain himself no longer, and, at the same time as kicking a lump of red brick with his dusty boot, he screamed .... "Jesus Christ ... Jesus Christ ...

Jesus Christ!!!"

Alan sat peering out from the back of the truck for a long time; just staring at the cloud of dust and smoke that he could still see hanging above the trees. As they drew further and further away, he started to think of his friends. How were they? Where were they? How many men had they lost? Who had they lost? He stared at the wooden floor of the truck. The men sitting around him were all quiet now. What would happen next?

Twenty long minutes ticked by until the truck slowed to walking speed, then turning sharp left, they followed a flint track that would eventually lead them to a barn that, until about thirty years ago, had been a saw mill. That's where they kept the truck. The men knew that once they had garaged it and shared out the materials and equipment that were left over, they would have to split up and all make their own way home on foot as best they could. A long day, and for most, a long night lay ahead of them, as they were now some distance from their homes. Following what had taken place over the last hour, moving around the village would become a nightmare over the coming days and weeks. The whole area would be swarming with Germans.

Frank, George and David had just emerged from the ditch on the far side of the field. Feeling relatively safe, they were walking slowly through a scrubby field that gently sloped down to a small stream that fed into the main river that ran under St. Michael's Bridge, when the noise from the explosion reached them. All three threw themselves to the ground, and then, a few seconds later, realising that it was the sound of the bridge being demolished they leaped up and embraced each other.

Grinning broadly, they stood in the middle of the field for nearly a minute, staring with satisfaction at the huge cloud of smoke and dust rising up above the trees in the distance. Soon, their senses returned, and they realised that standing in the middle of the field gawping at the sky was probably not the best thing to be doing. They quickly moved off towards the stream that they knew to be only another two hundred yards away. On reaching it, without a word, they each put down their guns, dropped their packs, pulled off their tunic tops and shirts, and cupped great hands full of fresh cold water over their heads, faces and shoulders. After another minute, they quietly dressed, picked up their gear and set off towards the main river.

The booming from the explosion was heard by everyone and everything within a radius of thirty miles. Grazing animals stopped and gazed skywards. Great flocks of birds took to the air in panic; farmers and villagers looked up from their work, fearing what it might mean. Commander Clay and his men, now deep in the woods, stopped abruptly and stared at each other as the sound of the explosion reached them. After a few seconds, the Commander spoke; "Bloody hell. Good old Alan. They did it!"

The men patted each other on the back, waved clenched fists in the air and then, more slowly now, moved on again, each one deep in thought. Henry was convinced that they had succeeded in their mission, and although he would have liked to have been able to see the demolished bridge for himself, he was sure, with the sound of such an enormous explosion, that the bridge was down. Now, he thought to himself, nothing would ever be the same again. Now, their lives would be changed forever. God only knew how the Germans would respond.

Joseph walked along behind Henry and the others. A shiver ran through his body as he recalled the smallest details of the day – for a moment he was back there again, leaning on the wall in Miss Estelle's garden; he could even smell and taste the acrid smoke that followed each separate shot. Tears trickled down his cheeks as he walked. He kept his gaze on the ground immediately in front of him, not wanting to make eye contact with the others. He suspected that his friends might be feeling the same too. As they walked on, Joseph found himself thinking about his parents, his little sister, his grandparents and their farm. He wondered what they had all been doing today and what they had thought when they heard the explosion; but most of all, his thoughts turned to Julia.

Chapter Six

JULIA

Julia was nine months younger than Joseph. They had known each other since their early years at Watersham primary school. When Julia started at the age of five years, Joseph was in the year above. She wasn't particularly aware of him in her early school days; he was just another one of the big boys, who charged around the playground at break times causing havoc amongst the first years. The teachers were always telling them off and trying to get them to calm down, but although they had some success in the constant battle of wits between exuberant young boys and the need for control by the authority, there was nevertheless an unwritten rule, followed by most teachers, that boys will be boys and that they need to burn off their excess energy by tearing about the place like maniacs.

Sometimes this led to collateral damage – usually in the form of a little five year old girl being flattened by a big six year old boy. Fortunately, Julia had never been on the receiving end of a collision in the playground and Joseph had never been directly involved in any serious harm to the little ones – but he loved to run wild with his friends, and Julia, although sometimes frightened by the big boys' rough play, was also excited by them.

It wasn't until much later, when Julia was ten and Joseph was nearly eleven years old, that they started to recognise each other as individuals.

"I'm sorry," Joseph said, as they bumped into each other in the school corridor one day.

"No," Julia replied, looking straight into Joseph's eyes, "My fault".

Joseph, for the first time, noticed her beautiful deep brown eyes and, without thinking, touched her gently on her shoulder and said, "Right, good, see you later then", and then turning, he was off again about his business. Julia stayed where she was, standing completely still, her eyes following his every movement as he made his way to the double doors that led to the playground: and then he was gone.

She suddenly felt self-conscious, looked at the ground and then lifted her head to look around her. No one was watching. No one had seen. She then realised that her mouth felt incredibly dry, and headed off towards the water fountain, situated at the other end of the corridor.

From that day forward Joseph kept an eye out for Julia and she looked out for him. Sometimes they would see each other on a Saturday morning in the village, or at church on a Sunday – although this didn't happen very often as neither family was particularly religious. The opportunity to talk was almost non-existent, and the most that they managed in acknowledgement was a quick wave, nod or very occasionally a half swallowed "Hello".

When Julia was thirteen, she took a Saturday morning job, working as a waitress at the little café in the High Street, The Green Tea Café. She loved it; for the first time in her life, she felt that she was part of the adult world, and best of all, she had some spending money.

Joseph and his friends – all young teenagers – were not the sort of boys who would normally frequent a posh little café in the middle of a country village. Both they and the regular customers would probably have found it uncomfortable and possibly embarrassing if they found themselves sharing the same watering hole. The usual clientele were middle aged, middle class women, whose husbands were professional people; bankers, solicitors, businessmen, doctors, land owners and some of the bigger tenant farmers.

Most of the women were regular customers, who, not being exactly run off their feet with work, and having more than enough help with the daily chores of running their households, found themselves with plenty of spare time for taking coffee, tea and occasionally lunch, with their similarly socially busy friends.

Julia enjoyed serving them as they were always pleasant and easily satisfied – as long as they were served properly – and they tipped well. She also liked serving them because if there was any gossip about, which there usually was, it was very difficult not to overhear what was being discussed. Because of this rich source of local knowledge and gossip, Julia found herself to be in great demand amongst her girlfriends and would often be hijacked by one or two of them, looking for the latest gems, before she could get more than twenty paces from the café on her way home.

The main topic of gossip at the moment concerned a young lady by the name of Rosemary Hemsley. She was 20 years old and was the only daughter of Stewart and Elizabeth Hemsley. They were smallholders who ran a little farm on the edge of the village. It was run down and was becoming more run down with every year that went by. Stewart Hemsley was more interested in music than farming; spending most evenings and too many lunch times playing the piano down at The Red Lion. The farming community had little time for him and he was rarely seen at farming events or markets. Mrs Hemsley kept herself very much to herself and didn't mix with other farmers' wives; in fact, she rarely mixed with anyone.

Rosemary, on the other hand, was very gregarious. She always had been, even at primary school, but strangely, she had very few real friends. She was too friendly. On reaching her fourteenth birthday, the village boys started to take advantage of her and many of them found that they could get her to do things that the other girls wouldn't. It was just heavy petting and often quick and clumsy, and although she thought that she was being nice to the boys, she soon picked up some unpleasant nick names. The village girls had far worse names for her than the boys did; one of the least hurtful being "the village bike."

Rosemary now worked at Smith's Dairy. Often, she would go out with Betty Ashton on one of the delivery rounds. This involved loading up crates full of pint and half pint bottles of milk, but they would also take an equal measure of ten-gallon milk churns with them on the milk round. Many customers would leave out a large jug on their doorsteps, and Rosemary and Betty would fill the jugs with a ladle, straight from the churns. On returning the jug to the doorstep, they would place a heavy saucer or saucepan lid, on top of the jug. Occasionally, a stray cat would get lucky and manage to knock the lid from the jug and help itself to a free breakfast, but on the whole, the system worked well. Some customers had two deliveries of milk during the day; one before breakfast and one during the early afternoon.

Smith's Dairy had the contract to deliver milk to the main German barracks, a few miles away at Tangmere Airfield. For a number of years before the war and until the German invasion, the airfield had been one of the most important Royal Air Force bases in the south of England. Rosemary liked to flirt with the German soldiers at the base, and would often dally a little longer than was strictly necessary. Betty hated going there, and liked to get in and out as quickly as possible. Rosemary liked the attention and was more than happy to spend a little time talking to the soldiers, even though she couldn't understand a word of German. Betty complained many times to her boss about Rosemary.

"What is it?" he asked one day. "Why are you always complaining about working with her?"

"Because she's a fucking slut," Betty replied, succinctly.

Although Rosemary's German was non-existent, she certainly understood what the soldiers meant when they spoke to her. One of the men, Sergeant Helmut Steiger, had good English and they had managed to have a few quite long conversations. She liked him a lot and felt excited whenever they met.

During one particular visit to the Barracks, Rosemary managed to slip away from Betty almost as soon as they started to unload the milk. Sergeant Steiger was waiting for her behind the warehouse. Rosemary ran to his arms. They kissed briefly, and, knowing that they didn't have much time, he pushed her gently back, holding on to her shoulders.

"Listen", he said "meet me tonight at the other side of the airfield." He stopped talking, turned her slightly with one hand and pointed with the other. "You see that small barn to the side of the trees? Meet me there at six o'clock this evening."

"I will," she replied. She looked back into his eyes as she stroked his face. "Wild horses wouldn't stop me."

Helmut smiled at her, turned her around, patted her bottom and pushed her away. "Off with you," he said. "I'll see you tonight."

Once a week, for the next six weeks, Rosemary made her way to the barn on the far side of the airfield where Helmut was always waiting for her. Their love making was wild and passionate. Rosemary had never experienced anything like it before. Her heart raced as she biked the four miles from her parents' smallholding to meet Helmut in the barn. After they had exhausted themselves, they would get dressed and then stand in the near dark of the barn, gently kissing and caressing each other. She never wanted to leave him, but when she did, she thought about him constantly and couldn't wait until the next time. She had never felt so excited. In fact, she was so excited that she couldn't keep her little secret to herself. One day, on an early morning milk round with Betty, Rosemary couldn't stop herself, and with little prompting from Betty, she shared much of the salacious detail about her affair with Helmut. Betty was horrified.

"You bloody fool Rosemary! You must be mad – you can't fall in love with the enemy! I don't know what they'll do to you if they find out!"

Rosemary, oblivious to Betty's words of warning, turned and looked her straight in the eye. "You don't know what it feels like. I can't stop myself."

As the weeks went by, Rosemary became even more indiscreet, until she had told so many people that almost every villager knew something of the scandal. Between them, the ladies who took refreshment at The Green Tea Café had pretty much the whole story; and where there were gaps in their knowledge, it didn't take long for them to be filled in by one or two of the women who had a bit more imagination than the others.

One early morning, as first light was breaking, Betty and Rosemary delivered milk to Hoe Farm, about two miles out from Watersham, and were driving slowly along the track back towards the main road. As they rounded a bend, they could see men standing in the lane up ahead of them. One of them waved them down, and Betty slowed the van and stopped right in front of them. As they stopped, Betty realised that the men were all wearing balaclavas and turned to say something to Rosemary. As she did so, one of the men opened the passenger door and spoke: "Out you get Rosemary."

Without thinking, Rosemary stepped out from the van and the man closed the door. On the driver's side, another man spoke to Betty through her open window.

"Drive on Betty."

A shudder ran down Betty's back as it suddenly dawned on her what this was all about, and then the man leaned in closer.

"Drive on Betty."

Betty half recognised the voice, but with the balaclava and the poor light she couldn't be sure who it was. She released the handbrake and slowly pulled away. She stared straight ahead and after about one hundred yards, she looked in her mirrors, but the lane was empty.

As two of the men held her arms firmly, walking her briskly from the lane and through an open gateway into a grass field, Rosemary started to cry.

"What are you doing? What's going on? Where's Betty? Where are you taking me?"

The men didn't reply, but they stopped walking.

"I'll scream; I'll scream so loud – the whole village will hear!"

There was panic in her voice now. As she finished her sentence, she took a deep breath and was about to scream, when another man, standing behind her, reached over her shoulders with a thin scarf and pulled it tight across her open mouth and quickly tied it off at the back of her neck. The start of the scream turned into a gurgling and gasping noise. As she struggled to control herself, the man's arms came back across her shoulders again, but this time with a thicker scarf; this he quickly secured over her eyes and tied off behind her. Her head dropped forward as the man released his grasp. She realised that she could just about make out some shapes through the blindfold. She tried to shout again, but only managed a few groaning noises. The men either side of her were still holding her arms very tightly. Someone a few yards ahead spoke: "Over here."

Rosemary's head drooped forward again, tears ran down her cheeks and saliva and snot started to dribble from her mouth and nose. They walked on for another fifty yards until they came to a hay barn. Rosemary realised that she was inside a building and immediately picked up the unmistakeable smell of hay.

She also caught the smell of tar as she was led deeper into the barn. They stopped walking, and she could sense someone standing in front of her. His hands came up to just above her breasts and she felt him pull at the buckles that held up her overalls. Rosemary nearly collapsed with the shock of what was happening.

"My God," she thought, "They're going to rape me!"

The men at her sides held her up and edged her slightly forward. As she moved forwards, she could feel her overalls slipping down her body, and as her feet came up against something solid in front of her, she felt her overalls slide down to her knees. She was terrified and stood shivering with fear, as she heard the men moving around her. Slowly, the two men at her sides released their grip slightly, and then they were pulling her arms forward – but she couldn't walk forward, as her lower body was up against something. As she was gradually bent over the hay bales, with her arms being pulled forward, she could feel the hay rubbing against the front of her thighs and her stomach. She felt her knickers being pulled down and she tried to scream again, but with the scarf pulled tight across her mouth, only a faint rasping noise came from her throat. She felt hopeless, and dark thoughts started to enter her mind.

"This is how it's going to be. They're going to rape me. They're going to take turns to hold me over the hay bales and take turns to rape me." She felt sick, and then another thought ran through her mind: would they kill her when they were finished with her? As a fresh shudder of fear ran through her, another man spoke.

"Rosemary; you know why you are being punished today don't you? It's because you're a collaborator. It's because of your affair with the German soldier, and this is what happens to young ladies who sleep with the enemy."

As the man finished speaking, Rosemary heard a strange noise and at the same time felt a sharp, stinging pain across her buttocks. She automatically pulled against the hands that were holding her, but they were expecting it, and held firm. She let out a cry; that although muffled by the scarf, sounded like the cry of an injured animal. Before she had time to recover, she heard the same noise again and the same searing pain shot through her body. She lifted her head and arched her back as the third stroke left its mark.

She gurgled, screamed, gasped, cried, writhed and shuddered as the fourth, fifth and sixth strokes hit hard across her buttocks and the tops of her thighs. Rosemary lay still, sobbing quietly, wondering what might happen next. Her backside and thighs were so numb that most of the intense pain had gone and she wondered how badly they had hurt her.

There was a different noise now. It sounded like something banging against the side of a bucket, and as the sound came nearer she was aware of the strong smell of tar again. Without warning, something was being poured over her head. It was heavy, warm and sticky. In an instance, she knew exactly what it was. It was the same stuff that her father had used to coat the corrugated tin roof of the old privy on the farm. It was pitch tar. She could feel it slowly running down the back of her neck, round her ears, along her forehead and down the side of her face to her chin, where great droplets collected and then dripped onto the hay bale beneath her face. The man spoke again.

"Can you hear me Rosemary?"

Rosemary nodded her head slowly and let out a whimper.

"You won't do it again will you? You won't be seeing any more German soldiers, will you?"

Rosemary shook her head as more tar dripped from her nose onto the hay bale.

Slowly, the men let go of her arms and she lifted herself slightly up onto her elbows. One of the men leaned over and loosened the knots on the scarves. Rosemary coughed and spluttered.

"Don't try to take them off yet" he said, "wait until we've gone."

Rosemary didn't move, but listened to the men's footsteps as they filed out from the barn.

After a while, there was nothing but silence. Slowly, she raised herself up and backwards, keeping her head tilted down as she did so, until her full weight was back on her feet. As she reached for the knots tied behind her head, she worried about the tar running into her eyes, and leaned forward even further as she very carefully loosened the knots and removed the scarves.

She lifted the underside of the thicker scarf to her forehead and wiped away as much of the tar as she could and then used the smaller scarf in the same way. More confident now; she lifted her head and stood up straight. As she did so, some of the feeling started to return to the tops of her legs, and she winced as the grazes started to sting again. She grabbed a hand full of hay from the bale in front of her and rubbed at her hair with it, repeating the action a dozen times until she felt that she had removed as much of the tar from her hair as she could. She shuffled back from the hay bales, turned slightly sideways and very gingerly bent down to pull up her knickers. She bit her bottom lip as she felt the stinging return to her broken skin. She then bent down again and pulled gently at the straps of her overalls with her tarry fingers, eased them carefully over her bottom, hitched the straps over her shoulders and clipped the brass hooks back over their buttons. She turned and looked towards the main door of the barn. The morning light was much brighter now and she walked very slowly towards it.

When Rosemary reached the door, she leaned against the heavy oak doorpost, took several deep breaths, and looked out across the meadow. It looked quite beautiful in the early morning light, and apart from the sound of a blackbird singing in the distance, the countryside was perfectly quiet. She stood stock still, trying to understand what had just happened to her. Tears ran down her face, mixing with the smeared tar and for the first time that morning, she thought of Helmut. She knew in her heart that she would never see him again.

After a few minutes, she stepped away from the barn and walked towards the gateway that led onto the lane. Slowly, she started off towards the village, heading for home. She knew that when she got back to the farm, her mother would have to cut off all her hair for her. Rosemary muttered to herself as she walked down the middle of the lane … "there's nothing more for it when you've got tar in your hair …. you've just got to cut it all off …."

Joseph didn't get into the village much anymore on a Saturday morning, as he was usually working on the farm, but every now and then he managed to get the day off and have some time to himself. He had heard that Julia was working at The Green Tea Café, and decided that he would try to have a chat with her, if he could arrange it so that they 'accidentally' ran into each other. He certainly didn't want this to happen whilst his friends were around, and he knew that there was absolutely no way that he would be able to bring himself to go into the café on his own. Anyway, how could they have a sensible conversation if he was a customer and she was serving him with his tea? Even worse, what if he was served by one of the other waitresses, leaving Julia looking on from the other side of the café in puzzlement? No, the answer was to catch her as she left at the end of her morning's work.

By the time that this particular Saturday morning came around, Joseph had given a great deal of thought to it. He guessed that Julia would probably finish work at about two o'clock. His plan was to occupy himself with his friends for the morning, pop in to his Aunty Rosie's – who lived in a small terraced cottage just off the High Street – for lunch, and then get back close to The Green Tea Café for about ten to two, so that he could wait for Julia to emerge from the front door. What might happen then he had no idea. He just hoped that he wouldn't make a fool of himself, and that if he did, if it all went horribly wrong, he prayed that none of his friends would be there to see it.

On the dot of two o'clock, Mrs Wilson, the owner of the café, nodded to Julia and another girl to indicate that their shift was over and that they could go home. They made their way to the old store room at the back of the café, where Mrs Wilson handed them their wages in little brown envelopes. They collected their coats, said their goodbyes to Mrs Wilson and walked through the restaurant, smiling at the last few remaining lunchtime customers. From his vantage point some thirty paces away, leaning against the patchwork bark of a plain tree, Joseph had not taken his eyes from the front door of the café for the last ten minutes. As the door opened, he pushed himself away from the tree, unfolded his arms and took half a step forward. He was aware that his heart was beating faster than normal, and that he was feeling even hotter and more flustered now than he was some ten minutes earlier.

Julia and her friend stepped out from the café, and for a couple of minutes, they stood chatting on the pavement. Joseph changed the weight on his feet from one to the other, folded and unfolded his arms, took a few steps forward and then stopped, not knowing quite what to do. Eventually the two girls stopped chatting. Julia's friend turned, waved and set off down the street, walking away from Joseph. Julia returned the wave and started to walk in Joseph's direction. Finally, having pulled himself together, he looked both ways and seeing that the road was clear, he crossed over to the pavement on Julia's side of the street. Julia was ambling along, looking casually across to the other side of the road towards a group of ladies who had stopped to talk on the pavement. When they were only five paces apart, Joseph called out her name – "Julia!"

She immediately turned her gaze towards Joseph, brought her right hand up to her neck and stopped walking.

"Joseph," she said "Joseph, it's you."

Somehow, he managed the last few steps and stopped in front of her. They stared at each other for what seem like an age, before Joseph managed to summon up a few more words.

"I just thought … I just thought that it would be nice to say hello," he stammered. "I mean… well, you know… I mean, we haven't really been able to talk for ages… I just thought… well, you know…"

"I know," Julia smiled. "I knew that you would come."

They stood perfectly still, about a foot apart, just looking at each other as people brushed past them on the pavement. Joseph's heart rate, which had been beating as hard as if he had run flat out for twenty minutes through the beech woods at home, was beginning to return to something like normal, and now, although he wasn't really sure what he might say or do next, he felt suddenly, strangely calm.

"You knew I'd come?" he asked.

"Oh", said Julia "I didn't know where or when. I didn't know it would be here, today, in the street. I just knew that one day you would come to see me".

"Oh," said Joseph.

Chapter Seven

THE OIL DEPOT RAID

The postman didn't push the letters through the Carter's letter box as usual, but knocked at the door instead. After a while, Granny Carter shuffled out from the kitchen, crossed the hallway and opened the door.

"Morning George" she said, "Have you so much post that you can't get it through the letter box this morning?"

"Morning Catharine", George joined in the joke. "Yes, you're so popular, you'll be having a separate delivery service soon," Then, stooping lower he added quietly, "Is Joseph here?"

Catharine wasn't at all surprised at George's request; in fact, she had expected it, as on the few occasions that the postman had knocked on the door, he always wanted a word with Joseph and Catharine knew why, but never asked.

"He's in the barn across the yard," she nodded.

"Right," said George, "I'll go and find him".

Joseph was loading a trailer with hay. George called out as he walked towards him - "Joseph!"

Joseph turned and, seeing George walking towards him, first rubbed his hands together and then on his trousers, took half a dozen steps towards him and held out his hand.

"Morning George, what's new mate?"

"There's a job coming up" George replied. As he spoke, he reached into his post-bag and pulled out an old map of the area. "You need to meet at seven o'clock tomorrow evening. Just here." He held the map up and pointed to a place that marked a spot in the woods that both men knew well.

"No problem" Joseph nodded, "Full kit?"

"Yes," George confirmed, "Full kit. It could be a couple of days."

The two men shook hands again and George turned and walked away.

Joseph watched him for a while, and then, as he reached the door, he called out "Be careful mate!"

Without stopping or looking back, George waved a hand in the air and shouted, "I always am!"

Joseph stayed where he was for a while, folded his arms, looked down at the dusty ground, kicked at an imaginary ball and thought to himself, "What will it be this time?"

After supper that evening, Joseph spoke quietly to his father whilst they dried the dishes.

"I'm sorry Dad, but I won't be around for a couple of days from tea time tomorrow. You'll have to get someone to cover my work for me. I'll get back as soon as I can."

Charles stopped drying the saucepan that he was holding and looked straight into his son's eyes. He knew better than to ask Joseph where he might be going, or why he needed time off at such short notice. They held each other's gaze for no more than a few seconds and then Joseph eventually dropped his gaze to the floor and said again.

"I'm sorry Dad."

Charles cleared his throat, carefully placed the saucepan on the draining board and flicked the tea towel over his shoulder. Then he put both arms around Joseph's shoulders and pulled him in close and hugged him like he used to when he was a little boy. Joseph closed his eyes and dipped his head in close to his father's, their stubbly faces rubbing against each other. Charles cleared his throat again and spoke softly into Joseph's ear.

"That's alright son, I know how hard it is – it's hard for all of us. But you're doing the right thing; just make sure you always come back safe."

Slowly they separated, patting each other on the arms, and carried on with the drying up. Mary, who had been sitting at the kitchen table looking through a recipe book, had looked up just as the two men had hugged. As they returned to the drying up, she slowly got to her feet, placed the book back on the shelf and walked off towards the sitting room. With every step that she took, another tear ran down her cheeks. By the time she reached the sitting room window, she was dabbing at her eyes with her hanky and struggling to control herself. She half lent against a curtain that hung against the wall by the window and looked out across the garden. It was a beautiful evening – so pretty, so still, so peaceful.

The next evening, Joseph made sure that he had left plenty of time to prepare himself before meeting the others in the woods. He ate a larger than usual supper and packed a bag with all the extra gear he thought he might need. He also packed a lunch bag stuffed full of enough provisions to get him through at least the next twenty-four hours. The last thing that he pushed into his back-pack was a large flask of tea.

At about six o'clock, he wheeled his bike over to one of the old chicken houses at the back of the farmyard, propped it up against the wooden side panels, and nipped inside through the half open door. It was very dark inside and smelt musty. He walked steadily through the shed, holding his hands out in front of him in case he should bump into something. Soon he reached the far end where there was an old feed bin. A small shaft of light penetrated the dark just to one side of the bin, which helped him to see where there was a gap between it and the end wall.

He reached behind the bin, quickly located what he was looking for, and pulled it out. His rifle was just as he had left it some two weeks ago: wrapped in hessian sacking and tied with twine. He carried the parcel carefully and made his way back towards the doorway that he could see easily now, as light poured into the dark chicken shed, dust particles dancing like snowflakes in the early evening air.

As Joseph emerged from the shed, he cast his eye around the yard to check that no one was watching him. Confident that he was alone, he hitched both straps of his kit-bag over his shoulders, quickly tied the still wrapped rifle to the crossbar of his bike, and rode off towards the footpath that led into the woods at the top of the farm. As Joseph prepared himself and set off, many other men from nearby farms, hamlets and villages were going through the same motions; all with the same thoughts going through their heads. Everyone hoping that they would be coming home again.

Joseph reached the rendezvous point twenty minutes early. He pushed his bike in behind a stand of hazel, leaned against an old elm tree and then stood absolutely still for a while, looking back along the four tracks that met in the clearing and listening to the sounds of the woods. He knew them so well that if there was a thing out of place, he would spot it immediately. He satisfied himself that there were no man-made noises, not even the sound of another bike nearby. He carefully unwrapped his rifle and tucked the hessian sack in his bag. There was the slightest rustle as a gentle breeze stirred the leaves at the very tops of the trees. Off to his left, perhaps at about twenty yards, he could hear the scraping of a blackbird in search of food as it raked through the old leaves that lay on the floor of the woods. Some distance away in the other direction, a black cap was calling, its pit, pit, pit call unmistakable to Joseph's ear.

Almost immediately, high in a beech tree only a few yards back down the pathway from where he had just come, another black cap started up in answer to the first one. Joseph would have been happy just to stand there, tuning in to the sounds of the woods and looking out for movement; not just from the birds but from animals as well. He knew from experience that if you just stood still for a short while in the countryside, it wasn't long before you were rewarded with the sight and sounds of the animals and birds that lived there.

Joseph leaned back harder against the trunk of the old elm, closed his eyes, crossed his arms and allowed his senses and his mind to wander off through the evening air that felt like a warm blanket keeping him and the woods safe. Now, a long way away to the North, he could hear the hammering of a greater spotted woodpecker, with echoes of the hammering bouncing off of other trees nearby. There was another rustling from the tree canopy just above him and to his right. He opened his eyes just in time to see a squirrel's tail disappear behind a leafy branch near the top of the tree. As he leaned forward slightly to try to catch another glimpse of the squirrel, he became aware of a faint new noise coming from back down the track.

It was not the noise of an animal or a bird moving through the woods, it was not the sound of leaves, twigs or branches moving in the wind; it was the unmistakeable sound of men coming towards him. Joseph quietly slid down the tree trunk, picked up his rifle and haversack and crawled on his hands and knees behind the elm tree. The sounds were much clearer now – probably three of them, and there was no doubt that they were coming his way. He peered from behind the elm tree, and as he did so, he automatically released the safety catch on his rifle with his right thumb, very slowly bringing it up to the best position for firing; changing the weight on his knees, pulling the stock into his right shoulder, slowing down his breathing and looking through the sights at the three figures who he could see through the undergrowth, but could not yet identify.

They were moving at a good pace, purposefully, as if on a mission, and about two yards apart – the man at the front had a rifle slung over his shoulder. Joseph took aim at his chest, held that position, and waited for them to come into full view. As they stepped into the dappled light of a clearing about thirty yards in front of him, he could now see clearly who they were – Alexander Miller, Albert Rose and Philip Greenfield. Joseph slipped the safety catch back on, stood up and, hitching the rifle over his shoulder, whistled softly so as not to startle his friends as he stepped slowly from behind the tree.

"There you are," said Alex.

"Where have you been?" asked Joseph, "And where are your bikes? I thought you were Gerry marching along the path. I had you in my sights for your last fifty yards you know."

"Sorry mate. We hid our bikes a couple of hundred yards back".

"Yes." said Bert. "And thanks for not shooting us this time".

"Think nothing of it mate", Joseph grinned.

Over the next ten minutes, others arrived at the rendezvous point. Brian Steel had been appointed leader, and up until this point, he was the only one of the twelve who knew what their mission was. After allowing a minute for everyone to greet each other, he called the men together.

"Right," he said. "It's going to be dark in about one and a half hours' time, so we need to push on as quickly as we can and cover as much distance as we can whilst the light is with us. I'll tell you now that we're heading East, and that our target is over twenty miles away. I'll give you the complete lowdown a bit later, but in the meantime, let's concentrate on covering some distance. Come on then."

Brian set off down the footpath that led off to the east, and the others fell in behind him in single file. Joseph noticed that a number of the men were carrying heavy back packs. "Explosives," he thought.

After about an hour they emerged from the wood and followed the path that tracked the edge of meadows, protected by tall hedges. They hadn't seen a soul so far, and now that it was late in the evening, and they were a long way from any villages, they were not expecting to run into anybody. Nevertheless, they didn't talk as they walked; they knew how far voices could carry on a balmy summer's evening. By the time dark started to fall, they had already covered about six miles, but being such a fine evening, it was quite easy to see where they were going. By a five-bar gate, where the path opened out onto a grass track, Brian called a halt and waited until everyone had gathered round.

"Now" he said, "Take a quick breather and then we'll do a couple more hours and see how we're going. If the visibility stays good, we'll push on through the night."

The men chatted quietly whilst they had a bite to eat and drank their tea. In less than ten minutes they were on their way again. Disturbed, three cock pheasants flew out from the low branches of a young sycamore tree just in front of them. They dipped and flew low across the meadow, gliding down into the protection of the long grass on the far side. Although, for one split second, the sudden clattering noise and alarm calls of the pheasants made a few of the men jump, it was the slightest of scares. These were normal sounds of the countryside at night, almost welcome in their familiarity.

Most of the men knew these pathways well. As kids, they had spent whole days wandering along the country tracks. Sometimes they would just walk. Usually they would carry food with them, simple things like bread and cheese and maybe an apple. Sometimes they had a lump of fruit cake as well. To drink they usually had cold tea or perhaps milk. In fact, what they had in their lunch packs was very similar to what their fathers took with them when they were working in the fields. Sometimes they would play games that went on all day. They never thought of danger, of getting lost or being attacked – they never dreamt that they would actually be fighting for their freedom, although many of the boys' games involved plenty of pretend fighting with sticks as guns – they certainly never thought that they would be walking through these fields at night, on their way to who knew what, not knowing whether they would all return home safe.

The next two hours passed without incident. Nothing unusual happened, they hadn't seen anyone and as far as they knew, no one had seen them. The light was still good and they were making good progress. At the end of a hedgerow, just before the pathway broke out across open down land, Brian brought his men to a halt again.

"Well done lads," he said. "Let's stop here for ten minutes ... everyone alright?"

A soft mumbled reply from some of the men indicated that all was well. Several took their flasks from their packs and poured a little more tea into their cups, others broke off some bread and cheese or a piece of cake and they all sat or stood in silence, wondering what awaited them at the end of their long march. Most of the men were smokers and were beginning to feel the effect of not having had a cigarette for a good few hours; but they all knew that no one would be allowed to light up out here.

You could spot the light from a struck match and smell tobacco smoke from a long way off. They knew that they would have to wait until they were deep in the middle of some woods.

Brian took out his map, and by holding it at an odd angle, he could just about pick up enough light to make out where they were. He turned to Alex, who happened to be standing next to him, and said in a soft voice, "That's about another five miles done – nearly half way now. Next time we stop, I'll tell everyone where we're headed." Alex just nodded as he pushed his flask back into his pack.

For the next fifteen minutes, they walked across open downland, with only the odd few pieces of stunted blackthorn for cover. They took great care not to crest the hill, reckoning that although they were out in the open, the chances of being seen at night against the rough downland background were slim. Never the less, they all felt a lot more comfortable once they reached the edge of a large beech wood that hung on the gentle south facing slopes of the Downs. As they walked in amongst the trees, still going east, they could just make out the sea, about ten miles to the south. A half-moon suddenly showed itself from behind thin grey clouds and the reflected beams danced and twinkled on the waves in the English Channel.

"That's pretty" Joseph whispered, to no one in particular.

For a few more miles, they were able to walk just inside the edge of the woods, with the moon and the sparkling sea as company. As they came to the end of the trees, Brian Steel held up his arm, indicating that they should stop. It took a minute or so for the men to come together again, and they then stood as one, waiting for instructions.

"Right" said Brian, "We're getting fairly close to our target now, so I need to tell you what our mission is. We're going to march for another few miles and then, as morning breaks, we're going to take shelter where we can, hopefully get some sleep during the day, and then tomorrow night, we're going to attack the fuel dump at Arningham. And when I say attack, I don't mean with all guns blazing. In fact, I mean the very opposite. We need to get in, plant our explosives, and get away as quiet as mice. As most of you know, the Germans have a huge stock of fuel there: petrol, diesel, kerosene and God knows what else. It's very well defended with security fences and lights, and of course, I'm sure there will be plenty of guards and guard dogs. So, any questions?"

The men had dozens of questions, but none that seemed worth voicing. Not at this precise moment in time anyway.

After checking his map, Brian led the way from the cover of the woods into countryside that was more open, but with a fair bit of cover from individual ash, oak and yew trees. There were also big tufts of rough grass, ancient ant hills and brambles with old man's beard interwoven between the giant thorny branches. All along a slightly raised bank at the top of the slope was a huge rabbit warren, and every now then, a rabbit could be seen bolting for one of the holes that stood out where the bare chalky earth caught the moonlight.

Walking was much more difficult now.

The men were spread out over a range of one hundred yards, all doing their best to stay within the shadows of the odd trees and scattered scrub. The uneven ground and the dappled moonlight made it difficult to pick out the best pathways, and the men stumbled as they made their way towards a large patch of dark trees that they could just about make out in the distance. After another mile, they reached the cover of Hanger Forest, a plantation of tens of thousands of larch trees. They had been planted by German prisoners from the Great War.

They were about forty feet tall, and hardly a shard of light penetrated through their great thick green branches. The forest floor was littered with pine needles that made walking much easier, although they now had a new problem – they could hardly see where they were going. Brian called to the men nearest to him to stop, and in turn the message was passed on up and down the line until they all collected together again. Brian counted the men as they came close and once he was satisfied that they were all together, he spoke.

"Listen" he said, "It's a bit tricky trying to walk through here in the dark; so, what I propose is that we wait here for an hour or so for daybreak. We might just get enough light then to see where we're going. We'll then get through to the other side of the forest where we'll settle down for the day and get some rest. Why don't you spread yourselves out a bit, take the weight off your feet and have a rest? You can smoke now if you want to, but don't forget, when we move on in the morning, it's no smoking again."

The men spread themselves out and sat in twos and threes. Most took out their tobacco and sat quietly rolling their own, but a few had ready-made Woodbines and lit up immediately. One or two opened up their backpacks and found something to eat, but most didn't this time; they were content just to sit, rest and smoke. Being country men, they were used to sitting and taking a break together. They and their forefathers had done it for centuries whilst working the land. They were also used to sharing – a piece of cake in return for an apple, some cheese for a hard-boiled egg. The old thermos flasks and flip top bottles were soon out again, but then after about twenty minutes, bags were strapped back up and they all sat in silence. They knew in their hearts that this was the easy bit. What they were all thinking about was what tomorrow night would bring.

Most of the men knew Arningham. Over the years, some had gone to the cinema there and a few of the men had played in the local football and cricket league games against the little town. It was a friendly rivalry that had gone on for longer than anyone could remember and was typical of the social life of villagers and small towns' people up and down the country. The men also knew Arningham's pubs very well. Joseph, even though he was not quite eighteen years old, had fond memories of drinking more than enough Arningham Best Bitter one summer's evening just before war broke out. A coach had delivered him and his teammates to the middle of the town for a game of cricket, and both teams had enjoyed a great evening in The Plough before they were taken home. It was well into the small hours by the time they arrived back in Watersham. Many of the men had fallen asleep on the coach, and it took those that were still sober enough some time to wake the last few and to get them started for their homes.

By five o'clock in the morning, the sun started to brighten the sky and the light beneath the canopy of the larch trees began to improve. At five thirty, Brian stood up, brushed the pine needles from his trousers, pulled his backpack on and swung his rifle over his shoulder. The men took their cue and got to their feet in readiness to set off. Brian waved his arm and they moved off together, spreading themselves out as they did so. Walking was very easy and very comfortable. They neither saw nor heard any movement for the next hour. Everything was quiet. Eventually, they could just make out where the forest ran out and the meadows that ran around the western edge of the town began.

Brian raised his arm again and signalled his men to join him. As soon as they were all close enough, he spoke quietly to them.

"That's more than close enough" he said, "In fact I think that we'll move back a bit to make sure that we're well out of sight."

He signalled for them all to move back and after about two hundred yards, he stopped and waited for the men to come close again.

"Right" he said, "This is far enough. Now spread out in a line at least ten yards apart, each one of you, get yourselves behind a tree, make yourselves as comfortable as you can, and get some sleep". The men peeled off and without further direction, each found a suitable tree. For the next half-an-hour or so, some settled down immediately to sleep, some wandered off deeper into the forest to relieve themselves and others sat with their backs to the trees, enjoying a little more to eat and drink. Eventually, with the exception of George Staples, who had volunteered to take first watch, they all slept.

After about an hour, George caught the scent of wood smoke drifting in from the town and during the next watch, Arthur Bourne heard a train pulling into Arningham Station at about eleven o'clock in the morning. At twelve thirty, Joseph heard dogs barking, but after a few minutes all was quiet again. At four in the afternoon, Alfie Moore, on his watch, heard a train pulling out from Arningham Station and so did most of the men, as they were nearly all awake now. At five o'clock, Brian took a short trenching spade that was strapped to his back-back and walked back into the woods to find a quiet place to defecate. After a few minutes, he walked back to the line in a different direction towards where he thought his last man would be, and finding Tony Smith wide awake, he greeted him quietly and whispered, "Pow-wow in fifteen minutes," and walked off towards the next man. After giving the same message to all his men, Brian walked back to his place near the middle of the line. All the men were milling around now. Some wandered off deeper into the forest with their trenching spades, some opened their packs and looked for refreshments, and others stood leaning against the trees. Most of the men were gasping for a smoke, but knew that they couldn't risk it.

The men gathered around Brian.

"OK, so as soon as it's dark, we'll be off" he said. "That will be in about four hours. When we set off, we'll go around the north side of the town, cutting across the railway line about half a mile away. Then we will head west and drop down to the back of the railway station. We'll hole up there until after midnight, and then get set to plant the explosives at the fuel dump on the south side of the station. I suggest that you get some more rest before we set off. After setting the timers on the explosives, we need to get as far away as possible as quickly as possible, and we will certainly be on the move until first light tomorrow morning. Should we get split up for any reason, make your way back home as best you can, but don't go directly home. Take your time. Only move at night and stay safe. OK. We'll talk again later."

With that, the men moved back to their positions and most settled down again to rest for a few more precious hours. The time dragged for them all. At about eight thirty, the light began to fade quite quickly and at nine o'clock Brian called everyone back together again.

"Right," he said, "we're going to move out. Make sure your bed is levelled out and that you haven't left any signs of us having been here. We don't want to leave any clues as to where we came from do we?"

"No Sir," they murmured in unison as each man walked back to check the area around his tree. At ten minutes past nine, Brian waved his men forward.

They walked in a line abreast for about half an hour until they reached the northern edge of Hanger Forest. Immediately adjoining the trees there were a series of small meadows with high hedges protecting them. Still staying under the cover of the last of the larches, Brian walked towards the hedge on the west side of the nearest meadow, indicating to his men to form a single file and follow him.

As they walked behind the hedge, the men automatically adopted their "be ready" march that they had trained so many times for: five yards apart, rifles and machine guns pointing at the ground, trigger fingers on the trigger guard, safety catches on. It was fairly slow going for the next twenty minutes. The grass and scrub behind the trees by the meadow had not been cut for a long time, making walking difficult. Once they came to the end of the series of meadows, they stepped over a rusty barbed wire fence, crossed a grass track and walked into a small copse. Having walked about fifty yards into the copse, Brian stopped and waited for everyone to catch up. After having checked their number, Brian set off again and the line of men followed on. They were only in the copse for about ten minutes before they came to the railway line. It was quite dark now and getting difficult to send signals up and down the line.

Brian waited until the men were close and then explained. "Look; we're vulnerable here. After listening and making sure that there's no train coming, we have to cross the line one at a time, get over that fence over there, cross that small meadow and then take cover in an orchard on the far side." The men looked where Brian was pointing, but had to take his word for it, as they could hardly see the fence on the other side of the railway line, let alone an orchard on the other side of the meadow.

Brian stepped out from the copse, walked over to the line and knelt down in the long grass. He listened for a while, heard nothing other than some sheep bleating some distance away, and waved the first man over. Joseph walked quickly past Brian over the line, climbed over the fence, and started on his way across the meadow. As he disappeared out of view, Brian waved George over, then Charlie Stewart, and then, one by one, the whole group – all the time listening for trains and any other noise that might mean trouble. After about three minutes, Brian himself followed the others and was pleased to see everyone grouped together under cover of the orchard.

"All present and correct" said Charlie Stewart.

"Well done" Brian replied. "Now follow me".

They walked diagonally through the orchard until they came to the side of a farm track. Growing in the next field was a tall crop of maize. Not far off, they could hear the sounds of diesel engines.

"Sounds like heavy trucks to me", Joseph whispered to the man next to him.

Brian spoke to Charlie who was standing nearest to him.

"Go straight across the lane Charlie, walk for one hundred paces into the middle of the crop, and then wait for the others".

Charlie looked up and down the lane, saw that it was all clear and set off across the lane, disappearing into the maize. One after another they all did the same until they found themselves standing in a group in the middle of the field with tall maize all around them.

Brian joined them and whispered, "We're going to stay here until midnight; so, make yourselves comfortable. The back of the railway station is only about three hundred yards that way." He waved in a general south-easterly direction.

The men started to push some of the maize plants over so that they could have a bit more room to sit down. Dogs barked in the distance. Joseph looked at his watch. It was only ten thirty.

The next hour and a half seemed to take all night to go by, but eventually, St. Peter's church clock chimed midnight. Brian stood up and spoke again.

"Now listen up. The boys with the explosives have already been briefed as to where and how to set them. It's our job to make sure that we give them all the help and cover that they need so that they can just get on with their job without worrying about getting caught. Ok? Right: follow me."

This time, walking through the crop wasn't quite so easy, as they had to cross the rows diagonally. On reaching the edge of the field, they could see the back of the railway station. They stood for a while just back in from the edge, still under cover of the maize. Brian walked a further forty yards to his left, until he came across a gap in the fence. He waited there and waved the others towards him. Brian leaned towards Tom Harrison and whispered instructions to him. Tom stepped forward, checked that it was all clear, bent low and walked quickly to the far end of the back of the station where some rough old hurdle fencing surrounded a storage area. He found a gap in the layered hazel and stared through.

From his position, he had a good view of most of the station on the other side of the railway line. There were dim orange lights emanating from three separate windows along the far side of the platform. Tom assumed that these were the main offices or guard rooms for the station. There was no one on the platform, no guards or any signs of movement, and as far as he could see, there was nothing moving beyond the station where he guessed the fuel depot was; although through the gloom, he could only just make out more orange lights in the distance. He listened for ten more seconds and then, being sure that all was clear, he waved the next man over.

After a few minutes, the whole platoon was spaced out for the full length of and behind the north side of the station. Brian walked along the line giving them specific instructions as to what to do next. After speaking to the last man, he turned and waved. James Miles took this as his signal and immediately worked his way to the end of the hurdles, along to the west end of the north platform and then, as quietly as he could, climbed over the low wrought iron fence on to the platform. He flicked the safety catch off on his sub machine gun and, keeping as low as he could, and remaining as tight to the wall as possible; he started to walk along it. He stopped for a while as he spotted one of his mates climbing on to the platform at the east end. He waved, although at this distance and in such bad light he couldn't make out who it was; but his mate waved back.

They slowly walked towards each other, all the time keeping one eye out for sudden movement from the platform on the other side of the track. Each man passed only closed doors and dark windows as they edged their way along the platform, until they reached a main office in the middle. By now, James recognised the other man as Eddie Brooks, a butcher's assistant from Mason's Butchers' in the High

Street in Watersham. They nodded to each other nervously as they both spotted the faint glow of a lamp coming from within the office and shining through the small arched glass panel above the doorway. James leaned towards the door and listened. From somewhere behind it came the sound of snoring. James felt some of the tension leave his body and he turned to Eddie and whispered: "Fast asleep."

The two men then retraced their steps, all the time keeping an eye on the opposite platform. After reporting back that all was clear, the men moved one at a time across the north platform and down onto the railway track and up to the edge of the platform on the south side. Brian detailed three men to take up positions here whilst the main group split in to two, with one half mounting the platform at the east end and the other half at the west. As they did so, somewhere on the other side of the station they heard the sound of a door opening, and for the first time they heard voices and dogs barked. All the men instinctively flattened themselves up against the walls. The three men down on the track trained their guns on the main ticket office doors in the centre of the south platform, any moment expecting guards and guard dogs to appear to see what the noise was about.

Nothing happened.

The dogs stopped barking, a door could be heard to close and all fell silent. Brian and his men began to breathe again. There were many more offices on the south platform, and lights could be seen through a number of the windows, but Brian guessed that at half past midnight, most of the occupants were asleep.

The two groups had now reached the southern side of the station where the main entrance was. There was a dim light burning over the main entrance. A tarmac concourse about thirty yards deep ran along the front of the station, where two German army trucks were parked. On the other side of the vehicles was a high mesh fence, and beyond that, seven large fuel tanks could be seen. Low strength orange security lights with overhead shades were fixed intermittently around the perimeter fence, and off to the right, inside the compound, was a large wooden building that looked as if it might double as a works office and a guard room. Brian guessed that this was where the earlier noise had come from, and that there were almost certainly guards and guard dogs inside. There was no way of knowing how many German soldiers there might be in the main station building, or whether others were billeted nearby.

Brian hoped that they would never find out. Following their earlier instructions, two men from each group took up positions near to the corners of the front of the station as the others moved quickly and silently across to the vehicles by the fence. Two more took up positions under the trucks, and the others spread out around the vehicles.

The six men carrying explosives slipped their packs from their backs and undid the straps. Whilst they prepared their explosives, Joseph and Alexander stepped out from the shadow of the trucks, removed heavy duty wire cutters from their packs and started to cut at the mesh fence. The clicking noise of the wire giving way to the cutters seemed to the men nearby to be like the sound of thunder. Each snip sent a shudder through their bodies – they all looked fearfully towards the door of the wooden building. The noise of the snipping seemed to go on forever, but there was no reaction from the dogs or the guards, and eventually a large piece of mesh fell to the ground, leaving a gaping hole in the fence. Joseph and Alexander stepped back into the shadows of the trucks and stowed the wire cutters back into their bags.

After a short silence, Brian tapped Stan Stiles on his shoulder. In response, he immediately ducked through the hole in the fence and walking as quickly as he could in a half-doubled position, made his way to the fuel tank on the far side of the compound. At five second intervals, five more men followed, each one targeting a specific tank. They each carried three sets of explosives with instructions to set two on each tank and to use the third, if they needed to, to cause additional damage. They weren't to use any explosives on the station itself. Stan and his team were well-trained and quick. Within minutes they had the explosives in position on the furthest six tanks and, as they fell back, two men attached more to the last tank, as the others made their way back through the hole in the fence.

Just as the last two men turned to make their way back, the door of the wooden building opened and a German soldier stepped out shouting something into the night air as two or three guard dogs started barking behind him. The two men still inside the compound fell to the ground, the men by the trucks pushed themselves harder back into the shadows and those that were able to, trained their rifles and sub machine guns on the soldier and the wooden building behind him. Those back at the station trained their guns on the office doorways, fully expecting all hell to break loose at any moment. The German walked slowly away from the building, and as he staggered and swayed slightly, Brian and his men realised that he wasn't armed. He was going for a pee. He stopped ten yards beyond the building and spent nearly a minute pissing against a silver birch tree. Whilst he did so, another voice yelled out from inside and the dogs fell silent again. The soldier turned, steadied himself and slowly walked back to the wooden building. After what seemed like an eternity, he eventually stepped back through the door and slammed it behind him. Immediately, the dogs started to howl again, and as they did so, Brian signalled to the two men still lying on the ground to get up.

As quickly as they could, Jim Bashford and John Steel ducked back through the hole in the fence. They strapped the last of their explosives to the three vehicles by the fence and, one by one, the men made their way back to the side of the station, across the first platform, down onto the tracks, across the north platform, down behind the station buildings and back into the maize. Alexander was the last man to reach the field, and as he did so, he noticed that the dogs had stopped barking and the station and the compound were quiet again. Somewhere in the distance, there was the distinctive sound of a heavy goods train.

The timers on the explosives had all been set as near as possible to fifteen minutes; but all the men knew that the timers were not as accurate as the manufacturers claimed, and that in reality, fifteen minutes could mean anywhere between ten and twenty minutes. Brian did a quick head count as they reached the middle of the field and having satisfied himself that they were all present, they moved off without delay. Alexander checked his watch as he set off. Three minutes had already elapsed. The men followed Brian as quickly as they could through to the other side of the maize field, across the farm track and back into the orchard.

As they emerged from the far side, Brian beckoned the men to him, and breathing heavily, said, "Now listen: things could get lively around here in a bit, so we need to push on, but keep your wits about you. Hopefully they will have no idea where we came from or where we have gone to, but just in case we were seen coming in, we'll go back a different way. We'll turn north now, straight up to the top of the Downs. Come on then." As he finished speaking, Brian glanced at his watch. He reckoned about seven minutes had already gone by since the timers had been set.

As they set off towards the Downs, the sound of a heavy goods train heading towards Arningham from the west could now be heard very clearly. Walking started to become more difficult as the climb uphill became steeper.

It was mostly scrubland on these slopes, long tufted grass, brambles, wind-blown blackthorn and hawthorn trees with occasional outcrops of white chalk breaking through the thin topsoil. The men had spread out as much as they could and were doing their best to keep close to what little cover there was, but if it wasn't for the fact that it was one thirty in the morning, with a lot of cloud cover, they could have easily been seen by any casual observer just happening to cast an eye across the side of the hill. A hundred yards from the crest they reached some heavier scrub made up predominantly of giant clumps of blackberry bushes that were about eight feet tall. As the men scrambled to find their way around these, the first of the explosives detonated.

Although the men had all been anticipating the explosion, they fell to the ground as one in an automatic reflex action. Each then turned to look back for the first time at the compound at Arningham. From their position near the top of the hill, they had a perfect view of the town, and as the first fuel tank went up in flames, the night sky lit up and the underside of the clouds began to glow orange and red. Only a few seconds went by before the second and then the third explosion echoed against the side of the hill. The colours reflected against the clouds doubled in intensity as a great pall of fire and thick black smoke rose up from behind the station.

More explosions followed, and large pieces of black debris flew high into the air. For perhaps another minute, the noise of the primary and secondary explosions seemed to be continuous and the noise was deafening. The night sky was now so light that it was easy to pick out individual landmarks around the town: the football field, the primary school, the high street with St. Peter's church and church yard at the top end were laid out in the fire light like a model village.

As the explosions and fire reached a crescendo, so the train that had been heard earlier pulled into the station. It was a heavy goods train with about thirty wagons full of coal. The driver, realising the danger, was trying to pull away again to get clear of the fire that was now threatening the station.

Great clouds of smoke and steam were coming from the engine as the driver did his best to get the train rolling again. Painfully slowly, it started to pull away, as burning pieces of debris fell all around. As the last wagon cleared the platform, yet more explosions reverberated against the side of the hill, and for the first time, uniformed figures could be seen on the north platform.

Brian stood up and called out to his men: "Come on lads; let's get out of here whilst we can!!"

The hillside was lit up as brightly as a fine English summer's day, and as the men stood to continue their climb up the last part of the hill, the attention of one of the German soldiers was taken for a split second as he spotted two or three tiny dots of reflected light bouncing back from the hillside. As he watched for another second, he was sure that he saw dark figures moving amongst the scrub near the top of the hill. For another moment, he stopped and stared, but as he did so, a great cloud of black acrid smoke drifted across the station, forcing him to jump down onto the line, where for the next few minutes he knelt choking and gasping for breath. By the time the smoke had cleared, and he had breathed in enough fresh air to stop coughing, the light on the side of the hill had dimmed and he couldn't even make out the clumps of brambles, let alone the silhouettes of moving men.

As the men crested the hill and started to make their way down the other side, one last enormous explosion echoed around the hillside. As the rumbling echoes died away, there was a strange flickering of light in the night sky like sheet lightning.

Now that the explosions had stopped, the noises of alarmed animals and birds could be heard all around the countryside. Cock pheasants were calling out from their perches in the hedgerows. Cattle were lowing in the valley below and sheep were bleating all over the hillside.

A large flock of pigeons flew over and then clattered

into the branches of a group of beech trees as they made the best of a bad job of trying to land in the near darkness. Brian looked at his watch. It was ten past two. Lights had come on at the few farmsteads that dotted the landscape below them and farm dogs barked.

Soon the men reached a chalk farm track. The whiteness of the path stood out clearly from the dark grassland through which it had been cut over hundreds of years. As they walked in single file, Joseph wondered how many times armed men had walked this track in the middle of the night before: perhaps the Royalists and the Roundheads during the English Civil War, King Harold's army that rushed to resist William the Conqueror and the Norman invaders, the Danish armies and Viking raiding parties, the Saxons, the Romans and British tribes. Now, here he was marching with a group of soldiers from the English Resistance, and Joseph wondered – who might be next?

They followed the track for about three or four miles as it led them lower and lower down into the lowlands on the north side of the hill. The countryside was quieter now, but there was the distinct smell of burning in the air. Alexander turned and walked backwards for a few steps and could see, against the night sky, still lighter than normal because of the fire, dark clouds of smoke hanging on the top of the Downs above them. He found himself thinking about the German soldiers and their guard dogs, and wondered what might have become of them – although he was pretty sure that he already knew the answer. He hoped that the steam train had made it to safety.

At three thirty the men reached mixed woodland four miles northwest of Arningham. Once they were deep into the woods, Brian called a halt.

"Take ten minutes".

The men were glad to stop and have a chance to catch their breath. Most drank first, draining the last from their thermos flasks and bottles. Some picked at their food, but no one felt much like eating. The craving for nicotine was becoming desperate for some of the men, and Brian knew that this would cause problems if they couldn't have a smoke soon.

"Listen," he said. "If we can march on until dawn, and find somewhere sensible to stop, you can have a smoke – but before that, we need to find drinking water to refill our bottles. It'll be a long time yet before we get home." Five minutes later they were back on their feet and spread well out as they headed west through the woods.

For the next hour and a half, the men walked in silence. Having come out from the woods, they had gone through a mixture of small meadows, some rough pasture, a large field of maize and another copse.

As the first signs of dawn began to break, they were walking along the edge of a recently harvested wheat field towards some farm buildings that stood on the other side of a lane that ran along its side. Checking all around, the men crossed the lane and walked into the farmyard. There were three, four wheeled horse carts in the yard, two empty and one piled high with straw. Four heavy horses leaned over their stable doors watching every move that the men made. Joseph and some of the others went to the horses and stroked their warm soft faces. The animals snorted their approval and nudged the men as they sniffed at their bags. Albert Rose undid his back-pack, took out a large apple, unsheathed a large knife from his belt and expertly cut the fruit into four. He then approached each horse separately, and, holding one hand flat, allowed each one to take their quarter of apple. The feeling of the horses taking the apple from his hand with their beautifully soft and sensitive lips was reassuring. It felt like a perfectly natural and normal thing to do – just as it should be.

The horses chewed on their pieces of apple as small drops of juice dripped from their mouths down the front of the stable doors. Some of the men stood and watched with big smiles on their faces.

Bert turned to see some of the others lining up to fill their thermos flasks and bottles with water. Philip Greenfield had found a mains water tap on the wall on the other side of the yard. After about fifteen minutes, the men had had a good drink and filled up every thermos flask and bottle that they had between them. Looking around carefully as they came back out onto the lane, they crossed back to the stubbly field and headed off towards some beech woods that stretched out from the far end of the field as far as the eye could see. By the time they left the field and entered the woods, the sky was much brighter. They walked on for another twenty minutes until Brian waved his arm in the air, indicating that they should stop.

"This will do" he said.

They were still a good fifteen miles from Watersham, but all the men knew that travelling during the daytime would be far too risky and that they would have to stay where they were until darkness fell, when hopefully they could push on home in one hit. Brian walked amongst his men for a while, telling them what a great job they had done and encouraging them to think about tomorrow.

"Just think" he said, "by this time tomorrow you'll all be tucked up in your beds". As he finished talking to each small group, his final words were "by the way, you can smoke now if you like." By the time Brian had finished his walk around, most of the men were enjoying their smokes. They followed the same routine as the day before, with one man taking a watch of about two hours before handing over to the next.

The day passed by fairly uneventfully. Occasionally, farm animals had been heard calling in the fields that bordered the woods, and on two or three occasions the sentries had heard the hum of engines – probably tractors and other farm vehicles.

At three in the afternoon, in the middle of Alexander Miller's watch, dogs could be heard barking some way off to the south. Alexander listened hard, trying to work out how many there were, and in which direction they were going. After ten minutes, he decided that there were at least three dogs and that they were moving from east to west along the hill to the south. Several of the men were awake now, and they were all listening to the barking in the distance. Alexander walked over to Brian, reached down and gently shook his shoulder.

"What is it Alex?"

"We can hear dogs barking in the distance Sir. It sounds like they're moving from east to west along the Downs. Could be a German patrol?"

Brian sat up and listened. "How long have they been making a noise?"

"Maybe ten minutes?"

Brian got to his feet, brushed himself down and pulled his jacket down straight. "Right" he said, "wake the men."

Alex quickly made sure that everyone was awake. After a few minutes, they were all standing in a group talking quietly about the barking dogs.

"Listen" said Brian, "it's probably nothing, but that could be a German patrol. Now I think that we'll move on a little bit further to the far end of the woods, where we'll wait for nightfall before striking for home".

The men were happy with this. They would all rather be on the move.

"By the way," Brian added, "no more smoking".

Several of the men cursed quietly under their breath. By about half past four they were nearly at the western edge of the beech woods. Brian called a halt and they stopped where they were, with a few forming little groups of twos and threes. They hadn't heard the dogs barking for some time now, nor had they heard any other noises that might concern them.

They all settled down and made themselves as comfortable as they could, most of the men choosing to sit upright against the base of a beech tree. They knew that they would have to stay here for a good few more hours until darkness came.

Charlie Stewart was the first one to spot the two figures in the distance, walking slowly straight towards them. Hand signals and hissing noises were quickly passed from one man to the other, indicating that someone was coming. They manoeuvred themselves carefully into better positions behind the beech trees, safety catches off and ready for action. As the two figures came into full view, Brian could see that they were just a couple of young kids out for a wander in the woods. He waited until they were almost on them and then stepped out from behind his hiding place. The two boys jumped and stood frightened and staring as the other men emerged from behind the trees. Brian walked up to them and spoke quietly.

"No need to worry" he assured them. "We're not going to hurt you. We're just out on a bit of a training exercise. Now tell me, have you seen any German soldiers today?"

"Loads of 'em!" the first boy said haltingly.

"Yes" agreed the second, "they're everywhere today. There's truck-loads of 'em. My Dad says it's because of the big fire at Arningham."

"OK lads" said Brian. "Now, the best thing that you can do is make your way home, and whatever you do, don't tell a soul that you've seen us. OK?"

"OK!" the boys said in unison, and with that, they turned and slowly retraced their steps. The further away they got, the faster they walked, until by the time they were a hundred yards away, they broke into a run and then disappeared into the woods.

"Right" said Brian, "even though I didn't want to move around too much in the day time, I think that we'd better get away from here. If those boys say anything, there's no knowing who might get to hear about it. Let's go."

As they crossed a track that divided the beech woods from a managed hazel coppice, they could hear the distant rumbling of vehicles further to the north.

"Probably German army vehicles" thought Joseph.

The roughly five acres of coppiced hazel woodland immediately in front of them had been cut down last winter. All the men were familiar with hazel coppicing and some of them had even worked at it for a while as a winter job on some of the local farms near Watersham. There were large piles of timber lined up near to the track, ready to be taken away for fence posts, props and for cutting up, for burning to make charcoal and for logging up for open fires and stoves. Most of the smaller stuff for hurdles, spars and bean sticks had already been collected up and taken away. After walking through the first open area of coppicing, they came to the next five acres that had been cut down some two winters before. Here, most of the hazel stools had sprouted a dozen or more fresh shoots that were now about two feet tall. Off to their left was a fully mature stand of hazel that many of the men guessed was due for cutting this coming winter and to the right an area that looked like it had last been cut about seven or eight years before. Straight ahead was another distinct patch that had new growth that was about eight to ten feet tall.

"Perfect for hurdle making" Tom Barnes said out loud.

Moving through this patch of hazel wasn't so easy. They knocked into the branches that had spread out from the base stools and now seemed to take up every bit of space. Often, the men had to turn sideways to get between two clumps. The next patch that they came to looked as if it hadn't been cut down for thirty years or more. Huge overgrown clumps of hazel dominated the area, and some stools had died and rotted back, leaving a great pile of papery looking dry rot on the ground. Other species were invading where they could, and in particular, small groups of young ash trees had gained a foothold.

A woodcock suddenly flew out from under Joseph's feet and peeled away like a brown arrow into the early evening sky. This had happened to these men hundreds of times since they were kids, but it still made them jump. Joseph took a deep breath, held it for a while and then exhaled slowly. Alexander caught his eye and gave him a knowing look.

As they emerged from the overgrown coppice there was a narrow forest track, and on the other side a plantation of what Charlie Stewart knew to be Douglas Fir. They were about sixty feet tall, and Charlie guessed that they had been planted thirty or forty years before. Walking was easy underneath these great trees, as most of the bottom branches had fallen off twelve to fifteen feet from the ground. There was a clear view for a long way through the forest. The men pushed on for about ten minutes and then Brian waved them to a stop.

"This'll do for an hour or two" he said. "We'll hole up here until nearly dark and then move off."

The men were pleased to stop again as they were tired, but deep down they just wanted to get home as soon as possible. Every now and then the noise of vehicles on the move drifted into the forest from some distance ahead.

At eight o'clock the light started to go and Brian and his men started off again, heading west. Twenty minutes later they were out from under the Douglas Firs and back into rough pasture as the ground rose and turned them back again towards the downland to the south. They climbed over a stile into a field that was being grazed by sheep. The creatures nearest to them looked up to see who these intruders were, but deciding that there was no danger, carried on grazing. The men walked in single file about six or seven yards apart and stayed close to the fence and the trees, behind the fence that gave them some cover and camouflage. They skirted two thirds of the field until they found another stile that led them along a well-used grass path that passed through clumps brambles and tall grasses and on towards some scrubland that they could see ahead of them. It was a beautiful evening, and the light was still quite good.

Eddie Brooks was on point duty and was walking steadily up front, eyes firmly ahead and sub machine gun pointing at the ground. As the pathway rose slightly and Eddie made his way around a slight bend, he suddenly threw himself to the ground and within a split second, the men following behind instinctively did the same. Fifty yards ahead of Eddie was a German soldier with an Alsatian dog on a lead. In the split second that Eddie had spotted them, he registered that the dog was looking directly at him. Immediately the animal became agitated and started to bark loudly. The soldier stopped and shouted at the dog to be quiet, totally oblivious to the fact that a group of armed men lay on the path ahead of him. Brian started to work his way along the path towards Eddie from about five places back, whilst the others rolled and crawled further to the left and right of the path. Joseph and Alexander managed to crawl some distance on their bellies off to the left to where there were four large oak trees. They each picked a tree, rolled through a patch of bracken until they were behind them, and slowly stood up.

From these new positions, they had a good view down the path, and they levelled their rifles towards the German soldier and dog, flicking off their safety catches as they did so. They both took deep slow breaths in order to steady themselves. The dog was still barking and pulling on the lead and the soldier was still shouting; and as he shouted, he started to slowly move forward again. Immediately behind him, three more soldiers appeared leading three more Alsatian dogs who were also pulling hard and becoming more excited with every step that they took.

The new group of German soldiers slipped their machine guns to the ready position as more came into view behind further away, and above the noise of the dogs and [sh]outing, Brian and his men could hear the sound of [the] vehicles that they assumed were troop trucks.

"how many more are there?" Joseph whispered to Alex.

As he spoke, they watched as the first soldier bent down to release the now totally over-excited dog. It took off like a greyhound leaving a trap, and accelerated at a tremendous speed down the path, rounded the bend and came screeching to a halt at the spot where he had seen Eddie only half a minute before. Eddie and Brian had both managed to roll about ten yards to the left. The dog sniffed and started towards Eddie, who was now lying in the bracken. He started to get to his knees as the dog raced towards him, and as it left the ground in a great leap, Brian gave a short burst from his sub machine gun and the dog fell stone dead in a great heap on top of Eddie, knocking him backwards onto the ground.

Within a split second of Brian firing, Joseph and Alex brought down the next three German soldiers and the three Alsatians bolted forward down the path away from their stricken masters.

The soldiers that were further down the path, and those still further back by the trucks, took cover and returned rapid fire.

Bullets flew above and through the undergrowth. Charlie Stewart raised himself on one knee and took all three of the oncoming dogs out with a long burst from his machine gun as they rounded the corner. They tumbled off into the bracken as their momentum carried them forward. Before Charlie could get back down again, a run of bullets struck him in a neat line across his chest. He fell backwards – dead before he hit the ground.

Brian's men crawled and wriggled their way left and right through the undergrowth, desperately seeking better cover. Eddie Brooks didn't move. He was lying face down and spread eagled in long grass behind a blackberry bush laden with huge ripe purple berries. Blood trickled down his face from a hole in his forehead where the fatal bullet had entered and from a larger hole at the back of his head where it had exited.

Brian was struggling to pull himself along, as he couldn't feel his right arm properly. Blood was soaking into his shirt and jacket from a bullet wound to the top of his shoulder, and he had to pull himself along on one side. After a struggle, he made it to a dry ditch and rolled himself in, still managing to hold on to his machine gun. Other men were in the ditch as well, and several were now managing to return fire from their improved positions. On the left, six men, including Joseph and Alex, had managed to reach the relative safety of a slightly raised bank that skirted a field of clover.

They were in a good position here. Behind the solid bank and slightly higher than the enemy, they now had a much clearer view of exactly where the soldiers were firing from.

The Germans started to fall back, and most of them soon reached the safety of the high banked road. The truck drivers had already moved on a further two or three hundred yards down the road, and were now leaning out from their half-opened doors awaiting instructions. Three or four of the soldiers started to make their way, half doubled up, along the road towards the trucks.

A badly injured man, blood running from an ugly wound on the side of his face, slid down the grassy bank, sat on the edge of the road and stared in confused bewilderment at the bank on the other side. Bullets still fizzed overhead.

Gradually, Brian and his men made their way back to the field of sheep, all of which were packed in a tight group in the southeast corner of the field, silent in their absolute terror. The men made their way as quickly as they could, back over the stile and into the rough pasture and then to the welcoming shelter of the Douglas Firs. Some two hundred yards in, they stopped. They didn't look like the same group that had passed this way only half an hour previously. Several of the men were bloodied; they were all breathing heavily and sweating profusely. Three men were missing.

Brian fell to his knees as the shock and loss of blood took its toll. He was shivering badly and felt sick. He couldn't think straight. Joseph and Alexander knelt down next to him. Joseph gently took the machine gun from him and slipped the backpack from his back as Alex held him steady. Between them they undid his tunic jacket and shirt, and as carefully as they could, eased his blood-soaked clothes from him. Philip Greenfield joined them and helped tie off a heavily padded tourniquet high up on his left arm. The bleeding stopped almost immediately. Phil then pulled out a syringe from his bag and, without ceremony, stuck the needle into Brian's good arm. Between them, they managed to get Brian's tunic top back on. Joseph offered Brian a drink from his water bottle. Brian took the bottle with his good hand, gulped down a few mouths full, tipped some water over his head and returned the bottle to Joseph.

"Thanks lads" he muttered.

Albert Rose had checked on the rest of the men and found that none of their injuries were serious; it was mostly cuts and grazes, although one of the youngsters, Micky Barnes, had a bloody gash on the side of his head where a bullet had cut a ragged furrow. He walked over to see how Brian was, just as Phil stuck him with the needle. His first sight of Brian confirmed what he already suspected and told him everything that he needed to know.

Bert Stubbs placed his hand gently on his friend's good shoulder. "Don't worry mate" he said quietly "We'll be alright; we'll get home safe." Then, leaning in closer to Brian, he said in almost a whisper "I'll take over now, shall I?" Brian didn't respond. He wasn't quite sure what was going on or where he was. He couldn't quite think why he was with these men or why they were standing and kneeling in the middle of these fir trees. He was feeling good though, although he had no feeling at all in his left arm – which he thought was strange – but there was no pain – which he also thought was strange. He wasn't shivering anymore; in fact, he suddenly felt very warm. He noticed a black beetle struggling to carry something over the forest floor of pine needles, and wondered if the beetle was warm too.

Bert waved the men over to where he stood.

"Right, I'll have to take over now. Here's the plan. We'll head off North from here in a minute, then we'll split into three groups and when we're a bit closer to home, we'll split down to ones and twos. We'll only travel by night and hopefully we can steer clear of any more trouble. OK: let's go."

Joseph and Alex helped Brian to his feet and pointed him in the right direction. The men split his kit between them, and they all set off again.

Chapter Eight

LONG WAY HOME

Joseph stopped at the edge of the wood and looked towards the old dairy that stood two hundred yards on the other side of the fence. The early morning light was beginning to improve, and he guessed that it must be about five o'clock. The countryside was still and quiet, with just the occasional sound of knocking coming from the cowsheds ahead of him. It was early morning milking time at the parlour, and he knew that the knocking was the sound of the cows banging against the metal barricades as they slowly moved down the aisle, waiting for their turn to be milked. Joseph could smell the sweet aroma of the parlour from where he stood. That comforting smell of warm milk; the smell of the warm cows themselves, and even the smell of their dung mixed with fresh hay and straw came to him. Hundreds, if not thousands of times, he had helped his parents and his grandparents with the milking back home.

He looked at the ground beneath his feet, wrapped his arms around himself and gave out an audible sigh. Homesick wasn't the word for it. Homesick was far too soft and sentimental a word. The feeling that was in the pit of his stomach right now was of a completely different order. It was more of a longing, but it was hard and sharp, like anger that eats away at your soul. Tears were running down his cheeks now as he thought about his lost friends, his family and Julia. He sank to his knees, his chin on his chest, his shirt soaking up his tears. For a minute or two he couldn't control himself, the rage inside was so painful that it flooded like burning oil over his whole body. All that he felt now was pure anger.

Gradually the tears subsided and he became aware of his shallow breathing. He slowly looked up towards the old dairy where cows were now beginning to emerge and make their way back to the meadows. He took a deep breath and shuddered. Wiping his eyes, he took more deep breaths and then, slightly unsteadily, got to his feet. He took a handkerchief from his trouser pocket, wiped his eyes again and quietly blew his nose, pushed the handkerchief back in his pocket and looked again towards the dairy.

He was tired and hungry and knew that he still had at least five miles to go.

It was about an hour earlier that he and John James had separated to make their own ways home, and at least three hours before that they had split from their group of three: Joseph and John James and Harry Foster. He assumed that by now, all the men would be on their own, slowly making their way home, although he guessed that Bert would still be helping Brian along. He hoped and prayed that Brian would make it back to the village, and knew that if he did, they would quickly find all the medical help that he needed. There were plenty of good doctors around who regularly risked their lives in patching up the Resistance fighters.

Joseph watched as one by one the cows came out from the milking parlour and stood waiting patiently by the main gate. He slowly moved towards the farm buildings, making sure that he was always under the cover of the branches that overhung the fields. They were mostly horse chestnut trees along the edge of the wood; their branches bowing down over the grassy field, but cut off in a straight line, as if by some great scythe, where the cows had reached up to browse on their tender leaves.

Within a couple of minutes, Joseph was at the gable-end of the main barn. He stood quietly for a moment and then carefully leaned against a boarded-up door and listened. He could just make out the voices of two men, and wondered if it might be the Fletcher brothers. Although he didn't know this area as well as he knew many others in the district, he was pretty sure that the Fletcher family farmed here. He knew Don and Frank Fletcher from their days together in the cubs and scouts. Don was a year older and Frank about a year younger than Joseph, so they were never best mates, but they knew of each other well enough.

He needed to know who was in the barn; he squatted down and waited. Every now and then there was the sound of movement from inside the building, and the distinctive sound of men's voices. He sat down with his back up against the boarded-up door, his legs sticking out between a stand of thistles. Although there were stinging nettles and docks as well as thistles growing tall all around this neglected piece of ground, the rabbits had made a good job of mowing the grass in between the tall plants and along the edge of the gable end of the barn. There were dry rabbit droppings all around, and brown ants were busy with the crumbly soil foundations of an ant hill. Knowing that he couldn't be seen where he was, and not wanting to risk showing himself to whoever was in the barn, Joseph decided that he would just have to stay put until the coast was clear. The first of the early morning bees were beginning to buzz about their work as the light levels and temperature began to lift.

Joseph guessed that it was about seven o'clock. He was

thirsty, hungry and tired. He'd run out of water and eaten his last small piece of dried out fruit cake at some point earlier in the night. He pulled his backpack across the short grass towards him and checked inside, just in case he'd missed something. He pulled out his old thermos flask, unscrewed the top and checked it. He looked at his empty water bottle. He pulled out and unrolled his water proof cape, catching the strange earthy and musty smell that always seemed to accompany outdoor gear, canvas bags and tents. For a few moments, the smell took him back to a scouts' summer camp on the Isle of Wight, some five years before. At the bottom of the bag were several boxes of spare ammunition for his rifle and three magazine clips for Brian's machine gun.

He looked across at the weapons that he had leaned against the wall. He'd been carrying Brian's gun since they'd dressed his arm in the woods. He thought of the Commander again, and wondered how much further his little group had to go before making it back to safety. He wondered how bad he was and, even if he made it, whether they could save his arm.

He thought about the men that they had left behind and wondered who would get the job of telling their families what had happened. He guessed it would have to be Bert.

He had fallen asleep, with his back to the wall of the barn and his chin resting on his chest. He woke suddenly as a heavy gate slammed – he felt the rumbling vibration through his back as it crashed against the other end of the building. He automatically reached for his rifle, but as he did so, he realised where he was and that he probably wasn't in danger. He could hear the sound of voices again, but this time, they were clearer and sounded as if they were coming from outside the barn. He could also hear horses' hooves on a hard surface, like cobbles or concrete. Joseph quickly crawled to the corner of the barn, half stood, and peered out. Don and Frank were standing in the yard, looking to the cows grazing in the distance. Joseph felt like calling out to them, but thought better of it. If the worst came to the worst, it was better that they didn't see him. If they didn't see him, they wouldn't have to deny it. The Germans were sure to be turning the whole area upside down and questioning everyone – especially young men.

After a few minutes, the Fletchers walked off down the farm track, leading the horse and cart home towards their farm. Joseph could make out six or seven milk churns on the cart and he guessed that they'd be going back for their breakfast. He could almost taste the bacon. As he watched the brothers disappear down the track, he found himself thinking again of his own family: in their kitchen, having breakfast, all together at the farm, and there was Julia sitting next to him at the table and there was his mother, frying pan in hand, asking who would like another fried egg, and there was Granny pouring tea from the big old brown tea pot. It seemed to him that Granny had been using the same brown tea pot ever since he could remember.

Once Joseph felt that the coast was clear, he collected up his things, walked slowly along the far side of the barn, peered around the corner to see that all was clear and then made a quick but silent dash through the gate and into the open end of the dairy. Ahead of him, beyond the milking parlour, he could see two great stacks of barley-straw and hay. He went straight to the haystack, took the empty water bottle and flask from his pack, and then, pulling great hands full back; pushed his rifle, machine gun and back pack into the warm hay and covered them over. He then went back to the dairy, knowing that there was bound to be water somewhere there. Sure enough, on a stand in the corner, there were four old dented milk churns, two were empty but two were almost full to the brim with water.

Joseph guessed that the brothers brought fresh water down to the dairy once a day in the churns, but that they would milk the cows twice a day and take the churns full of milk back with them to the farm each time. Joseph picked up a battered old white enamelled quart jug that was hanging from a nail and sniffed it. After swilling it once and tipping the water on the chalk floor he refilled it, hand shaking, and then, lifted it to his lips and drank long and slow. The water was still cool and fresh. After drinking his fill, he filled his bottle and flask, filled the jug again, and slowly tipped the water over his head, rubbing his hair and face with his free hand as he did so. He repeated this twice more, then rinsed the jug and placed it carefully back on its nail. He shook his head and ran his hands through his hair several times, removing as much of the water as he could. Tiny rivulets trickled down inside his shirt as he stood in the middle of the dairy, waving his hands in the air in an attempt to dry them.

As he did so, he noticed, for the first time, dark brown patches on the backs of his hands, on the cuffs of his shirt sleeves and on the arms of his coat. He walked back towards the main opening at the end of the barn, where the light was better, and held up his arms to get a better look. It was blood – Brian's blood. It wasn't brown at all, but red; and it was caked onto the back of his hands and on his clothes.

"Shit" he said out loud, and then, realising that he had spoken, walked to the end of the barn and, leaning against one of the great upright oak beams, peered outside. Everything was quiet apart from a cow lowing in the distance. Joseph stood there for several minutes, thinking back over the events of the last few days and then, feeling totally exhausted, he went back to the churns, picked up his bottle and flask and made his way back to the haystack. He pulled some more hay out, settled himself down, pulled the hay back over himself, wriggled a few times to get comfortable, closed his eyes and fell almost instantly into a deep sleep.

He dreamed of Julia. He was sitting in a warm bath, fully dressed, and Julia was standing next to the bath and leaning over him, pouring water from a great white ceramic jug as she bathed him. The colour of the bath water was deepest red.

Sometime around late afternoon, Joseph awoke to sounds coming from outside the barn. He pulled some of the hay away from his face and looked out from his hiding place. As he stirred, unseen rodents rustled in the hay beneath him. As he looked out, he saw exactly what he knew that he would see – cows were milling around by the gate, arrived ready for milking time. He knew then that the Fletcher brothers would be arriving at any minute for the afternoon milk. Sure enough, ten minutes later, the men walked into the dairy and started the routine that they had been practicing since they were kids.

They fetched the cows in two at a time, using a short rope halter, and tied them up to metal bars fixed to the side of the dairy. In front of the cows were two separate wooden racks filled with hay that the cows immediately started to pull at with their great tongues and then chew, happy and content with the world as the brothers got on with the business of milking them. The routine was simple and straightforward; two cows in, milk them, empty the milk from the buckets into the churns, lead those away and bring in the next two.

Repeat.

Joseph kept absolutely still, watching every move, and being amazed that what he was watching was almost identical to what they did back on his father's farm. He wondered how many people were milking cows in England right now, and who was milking the cows back home. He'd been gone a long time. He knew they'd all be getting worried. He wondered what they had heard. Had news reached them yet? They must have all heard about the great fire at the oil depot. They must have heard about that, the next morning, surely – but what about the rest of it? Did they know about Charlie and the others? Did they know about Brian? And did they know that he, Joseph, was alright?

It took the Fletcher brothers just over the hour to finish the milking, and at the end of it, they loaded up the churns onto the cart, let the cows back out, and then started off with the horse and cart back towards the farm. Joseph waited for about five minutes and then pulled himself out from the haystack; rubbed himself down and walked slowly across to the far side of the barn and looked out, just in time to see them disappear down the end of the lane. He returned quickly to the haystack, retrieved his knapsack and guns and, looking all around, made his way out from the front of the barn towards the meadow where the cows were grazing.

Keeping hard against the hedgerow, he walked along the side of the meadow, aiming for a copse that stood at the far end. The cows looked up at him as he passed them, and stood watching him, quietly chewing the cud, as he climbed over a barbed wire fence in the corner of the field and slipped quietly into the safety of the copse. In another hour or two it would be dark again.

Joseph sat on the ground in the middle of the copse with his back to a field maple tree. He had a good view in all directions from where he sat, and every now and then he looked around to check that there was no one around.

A pair of magpies chattered away up ahead, but otherwise the countryside was quiet as the light of the day began to lose its strength. There was a light breeze blowing in from the southwest, and on the wind, Joseph caught the faintest smell of smoke. It wasn't troubling or alarming – it wasn't acrid, like oil or tar burning. It wasn't the smell of plastic or rubber. There was nothing electrical or mechanical about it, and there was no hint of coal or charcoal in the air. He had experienced the smell of straw burning a hundred times and was used to great bonfires of tree branches and hedge cuttings on the farm and in the woods when the farm workers and foresters caught up with their winter work and coppicing.

Eventually the smell changed to that of a good old

fashioned garden bonfire, a bit of a mixture of everything, with just a little too much vegetation, making the fire burn slow and cool, with the maximum amount of heavy, damp smoke being produced. Joseph had had plenty of bonfires like that himself. As he rose to his feet and picked up his guns, a big red dog fox appeared out of the descending gloom, heading straight towards him. Joseph stood stock still. The fox got to within about fifteen yards of him before realising that he was there, and then shot off at right angles as fast as he could. Joseph waved Brian's machine gun in the air after him and smiled to himself. The fox kept on running.

It took Joseph five minutes to walk to the southwest corner of the copse, and, reaching its edge; he stopped, checked his bearings and then set off almost dead west along an old forest track that ran along the edge of an overgrown hazel coppice. Off to his left, there was fresh growth on about ten acres of hazel stools that Joseph guessed had last been cut only two winters previously. As he walked along the track, he was surprised to hear the sound of nightjars chirring up ahead. Usually, by early September, they'd raised their young and all flown back to Africa, but clearly, there were a few dawdlers still around. The chirring got louder as he came to the end of the open coppice and he stopped for a while, hoping that he might see one flying – but the light was so poor now that it would have been difficult to see one even if it flew right over his head. He could just about make out a lone ash tree, thirty yards away, one that the foresters had obviously left standing on purpose as a good roosting tree for birds like nightjars.

He guessed that was where the one he could hear was calling from, but it was too late and too dark to hang around here anymore; he needed to get on.

As he crossed one forest track after another, he began to recognise landmarks all around him. He knew these woods pretty well and reckoned that he was less than four miles from home now. A little further on, the coppiced hazel woods came to an abrupt end, as the terrain started to climb back up the side of the Downs. Walking was more difficult now, as in the dark, with huge beech trees all around making it even darker, the rising, uneven slope was less easy to negotiate. Off to his right, a large herd of deer, startled by Joseph's noisy footsteps, suddenly took fright and crashed off between the trees, some of them barking like dogs as they went. Their sudden noise made him jump and he stopped and looked across the side of the hill, just able to make out the white rumps of the last of the Fallows as they disappeared into the darkness.

He stood still for some time, frustrated with himself for not seeing the deer before they saw him. It was a mistake, and he realised that he had been pushing on too hard. He set off again, moving more carefully now, and after another twenty minutes he had reached the top of the hill where the downland levelled out. Walking was much easier now, and to make it easier still, the beech trees had been thinned to their final densities by the foresters, allowing in more light, so it was much easier to make out the lie of the land. As he moved steadily forward, now turning slightly more towards the southwest, there was a sudden break in the cloud cover and moonlight filtered down through the trees. Although not many of this year's leaves had dropped yet, there were plenty of last years on the ground and Joseph, thinking back to his childhood, felt like kicking them into the air; but thought better of it. He knew that he needed to stay alert. It was better if he could make it home without anyone hearing or seeing him.

After the beech woods, there was a chalk track that ran for a half mile gap across open downland, with only some short wind-blown oak trees and a broken hedge on one side for cover. Joseph had been thinking about this for the last hour or so. He knew that if he didn't go this way he would have to walk further south through the beech woods, down the other side of the hill where he could pick up some good cover through some mixed woodland.

Then, turning north, he could approach their farm from the south, through more woods that bordered their land. He reckoned that the detour would add at least a further four miles – perhaps another two hours on this terrain in the dark.

Standing under the cover of the last of the beech trees, he thought through his options again. He decided that he would go for the shortest route, and taking one last look around, set off along the chalk track.

He walked more quickly now; conscious of the open downland on either side of him, and of the moon shining much brighter. In fact, the light was so strong now that the whiteness of the chalk track stood out as clear as day from the dark cropped grass that ran down the middle and to each side of it. Joseph turned as he walked to check around him, and as he did so, he realised that the moon was casting a clear shadow behind him – it was even lighter than he thought. Where it was possible, he stepped off the track and walked as closely as he could to the small groups of trees and the broken hedgerow on the north side. Any cover was better than none. Half way across, Joseph looked to his left and to the south.

There, across the top of the beech trees, over the coastal plain, about fifteen miles away, the English Channel shone and sparkled in the moonlight. The sight was so beautiful that he nearly stopped in his tracks. He thought back to a few days earlier when they had all marvelled at a similarly spectacular view. Things had changed a lot since then; he didn't know how many people had died in the war over those few short days, but he knew for sure that some of his friends would never see such a sight again. He turned and looked straight ahead, picked up his pace and marched as quickly as he could towards the dark trees that stood at the end of the open down-land.

When he reached the welcome cover of the trees, Joseph was out of breath and could hardly see a thing under the dark canopy of the firs. He leant against an old gatepost by the edge of the track, its gate long gone, and waited for his breathing to come back under control. Gradually his eyes began to adjust to the strange light and as his breathing calmed, he stood perfectly still and listened.

A fox barked in the distance and even further away he could hear the alarm call of a cock pheasant, but even if it was someone out and about in the woods causing the pheasant to be alarmed, it was a very long way off to the northwest and nothing to be worried about. He stood listening for two full minutes, but heard nothing else that concerned him. He hitched up his backpack, readjusted his rifle on his shoulder, shifted the weight of the machine gun across his right arm and started off down the chalk and flint stone track that ran between the fir trees.

After about twenty paces he realised that the sound of his boots striking the hard flints under his feet was too loud. He left the track and walked on the pine needles that lay thick on the forest floor beneath the trees. These were Sequoia Firs. He remembered that his grandfather had told him that they had been planted in 1880, when he was a boy. Joseph felt a shudder run through his body: thinking about Granddad reminded him that, with a bit of luck, he'd be home with his whole family around him again in about half an hour.

He walked on until he came to the bottom end of the pine forest, where there was a wide-open gap before the next beech woods started on the other side. This was one of his favourite places in these woods. This was where he had watched as they culled the deer and where his father had first allowed him to fire a rifle. He looked along the edge of the trees to see the deer seats still standing there, looking inviting in the moonlight. This was certainly a special place; but there was no time to dwell on it now. After looking up and down the opening several times, Joseph stepped out from under the fir trees, at first crossing some rough grass, and then, following a deer track, he walked straight through a patch of brambles, skirted around some stinging nettles and entered the beech woods on the other side. He stopped walking fifty yards in and stepped behind the trunk of a large beech tree.

He looked back at the open gap that he had just crossed. Moon beams were shining into the gap and it appeared as if a giant search light was shining down through the trees and onto their branches, throwing their black shadows in diagonal lines amongst the shining beams. Joseph forced himself to look away and started off again for home. There was only about a mile to go now.

He kept away from the main forest paths and instead walked along the animal tracks that dissected the forest. Only local men and boys would think of following deer tracks in the middle of the night; strangers would stick to the main routes. Joseph knew these woods like the back of his hands and so he pushed on more confidently now, stopping every now and then to listen. At one point, he could hear another small herd of deer moving around not far off to his right. He knew that this part of the woods was one of their favourite places to gather. There were a lot of ancient yew trees in this area, some of which had been badly damaged decades earlier, probably when they were trying to clear the land before planting the beech forests. Some of the yews had been badly burned on one side, leaving them stunted and lopsided; others had been half uprooted and left for dead, prostrate on the ground. A few though had managed to survive, turning their upwardly facing branches into main growing points. Once, about three years ago, he had managed to creep up to this spot and had watched a herd of fallow deer for more than an hour. The deer, both fallow and roe, loved standing here amongst these giants, and from time to time they would nibble away at the lichen that grew on the bark, presumably getting some additional food supplement that only lichen could provide.

From this point, the beech woods fell gently away towards the first of the meadows that surrounded the farm. Joseph took his time, and on reaching the barbed wire fence of the first meadow, he stopped and peered out across the fields. In the distance, even though the moon had slipped back behind the clouds again, he could just about make out the outline of some of the farm buildings. He decided not to climb over the fence at this point, but instead to follow it.

He remembered helping his father and grandfather put this fence up about ten years ago, and he particularly remembered this section. It was just here that his father had decided to turn the line of the fence away from the edge of the meadow, and enclose part of the mixed woodland behind it so that the animals would have somewhere to shelter. This meant that he was able to follow the fence, but stay under cover for four hundred yards, until it brought him out to a grassy track that led to the back of the farm buildings. He stood there for a while, listening and sniffing the air. His senses told him that all was well, and so, slowly, he started off down the track.

After about a hundred yards, he turned sharp right, following a narrow path that took him into a small copse that ran along behind the farm yard. He had a good view of most of the farm buildings from here, and the rough lawn that separated the farm yard from the vegetable garden and the house. He could just about make out a dim light coming from the kitchen window. He watched and listened for a while and then moved on to the next vantage point. After about twenty minutes, he had completed a full circle around the farm buildings and house, and found himself standing behind the main barn that faced the farm yard.

He satisfied himself that everything was normal, and

decided it was time to get rid of his weapons. Quietly opening a side door on the barn, he slipped inside and felt his way across to the far side where he found the potato store. Putting down his guns and backpack, he moved five or six bags of potatoes to one side, stood the guns up against the next row of bags, stuffed the back pack in beside them, lifted the first lot of bags back to their original position and threw a load of empty hessian bags over the top of the full ones. He would move the guns and the bag again tomorrow; as soon as he got the chance. Satisfied that everything was in order, he felt his way slowly around the edge of the barn until he reached a small side door. He opened it quietly, listened for a moment, looked out, and then slowly walked across the farmyard. From his stall in the far corner of the farmyard Billy, the Hereford Bull, watched Joseph's every move, but remained silent.

It seemed darker than ever now. He made his way up the garden path until he was within only a few yards of the kitchen window. He could clearly see Granny sitting at the kitchen table reading a book, and above her head he could see the kitchen clock. It was nearly ten o'clock. He walked across the lawn looking in the other windows as he went, but he couldn't make out much as the rooms were either in darkness or had their curtains drawn. As he walked past the front door and then came to the sitting room window, he stopped, moved in closer and peered in through a small gap in the curtains. He smiled as he saw Mum and Dad sitting in their arm chairs next to the open fire. He pulled away and headed straight back to the kitchen door.

He lifted the latch as quietly as he could and stepped inside.

Granny looked up from her book and stared at Joseph.

"My God," she said, "My God you've come home safe! Joseph... Joseph... Joseph!!"

She couldn't say much more. Tears filled her eyes and

she fought to catch her breath as she started to push her chair back. In the time that it took her to stand, Joseph had crossed the room and rounded the table, and they flung their arms around each other with Joseph whispering, "There Gran… it's alright. I'm home now… I'm sorry I… it was too long… I should have… I'm alright. I'm home now…"

Charles called out as he made his way from the sitting room. "What's up? Are you alright? I'm coming."

"Joseph!!" he cried a moment later as he entered the kitchen. "Mary, come quick, it's Joseph! For the love of God, it's Joseph!"

Joseph and Catharine gently released each other and Joseph stepped out from behind the table into his father's arms. They held each other tight and gently swayed from side to side in the middle of the room.

Seconds later, Mary ran into the kitchen and embraced Joseph and Charles together. Joseph lent down and kissed his mother on her head, and Mary, with tears running down her face, mumbled; "Look at the state of you… my God Joseph! Where have you been? Joseph… Joseph… for God's sake…"

Catharine made her way to the kitchen range, slid the big black kettle onto the hot plate, opened the vents on the fire, picked hold of an oven glove, grabbed the fire door handle with it and swung open the door. Briefly, a bright orange glow showed itself, before Catharine covered it with two more logs from the basket by her feet. As she closed the door, Harold walked into the room beaming.

"Just came to see what all the fuss was about!" he laughed as he too threw his arms around the three of them still swaying in the middle of the room.

Lily was screaming before she reached the kitchen. "Joseph! Joseph! Joseph!" She crashed into her brother's back, pushing her arms around his waist as she cried out his name.

Slowly the crying subsided and they all sat down around

the kitchen table, leaving Catharine standing by the range, waiting for the kettle to boil.

They all stared at Joseph. He looked like he had been through a hedge backwards. His hair was a mess, he had five days' growth of stubble and his face was dirty. His clothes were filthy, as if he had been rolling in mud. Charles had already realised that a lot of the stains were not dirt, but blood. No one wanted to ask the obvious questions, and eventually Charles said, "Let's get one of Gran's cups of tea inside you and then we'll get you cleaned up." As he finished his sentence; the kettle started to whistle.

Chapter Nine

THE POST OFFICE

George Marsh had grown up in Watersham and had been to school with many of the young lads who were in the Resistance. He knew Joseph and Alexander particularly well and had played in the same school and village football and cricket teams as them. Their parents and grandparents all knew each other, and at harvest time, he and his family had often helped out on their farms. He had worked for the Post Office from the age of 15, and over the last few years, he had become very well known to just about everyone in the village and surrounding farms. In his short time as a postman, he had delivered mail on each of the three rounds that were centred on the village post office, and claimed to know the names and addresses of every single person living in the district.

He knew much more than that though.

He knew pretty well what everyone was up to, and he was always one of the first to know the latest gossip. People liked to talk to George, especially those who lived a long way out. To many people, he was their main link with the village.

George wasn't a gossip himself though, and kept most of what he was told to himself, but if asked a direct question by a villager, he would usually give a direct answer – but only if he was sure of his facts.

George was a creature of habit. Every day except Sunday, his alarm clock would ring at 5:30a.m. and he would jump out of bed, pull on an old dressing gown, push on his slippers and go straight down to the kitchen. Tabitha the cat slept in the kitchen, in her bed next to the wood basket, and most mornings, she would hear George getting out of bed and would stretch, walk across the kitchen floor and sit waiting under the kitchen table, as he opened the door. They always greeted each other and Tabitha would rub herself against George's legs as he opened up the flue plate on the kitchen range and riddled the grate. He lifted the ash tray out, and as he opened the back door, Tabitha did what she always did; she shot between his legs and ran out into the back garden.

George walked a few paces to where the ash bucket was and tipped the warm ashes in. He looked around for a few seconds to check the weather. Not bad; fairly overcast, but dry. As a postman, he was always pleased when the weather was dry; it made his job so much easier. He went back in, slid the ash tray back, opened up the fire door, picked up three good sized logs from the log basket and pushed them on to the gently glowing embers of the fire and closed the door. He weighed the kettle in his hand, decided that there was plenty of water inside, and slid it onto the hot plate on the range. As he did so, he could hear the satisfying sound of the fire drawing as the flames caught on the dry logs.

George ran back upstairs to get himself ready for the day. By the time that he came back downstairs again, dressed in his postman's uniform, the kettle was singing away and Tabitha was meowing at the back door. He let her in, took the teapot over to the range, picked up the kettle, poured a small amount of steaming water into the pot, and swirled it around a few times as he walked back to the sink and tipped it away. As always, he put four big spoons full of tea into the teapot, returned to the range and filled the teapot to the top with more steaming water. As he set the teapot on the table, he could hear his mother's footsteps on the stairs and as he started to lay the table, she came into the kitchen.

"Morning George" she said as she made her way to the larder. "Fancy a couple of nice boiled eggs for breakfast? There's no bacon I'm afraid. I can't get any more until next week, as I've run out of coupons."

"Boiled eggs would be great" said George.

Margaret got on with boiling the eggs as George made himself a cheese sandwich for his lunch. He wrapped it in greaseproof paper and put it into his lunch bag that was hanging on the back of the kitchen door. He picked up his thermos flask that was on the window sill by the sink, took it to the table and poured in some milk and added one tea spoon of sugar, then lifted up the tea pot and carefully poured tea in until it was nearly to the top. He screwed the top on, walked across to the kitchen door and slipped the thermos into his lunch bag. As he returned to the table to pour the tea, his father walked into the kitchen.

"Good morning George. What's the weather like out there?"

"Morning Dad. It's not too bad actually – Tea?"

One minute later, the eggs were ready and they all sat down to eat.

At exactly 6:15, George stood up and made his way to the door, grabbed his coat and lunch bag and opened the back door. "See you at tea time" he said.

Margaret and Tom looked up. "Yes – see you later".

George took his bike from the lean-to and set off for the Post Office. At 6:25 he arrived at the side gate, pushed it open and leaned his bike against the wall. He could see through the window that a light was already on in the sorting office and guessed that the Post Mistress, Olive Tindall, was already on the move.

He opened the main door, walked around the four full mail bags that had been delivered earlier from the main sorting office at Chichester, and called out "Morning Olive!"

Olive came in through the door on the far side that linked the sorting office with her house and said, "Morning George. You're the first as usual. What's it like out there this morning?"

"Not bad at all. Quite dry actually", said George as he started to pull the mail bags across the floor to the sorting desks.

The Post Office was not only the local sorting office for Watersham, but for the smaller villages of Banstead, Fordwater and Fieldwell. He lifted the bags on to the desks and emptied them out. As he folded up the last of the bags, the door opened and two more postmen walked in: Walter Adams and Arnold Collins. Good mornings were exchanged all around and the men started to sort the letters and parcels. A minute later, the last two postmen arrived: Billy Turner and Sid King. They all got on with their work and by 7:15 they had finished and started to sort out small bundles of mail into the correct order for their delivery rounds.

"I'll get the tea" Olive said as she turned and made her way back to her kitchen.

After a few minutes, the men loaded the last of the mail into their delivery bags and started to tidy up. Sid opened the side door and carried his bag over to where he had left his bike and started to tie it on to the front carrier. In the street outside, there was the unmistakable sound of a truck pulling up and just after that, the sound of a car stopping. Sid looked up as he heard raised voices in the street and the sound of heavy boots on the pavement outside. The side gate suddenly burst open and four German soldiers pushed their way into the yard and stopped right in front of Sid. One of the soldiers pointed to the side door of the sorting office, indicating for him to go back inside. Sid didn't hesitate and quickly walked back in with the soldiers following behind.

The other postmen looked up and stopped what they were doing. The German soldiers didn't speak and stood at ease just inside the doorway, leaving the door open. After an awkward silence, George cleared his throat and spoke.

"Can we help you?"

There was no answer. The soldiers just stared at George. As he was wondering whether to repeat the question, there was the sound of footsteps in the yard and a German Officer stepped through the doorway and closed the door behind him.

"Good morning" he said in perfect English.

The postmen hesitatingly replied "Good morning" and looked at each other for reassurance, just as Olive arrived back in the room carrying a large tray with a teapot, cups, saucers, milk and sugar on it. She stopped in her tracks as she spotted the soldiers and gently placed the tray down on the desk nearest to her.

"Well gentlemen, to what do we owe this pleasure? I'm Olive Tindall, the Post Mistress".

The Officer took off his hat and replied directly to her.

"Good morning Miss Tindall. My name is Captain Jan Muller; I need to ask you and your postmen some questions. Is there anyone else in the building?"

"No" Olive replied, "There's no one else here". Then trying her best to remain calm she added, "Perhaps you and your men would like some tea? I can easily get some more cups if you'd like… that is if you like tea…"

"Thank you" the Captain said, "I'm sure that we would all like some tea".

Olive smiled at him, turned, and headed off towards the kitchen. Captain Muller nodded at one of the soldiers and indicated for him to go with the Post Mistress. The soldier pushed past the postmen and followed Olive into the kitchen.

When they returned to the sorting office with Olive carrying more cups and saucers, George had already started pouring the tea.

"So" said Captain Muller, "here we are". He slowly walked across to where the tea was, waited a few seconds for George to finish pouring and took one of the cups. He tasted the tea. "Excellent" he said. One by one, everyone took a cup, and for a while, all was quiet.

"Now" said Captain Muller, "what we need to know Miss Tindall is which of your postmen are working with the Resistance?"

Olive nearly choked on her tea, and she struggled to get her cup and saucer back to the tray without spilling it.

"What a question!" she exclaimed. "None of these postmen have time for the Resistance. They're too busy with the mail!"

The Captain put down his tea, folded his arms and looked directly at Olive. No one else spoke and there was an awkward pause until the Captain spoke again.

"So, you think that they know nothing, do you?" As he spoke, he slowly turned his gaze away from Olive and looked each of the postmen in the eye. Arnold took half a step forward and started to say something, but Captain Muller raised his hand immediately, indicating that he should stay quiet. Arnold looked around at the others, who were now all looking at the floor, and decided that the Captain was probably right. It would be best to say nothing.

"Miss Tindall. I will ask you once again. Which of these men works for the Resistance?" The Captain left the question hanging in the air as he walked slowly around the room, purposely walking very close to the postmen and then stopping right in front of Olive. "Well?"

Olive looked the Captain straight in the eye and spoke again. "I've already given you my answer."

Captain Muller turned on his heels, walked sharply over

to Arnold and stood in front of him.

"So – you had something to say?"

"Yes" stuttered Arnold, "I was going to say…I just wanted to say… to say… we don't know much about the war… we just get on with our work here Captain. We're just postmen you see… we're just ordinary postmen."

The Captain turned on his heels again, but this time to face his soldiers. "Take this man to the truck" he said.

Without hesitation two soldiers stepped across and stood next to Arnold. One turned and started to walk out of the room and the second gave Arnold a gentle push and they followed on. Arnold said nothing, but the others started to object immediately.

"You can't do that!"

"Where are you taking him?"

"He hasn't done anything wrong!"

Miss Tindall reached out and grabbed the Captain's arm. "Please don't take Arnold!" she said, "Honestly, he doesn't know anything!"

The Captain looked down at Olive's hand on his arm and she slowly pulled back.

"I'm sorry," he said as he lowered his voice to almost a whisper so that only Olive could hear, "but I don't have any choice. I have to take someone in for questioning. You can blame your Resistance fighters for doing so much damage and killing so many of our soldiers."

He turned and walked sharply out of the room with the other two soldiers in close order behind him. The Post Mistress and the remaining postmen didn't move or speak until they heard the sounds of the German truck and car pulling away. George was the first to break the silence.

"Where the hell are they taking him? He doesn't know anything!"

Olive Tindall walked across the room and closed the door to the yard.

"Listen" she said, "We had better carry on as normal. They might be watching us. Watching to see what we do. Watching to see if we are going to go running off to tell someone what's just happened. So, we'd better carry on as normal. Alright George – you know who to get messages to don't you? You can do that on your round, can't you?"

"Yes" said George, "Yes – of course I can". He slowly walked over to where Walter, Billy and Sid stood. They hadn't moved or spoken since the German soldiers had arrived in the sorting office. They were all in shock. "It's alright" said George as he patted each man on the arm. "Don't worry, Arnold will be alright. They won't hurt him. He doesn't know anything. They'll be dropping him back here in no time".

Olive listened to what George was saying, and seeing how shaken they were, she walked over to join her postmen.

"Come on," she said gently, "let's get on with our work and get these letters delivered. They're not going to deliver themselves, are they?" She too found herself patting the men on their arms.

Sid spoke as he went towards the door and reached up to take down his coat. "You're right: we ought to just get on with it... that's the best thing to do".

Walter followed straight on with just a few succinct words. "Yep, it'll be for the best."

Billy looked over at George and said, "But what do we tell people? What if they ask?"

George looked at Olive and then spoke again.

"Don't say anything. Don't say a word. Nothing happened here this morning – right? Nothing happened here. I'll get a message to those who need to know."

Everyone nodded in agreement and the men started to prepare themselves for their rounds.

"Oh" said Billy, "What about Arnold's round? Who's going to do it?"

"Don't worry" replied Olive, "I'll get one of the Post Office girls to help me do it, once I've opened up and got everything settled. Mary and Jenny will be here at about half past eight".

Minutes later, the postmen pushed their bikes out from the yard, through the side gate and then set off on their rounds.

George carried on with his round exactly the same way as he always did. He started at Park House School. There was always a lot of mail for the school, and this morning, he was pleased to have a good pile to hand over to Miss Hetherington, the school secretary. She was always at her desk in reception, bright and early.

"Plenty for you today Miss Hetherington" he said, as he placed the pile of letters onto the highly polished oak table that she used as her desk.

"Thank you, George" she said as she looked up "Not a bad morning this morning?"

"No. Not too bad at all", replied George, and then turning back immediately he added, "Good day to you. See you tomorrow".

"Yes", said Miss Hetherington, "Tomorrow's another day".

George thought to himself as he took hold of his bike, turned it around and set off back down the drive. "Tomorrow certainly is another day. Let's hope it starts off better than today did".

George delivered letters to the outlying houses and cottages on the edge of the village and then started to make his way uphill towards the farms and farm workers' cottages to the north. It was already nine o'clock when he reached Hill Farm. He didn't actually have any post for the Carters this morning, and just in case he was being watched, he pulled a large brown envelope out from his bag as he walked towards the door; to make it look as though he had something for them. He knocked on the door and waited, casually looking around as he did so. After a while, Granny Carter opened the door and greeted him.

"Morning Mrs Carter" said George, "Is Joseph around?"

"He and his dad were over near the big barn a few minutes earlier", she replied. "Right", said George, "Thanks, I'll go and find them".

Before he turned, he slipped the envelope back into his bag. Granny Carter stood with the door half open as she watched George make his way back down the kitchen path. As he reached his bike, he spotted Charles and Joseph in the yard by the big barn. He waved at them and they waved back. He collected his bike and wheeled it across to the farm yard.

"Morning", Charles called out as George walked towards them.

"Morning, but not good", said George in a quiet voice.

Joseph and Charles could tell immediately from George's tone of voice that something was wrong.

"What's up?" asked Joseph.

George then spent several minutes explaining exactly what had happened at the Post Office only a few hours before. At the end, with his voice shaking slightly, he said "So that's it really. Christ knows where they've taken Arnold or what they're doing to him. But the thing is, you need to know what's happening. You need to know what's going on. You need to let your guys know and someone must speak to his family. I don't know what else to do really?"

"Don't worry George" said Joseph, "I'll make sure that the message gets to the right people".

"I know you will" replied George, "I just hope that they don't hurt Arnold. He doesn't know anything – you know." He paused, then, "Listen – I'd better get on, in case anyone has been following me. Good luck. Look after yourselves. I'll see you later".

"Good man George" Charles said as they shook hands.

"See you later mate" said Joseph.

"Right" replied George. "I'll be off".

Half an hour later, George stopped by the pond outside Peach Cottage. There was a seat there that looked out across the fields that fell away down to the Coastal Plain. He leaned his bike against a hedge, took his lunch bag from the carrier on the front of his bike, walked over to the bench and sat down heavily. He looked out across the fields as he undid the wrapping on his sandwiches. It felt like an age had gone by since he wrapped them this morning. He ate his lunch in deep thought, wondering where they had taken Arnold and what they were doing with him. As he finished his sandwich, he heard a vehicle coming down the road and looked up to see a flat-bed truck being driven by Joseph. Neither of the men acknowledged one another, but George knew that Joseph would be on his way to find Commander Clay.

The rest of his round continued without incident and at half past two in the afternoon, he arrived back at the Post Office, leaned his bike against the courtyard wall, un-hitched the mail bag from his bike and carried it into the sorting room. Walter was there ahead of him and as they greeted each other, Olive came in from the front Post Office.

"Any news?" she asked.

"No. Nothing new" replied George.

"No. Nor me" Walter said as he shook his head.

"No" said Olive, "only a few general mutterings from one or two customers during the day, but nothing at all about this morning." And then moving closer to George, she said "Did you manage to get a message out George?"

"Yes" said George as Billy stepped into the room. "Anything to report?" he asked.

"Not really" replied Billy, "only a couple of German trucks parked in Dairy Lane first thing. But when I came back that way just now, they were gone".

Ten minutes later, Sid arrived back, but had nothing to report.

"Kettle's just boiled" said Olive. "Come in for a cuppa". She walked towards the kitchen and the postmen followed. They sat around the kitchen table and Sid spoke first.

"What about Arnold's family?"

"Don't worry" replied George, "I'm sure that Mrs Collins and the kids are being looked after".

The truth was that he didn't really know any better than anyone else what the situation was, but he desperately wanted to reassure everyone that everything was going to be alright. As they sat drinking their tea, they all wondered where Arnold was.

Arnold could taste blood and dust in his mouth as he regained consciousness. He didn't know how long he had been lying on the floor, but as he opened his eyes, he remembered where he was. He was in a barn with an earth floor. From his position, he could see daylight quite clearly through a large gap under the double doors ten paces to his left. He coughed and spluttered and raised himself onto his elbows, coughed again and spat blood onto the floor.

"Stand up!!" shouted a German voice from behind him. "Stand up, you idiot!"

Arnold swayed as he pulled himself up onto his knees. As he started to get to his feet, a sharp pain shot down through the side of his rib cage and he could feel blood dripping from his nose. He steadied himself and caught his breath as an unseen hand took hold of his left elbow and slowly guided him towards a kitchen chair a few yards away.

He held on to the side of the back of the chair and slowly lowered himself to the seat. He suddenly remembered that this was where he had been sitting earlier, before he blacked out following a rain of punches from his interrogator's accomplice. Arnold lifted his head and looked at the man who had helped him to his chair. It was the same man who had punched him so hard and so many times throughout the morning. He wasn't in uniform and neither was the man who had asked him so many questions – most of which he didn't understand or had no knowledge of. He thought that that was why they had knocked him about so much. He had irritated them with his ignorance and stupidity. They had got angry with him when they realised that he really didn't know anything about the Resistance.

Since Captain Muller and the German soldiers had left him in the barn with the Gestapo, Arnold had felt totally alone. Once they started knocking him about, he was sure that they would kill him.

He hadn't told them anything, because he didn't know anything. He didn't know who the leader of the Resistance was. He didn't know any members of the Resistance. He didn't know where their headquarters were and yes, he was sure that none of his fellow postmen were members of the Resistance. Now that they had stopped asking him questions and stopped hitting him, he wondered what they would do next.

Herr Gartner walked up to Arnold and bent down to speak to him.

"You are clearly a very stupid man – Arnold. You really don't know anything, do you? I am not surprised at all that the Resistance don't include you in their plans and their secrets." And then he suddenly straightened himself, looked up at the roof of the barn, raised his voice and screamed. "You... are... too... fucking... stupid!!"

He took several deep breaths, looked across at his accomplice and said very loudly in German "For Christ's sake, take him out of my sight. Take him back to his bloody little Post Office!"

Twenty minutes later, a German staff car stopped outside the Post Office and Arnold was unceremoniously pushed out. He stumbled and fell to the pavement coughing blood as the car pulled away. An elderly man, who had been walking on the other side of the street, crossed over the road as quickly as he could and knelt down beside Arnold.

"My God" he cried, "What the hell has happened to you man?"

Arnold couldn't speak. The pain in his side was too severe and he was still coughing.

George appeared at the side gate.

"Arnold! Arnold! Oh, for God's sake, Arnold!!" he cried. He started towards him, and then, realising that they would need help, he turned, pushed open the side gate and shouted as loud as he could, "Quick! Quick – we need help out here! It's Arnold!!"

He then turned back to the pavement, dropped to his knees, pulled off his jacket and draped it over Arnold's back and shoulders. Arnold was on his hands and knees, struggling for breath.

Within seconds, Olive, the postmen and the Post Office girls, Mary and Jenny, were all out on the street. Mary turned pale when she saw the blood dripping from Arnold's nose and mouth onto the pavement, and turned away.

Olive saw her and called out "Mary, get back inside quick and get the kettle on the boil!"

Mary put her hand over her mouth as she gagged, and she ran back inside towards the kitchen.

"Sid", George shouted, "Get a table top out here as quick as you can!"

Sid and Billy ran back into the sorting room and picked up one of the trestle table tops that was leaning against the wall with half a dozen others.

Before the war, they had used them at Christmas time when there was always a lot more mail to sort. They carried the table top back out to the street and laid it down by Arnold's side. George and Walter helped Arnold over on to his side until he was somewhere near to the middle of the table top.

"Jenny!" Olive called out, "Go and see if you can find one of the doctors down at the surgery, and if you can't, get one of the nurses to come!"

Jenny started off down the street.

"On the count of three," George said, as the men readied themselves to pick up the table top with Arnold on it. "One... two... three."

"Jesus Christ!" he whispered a moment later, as they gently placed the table top on one of the sorting desks. "What the hell of they done to you Arnold?"

Olive leaned forward, placed her arm around Arnold's head and shoulders and whispered in his ear, "There, there Arnold. You're alright now. You're safe. We won't let them hurt you anymore. The doctor is on his way".

Arnold was calmer now; he had stopped coughing, but was making strange gurgling noises, as more blood dripped from his mouth. Mary arrived carrying a bowl of hot water and tea towels draped over her shoulder and put them down on the next sorting desk. Olive quickly took one of the towels, soaked it in the hot water and started to wipe away the blood and dirt from Arnold's face and neck. Mary took one of the heavy over coats from its hook and very carefully covered Arnold with it.

"Thanks ...." Arnold muttered.

"Mary" Olive said, "Can you get down to Arnold's house and tell his wife Elizabeth what's happened? George, could you go with her please?"

"Certainly", George said as he followed Mary from the sorting room. As they stepped onto the pavement, he turned and looked back up the street to see Jenny and Doctor Evans hurrying towards the Post Office.

When they arrived at the Collins' house, they were met at the door by Mrs Stewart, the Collins' neighbour. She had been with Elizabeth nearly all day, since getting a message from Commander Clay's wife that Arnold had been taken away for questioning.

"Any news?" she asked quietly.

"Arnold's back at the Post Office" Mary replied, "but he's in a bad way."

Mrs Stewart stepped aside to let Mary and George into the house. Elizabeth was sitting at the kitchen table with her three children, and they all looked up as Mary and George walked in.

"Elizabeth", Mary said, desperately trying not to burst into tears, "Arnold's back at the Post Office, but he can't come home right now. Would you like to come with us?" George and Mary smiled at the children as they looked blankly at them, not understanding what was going on.

Elizabeth pushed her chair back and stood up. "Right" she said, gently stroking her children's hair, as she walked around the table. "Now don't you worry; I'll be back with your dad soon. Mrs Stewart will keep an eye on you for a while – won't you Meg?"

"Yes" said Meg Stewart, "We'll be fine, won't we children? You get off and see Arnold. Don't you worry yourself about the kids; they'll be fine with me."

Elizabeth took her coat from the back of the kitchen door and followed Mary and George out into the street. She placed her arm through Mary's and twenty paces away from the house, she stopped and said very quietly, "So, how is he? Have they hurt him? Have they killed him?"

Mary looked straight into Elizabeth's eyes and held tight to her hands "Elizabeth – they've knocked him about pretty bad, I'm afraid; it's not good, but Doctor Evans has just arrived to help."

Doctor Evans took less than a minute to determine what Arnold's main problem was.

"Broken ribs and a punctured lung" he said quietly, as he looked up at Olive. "This is very serious. We need to get him to hospital without delay. He's also got a broken nose and possibly a fractured jaw; that won't kill him, but the punctured lung might".

Olive turned to Sid and was about to speak as Elizabeth, Mary and George stepped through the door.

"Jesus Christ!" Elizabeth screamed, as she saw Arnold on his side, dribbling blood and making shallow gurgling noises "What in heaven's name have they done to you?"

Arnold looked at his wife through half closed eyes and started to lift a bloodied hand towards her. Elizabeth grabbed hold of his hand and bent down to kiss his damp forehead. Olive walked over to George, reached for his elbow and firmly guided him back towards the outer door.

"This is serious" she said, "he's got a punctured lung and we need to get him to hospital a bit quick. We need transport."

"Leave it to me" George replied, already turning to go.

Ten minutes later, George arrived back at the Post Office driving a van. Within two minutes, they carried Arnold on his makeshift stretcher and gently slid him on the trestle table top in to the back of the van. Doctor Evans jumped in the back of the van beside Arnold and Elizabeth climbed into the passenger seat. George started the engine as Sid closed the rear doors of the van and banged hard on the side panel of the van to indicate it was safe for George to drive off.

Olive, Sid and the others watched as the van pulled away. No sooner had it moved out of sight, a German staff car came into view from the other direction. The Post Office staff watched as the car slowed and came to a standstill right beside them. The passenger door opened and Captain Muller stepped out.

"What is going on?"

Sensing that this was not a good place to be, the staff slowly, but purposely, moved into the yard and then through to the Post Office sorting room. Olive followed them to the yard and then turned and looked the Captain straight in the eye.

"Are you saying you don't know?" she said, raising her voice and taking half a step towards the Captain.

173

"No" he said, now feeling slightly unsure of himself, "Tell me, what has happened?"

Olive leaned closer to Captain Muller and jabbed a finger towards him. "Your thugs beat poor Arnold to within an inch of his life – the bastards!"

"I'm sorry" replied the Captain, "I hope that you know that that was nothing to do with me or my soldiers – we had our orders".

"Yes!!" Olive screamed, "But you were the one who handed him over to the thugs!" She jabbed her finger into Captain Muller's chest. "I'll never forgive you or any of your bloody soldiers!"

Captain Muller took a step back and straightened himself.

Olive cleared her throat and spat on the floor next to the Captain's boots. "You've made plenty of new enemies today" she said, as she turned and slowly walked back into the main Post Office, slamming the door behind her. Captain Muller stayed where he was for a while, staring at the Post Office door, and then turned away sharply and marched back to his waiting car.

It took George about thirty minutes to drive to the hospital in Chichester. Throughout the journey, Arnold gurgled and spluttered as he lay on his side, struggling to breathe. Every now and then he had coughed violently, spraying blood on Doctor Evans' clothes and across the floor of the van.

Elizabeth Collins spent most of the journey kneeling on her seat and reaching back towards Arnold, stroking his hair and reassuring him and herself that everything was going to be alright. Doctor Evans did his best to comfort Arnold as much as he could and made sure that he stayed lying on his side, so that the blood couldn't build up too much in his punctured lung. He was more concerned with every minute that went by and at about the half way stage, he could feel that there was an unusual swelling in Arnold's abdomen. He didn't mention it to Elizabeth.

George pulled up by the main entrance to the hospital, and he and Elizabeth jumped out from the van and ran around to open the back doors. Doctor Evans stumbled out from the back of the van, straightened himself up and ran into the hospital calling for help. Almost immediately, two hospital orderlies arrived and started to gently pull the table top back towards the rear of the van. George and Doctor Evans took hold of the top end of the table and the four men slowly walked Arnold into the hospital. Elizabeth walked alongside the make shift stretcher, her white face betraying her fear.

They placed Arnold's stretcher straight on top of a bed inside the first examination cubicle that they came to, as the duty doctor and two nurses hurried over. Doctor Evans took three or four steps towards them and, making sure to keep his voice low so that he couldn't be overheard by Elizabeth, he quickly introduced himself to the doctor, explained what had happened, what his prognosis was concerning the suspected punctured lung and what his concerns were about Arnold's swelling abdomen.

"Thank you" Doctor Freeman said, as he left Doctor Evans and joined the nurses who were already attending to Arnold. Doctor Freeman nodded to Elizabeth and George as he moved in closer to examine Arnold, whose breathing was now very shallow. He was still lying on his side, perfectly still, as a mixture of blood and saliva dripped from the corner of his half open mouth – like stretched red treacle, sticking to the dark varnished wood of the trestle table top.

Doctor Freeman held his stethoscope and listened; first to various positions on Arnold's back, and then, as far as he was able to, to his chest. The nurses hovered around, dabbing at Arnold's face with towels and loosening his clothing as Elizabeth, George and Doctor Evans stood back, watching Doctor Freeman's every move. Every now and then, the two doctors would catch each other's eye, and with the slightest facial movement, imperceptibly exchange some piece of crucial information.

Doctor Freeman carefully opened Arnold's blood-soaked shirt and gently felt his abdomen. It was badly swollen, and as he felt further round to the side, Arnold cried out in pain. As Arnold cried out, Elizabeth jumped up and George only just managed to grab her arm in time to stop her from running to Arnold.

"Now, now" he said "it's alright – it's alright – the doctor and nurses will look after him. We must just keep back out of their way for a bit longer, whilst they decide what to do."

Doctor Freeman spoke quietly to the nurses as he continued his examination. As soon as he finished, one of the nurses hurried off towards the main office. Doctor Evans watched as she entered the office, and through the great windows that looked out into the waiting room, he saw her go straight to the telephone.

After two minutes, the nurse returned to the examination cubicle and spoke quietly to Doctor Freeman. Doctor Freeman nodded his understanding, picked up a towel, wiped as much of the blood from his hands as he could and turned to walk the few steps to where Elizabeth, George and Doctor Evans were waiting. He looked straight at Elizabeth and spoke quietly and slowly.

"There's no good news I'm afraid. He's in a bad way. There's at least one broken rib on his left side and a punctured lung. He also has a badly damaged jaw and a number of other minor injuries; but what's of most concern is the severe swelling to his abdomen. There's certainly some serious internal bleeding going on and it's possible that he has damage to some vital organs – the liver for example. I've called for the emergency surgical team, and they're on their way. They'll be here as quickly as they can. The only thing that we can do is to get him into theatre and try to stop the bleeding. I'm sorry that I can't give you better news; but there it is."

Elizabeth slowly bowed her head, lifted her hands to her face and quietly began to sob. Not wanting Arnold to hear her, she turned to face the other way. Doctor Evans turned with her and placed a comforting arm around her and Elizabeth leaned her head into his shoulder. Doctor Freeman turned back to his patient as two orderlies dressed in brown hospital coats arrived to take Arnold to theatre.

Doctor Evans spoke to Elizabeth.

"Let's go over to see Arnold, shall we? Only we won't be allowed into the theatre."

Elizabeth pulled a handkerchief from her sleeve, wiped her eyes, and, still with Doctor Evans supporting her, walked back towards where Arnold lay. His breathing was now shallower than ever and his eyes were completely closed. She bent down and kissed his forehead and ran her fingers through his matted hair.

"I'll see you again soon my love."

Arnold's eyelids flickered slightly, but otherwise there was no response.

Elizabeth, George and Doctor Evans made their way slowly, in total silence, towards the canteen. More tears ran down Elizabeth's face as they walked, and every now and then she dabbed them away and gently sniffed. Elizabeth and George sat at a table, as Doctor Evans went off in search of a pot of tea and some biscuits.

Back in the village, Olive called round to see George's parents to explain where he had got to. Afterwards, she went back to check that everything was alright with Mrs Stewart, who was still looking after Elizabeth and Arnold's children.

George glanced up at the clock that was on the wall above the serving counter.

"Blimey" he said to no one in particular, "It's just gone half past six".

They sat quietly drinking their tea, until twenty minutes

later, when Elizabeth asked if anyone knew where the toilets were. Doctor Evans pointed back towards the waiting room.

"I think that they're on the other side of the main doors", he said.

For the next hour or so, small talk wasn't easy. No one wanted to talk about the day's events; they all just wanted to know how Arnold was.

At about half past eight a nurse who they hadn't seen before, came into the canteen and walked straight up to them.

"Mrs Collins?" she said in a gentle voice.

"Yes", said Elizabeth as she started to stand "How's my husband – Arnold? Is he alright? Have they finished the operation? Can I see him?"

The nurse patted her gently on her arm, said "Follow me please", and immediately turned to go.

Elizabeth picked up her coat and hand bag and walked quickly after the nurse as Doctor Evans and George stood and followed. The nurse led them to the main office where Doctor Freeman was waiting for them.

"Please sit down" he said. Once they were all seated, Doctor Freeman leaned towards Elizabeth, reached out and held both her hands in his.

"I'm so sorry to have to tell you this Mrs Collins, but your husband died at twenty past eight this evening. I'm afraid that there was nothing that we could do to save him".

Chapter Ten

JOSEPH AND JULIA

Since making it safely back home, Joseph had spent ten days working hard on the farm, helping his father catch up with the early autumn work. He had told Charles as much as he dared to about what had happened, but had only given away the absolute minimum to the rest of the family. He was very nervous about saying too much – you never knew when someone might unintentionally say something to the wrong person – not everyone knew when to keep their mouth shut.

Word had reached him about his friends. They'd all made it home safely, including Brian, and as far as he knew, the Commander was alright; he'd been patched up and had gone up country somewhere to recuperate at his sister's. The German patrols had been a lot more active since the oil depot fire, and they'd spent a long time questioning people in all the local villages. There were rumours that four or five people had been taken away for questioning; but nothing was certain. Everyone was nervous, that was for sure. People didn't stop to talk to each other, the pubs were closed and after tea time, the streets were empty.

By the next weekend; Joseph was determined to see Julia. He had to; he was desperate to see her. On the Thursday morning, he was just finishing his breakfast, when he heard the rattle of the letter box. Jumping up and yanking open the front door, he ran down the path and caught up with the postman by the front gate.

"Morning Georgie" – Joseph offered his hand.

"Morning Joe," George replied, as they shook hands firmly. "Are you chasing me with a love letter to post?"

"No," Joseph replied, returning the postman's smile, "But I'd like to get a message to Julia if I can. I don't want to put anything in writing though."

"No problem," George nodded. "What do you want me to tell her?"

"Tell her," said Joseph, "That I'll be waiting by the war memorial at nine o'clock this Sunday morning."

"Anything else mate?"

"No," said Joseph, "That's all."

"Right," said George. "I'll make sure she gets the message."

They chatted for a few more minutes and then Joseph, looking back and waving his arm in the general direction of the farm, said, "Well, this won't get the pigs fed, will it? I'd better get back. Thanks for taking the message mate."

As he spoke he patted George on the arm. They shook hands again; this time more firmly and for longer.

George looked straight into Joseph's eyes and said "Good man Joe, good man. For God's sake, be careful man. Be careful. We can't afford to lose you, you know."

"Don't worry" Joseph replied solemnly, "I'll be careful; and thanks again for taking the message."

The two men parted and Joseph watched as George pedalled away.

Without looking back, George waved his arm and

shouted "Don't come running to me if you break your leg!"

Joseph laughed and shouted back "Get on with you!"

As he turned and walked back to the house, he was already thinking about Sunday and seeing Julia again. He was sure that she would be there.

Early on the Saturday morning, Joseph and Lily were in the dairy, milking the cows. For the first half-an-hour, they didn't say much. That was normal. At half past five in the morning, there wasn't much to be said; they were still half asleep. There was the odd comment about the weather and a few words about one of the cows that had a slight limp, but other than that, they both got on with their work without talking. Suddenly, Lily stopped milking and sat upright on her stool; a single tear ran down her cheek and as she wiped it away with her sleeve, she called out Joseph's name.

Joseph looked across at her - "What is it?"

Lily sniffed as she felt more tears coming. "Joseph" she said again, "You will tell me all about it one day, won't you? I hate it when you're away like that. I get frightened you see. We all do."

Joseph stopped milking and stared at the ground.

"I know" he said. "We're all frightened. It's a bad time for everybody right now. But it'll be better one day, I'm sure it will."

He looked up at Lily and smiled. She looked back as more tears ran down her face. Using both sleeves this time to dry her eyes, she smiled at her big brother, the way that she had always done. Realising that the milking had stopped, the two cows standing in front of them were becoming restless, and so they returned to their work.

After finishing the milking and tidying up; they walked arm in arm back towards the house, looking forward to breakfast. They walked slowly across the yard until they reached the path that led up towards the back of the house, where Lily pulled on Joseph's arm and they stopped.

"Dad says you're off to the village in the morning. Will you be seeing Julia?" She had thought long and hard about asking this question, and although she was desperate to ask it, she didn't want to pry. She loved the idea of her big brother having a girlfriend; in fact, she was excited by the very thought of it. She didn't really know Julia, and couldn't remember actually talking to her at school or in the village as the big girls and the younger ones tended not to mix, but she certainly knew all about her. Over the last few months, as Lily realised that Joseph was seeing her, she had already imagined the engagement party and the wedding and, to her mind, the best bit would be gaining a big sister to share her secrets with.

"I might be" Joseph teased, "But that would be telling, wouldn't it?"

With that, he ran his hand gently through Lily's hair, turned and walked towards the kitchen door. She followed, smiling.

Joseph was early. It was only twenty to nine and he was already standing by the war memorial. It was quiet. A few people were making their way towards the church and on the other side of the low flint wall that bordered the church yard. An elderly lady, carrying a bunch of flowers, was picking her way amongst the grave stones. Joseph watched her. After a while she stopped, stood for a moment and then bent forward. When she stood up again, the flowers had gone, and she stood perfectly still, her arms folded in front of her and a large black leather bag swinging from the crook of her arm. Joseph recognised her as one of the elderly ladies who lived in the village, but he didn't know who she was or whose grave she was tending. Behind him, he heard a car and turned to look.

A black Mercedes was coming down the street towards him.

He leaned against the low flint wall and tried to look

relaxed and unconcerned as it drove slowly past him. The German officer sitting in the front passenger seat looked directly at Joseph, and for a few seconds their eyes met. One of the men sitting in the back of the Mercedes also looked directly at him, and Joseph straight at him – it was Arthur Williams. Arthur turned his head and looked the other way. Joseph made a mental note to tell Commander Henry Clay that he had seen Arthur in the back of a German staff car. The vehicle continued on its way and Joseph turned and looked back across the church yard, letting out a deep breath and blowing out his cheeks as he did so.

The lady who had been tending the grave was walking away now, and as he watched her, he took a few steps away from the memorial, pushed opened the heavy wooden gate and walked slowly along the path that led to the main entrance to the church. He stood on the path for a while, watching as the woman went through a gate at the far end of the church yard and disappeared down a path behind a thick laurel hedge.

Joseph looked around and saw the bunch of bright yellow chrysanthemums that she had been carrying, lying on a grave twenty paces to his right. He walked over and read the inscription on the headstone: In loving memory of John Henry Clay – 1881 to 1918 – who fell in the Great War. Forever missed by his beloved wife Elizabeth, son Henry and daughter Louisa. This was Commander Henry Clay's father's grave – the lady he had just seen leaving the flowers must be John Henry Clay's widow and Henry Clay's mother. He read the inscription once more and then headed back to the war memorial.

A few more people were walking up to the church now, and Joseph nodded to them as they passed. As he reached the gate, he looked back towards the church clock. It was five to nine. As soon as he got back to the memorial, he looked down the list of names that were so familiar to him. Third from the top was the name that he was looking for: John Henry Clay.

He looked up and down the street, and there, walking towards him, waving at him, was Julia. He stood rooted to the spot, a huge smile on his face, watching her every beautiful step as she made her way towards him. She stopped in front of him and they both said quietly and in unison "Hello."

For a while they just stood there, holding hands and staring into each other's eyes. Several people brushed by them, but they didn't notice.

The church clock struck nine and Joseph said "I knew you'd be here."

"Yes; I thought you would be too" she replied.

He stepped out into the road and gently pulled Julia after him.

"Come on" he said, "Let's get out of here."

"Where are we going?" she asked.

"No idea" he answered.

They walked in the middle of the road, holding hands, and after ten minutes, they had reached the outskirts of the village. Three men on bikes appeared and the last of them let out a loud wolf whistle as he rode passed them. Joseph didn't react, but Julia blushed slightly and looked at her feet.

"Take no notice" laughed Joseph, "He's just jealous."

They walked on a little further and then turned off from the road along a path that led to open fields. The entrance to the field was by way of a wooden stile. They walked in single file along the narrow path and on reaching the stile Joseph suddenly stopped, turned, put his arms around Julia's waist, pulled her in close and kissed her.

Taken completely by surprise, Julia pushed him back for a few seconds and then, wrapping her arms around his neck, she gave way and they kissed again. They each pulled the other in closer and kissed harder, their mouths wide open and pressed together, their eyes tight shut, holding on for dear life until, after what felt like an age, their lips leaned against each other, their noses still caught their breath.   Joseph moved his f̲ away from Julia's and said "I was worried I'̲ again and I couldn't bear it. I've been thinking the time."

Julia started to weep. "I didn't know where ⌐ were, or if you were alright. When the news came in about the oil depot, everyone was so worried, and then a few days later when news broke about the men that had been lost from the village… well… I…I didn't know… I didn't know what… I didn't know what to think… I thought it might be you that was … you know…"

She looked down at the ground as tears ran down her face and dripped onto the dry soil between her shoes. Joseph gently lifted her chin up with his fingers and kissed her softly on each cheek. He could taste the salt in her tears.

"You mustn't worry about me" he whispered, "I'll always come home to you. You know that, don't you?"

Julia didn't answer. They both knew that it didn't work like that. Julia wondered to herself just how many millions of times over the centuries soldiers had made that same promise to their sweethearts. They kissed again; gently this time.

Chapter Eleven

THE PICNIC

Julia had been looking forward to today for a long time. Even though summer had long gone, the weather had been fine and dry for weeks, and this morning, although fresh and autumnal, it was bright and sunny by eleven o'clock, without a cloud in the sky.

Joseph had promised to meet her by the war memorial at half past eleven. Although he would normally work on the farm until four o'clock on a Saturday; today he had done a deal with various members of the family so that he could have the best part of the day off. He had stopped work at half past ten, rushed indoors for a wash and brush-up, changed into his smarter clothes, grabbed a big slice of his mother's fruit cake as he shot through the kitchen, shouted cheerio as he picked his coat from the rack and bolted through the back door. He ate the cake as he pedalled hard down the road towards Watersham. At twenty-five past eleven he rode up onto the pavement next to the war memorial, jumped off his bike, pushed it through the church yard gate, along the path and round to the back of the church where there was an old wooden shed that held the wheel barrows; hand tools; fag hooks and scythes used by the small team of elderly men who kept the churchyard trim and tidy.

There were already two other bikes leaning against the far side of the shed next to the huge yew tree that grew there; this was a popular place for the young men of the area to leave their bikes. Joseph wheeled his up next to the others, and headed off back to the war memorial. No sooner had he got there than Julia appeared, waving, a little way off down the street. She was carrying a large wicker basket. Joseph smiled and waved back.

As soon as Julia reached him, he held out his hand and took the basket from her, kissing her on the cheek.

"Hello sweetheart."

"Hello Joe. Aren't we lucky with the weather?"

Joseph looked up at the clear blue sky and smiled. They linked arms and set off to walk out from the village. Just before turning off into the woods, they stopped and stood hard back to the side of the road, waiting for a small convoy of German trucks to pass. As the last one went by, a soldier, sitting by the tailgate, waved at them. Joseph and Julia automatically gave a half wave back, looked at each other and then turned towards the woods.

They'd walked this path before.

"Let's go right to the top," Julia suggested enthusiastically.

"Suits me," Joseph agreed.

The path through the tall beech trees rose steadily as it followed the contours of the side of the hill that would eventually lead up to the open grassland at the top of the Downs. This part of the woods, not far from the village, was known to just about every villager. The school teachers brought the kids here for nature lessons, young mothers walked here with their little ones, older people liked it because it was quiet and the walking wasn't too difficult, and kids out and about without their parents could safely mess about here. It had been like this in the beech woods for as long as anyone could remember

Pretty soon they were on a much steeper path, and after a while they stopped to take off their coats and catch their breath. Joseph put down the picnic basket and Julia leaned against him as they both looked back down the path towards the village. It was much warmer now, nearly as warm as a good English summer's day. There was no wind, but leaves were gently falling from the great beech trees like giant coloured snowflakes; bright vibrant red, orange and yellows caught in the midday sun. They both watched for some minutes without speaking, soaking up the magic.

Eventually, Julia sighed: "Beautiful: just beautiful."

"Just like you," said Joseph.

She turned to him, dropped her coat and slipped her hands around his waist. Joseph let his coat fall too, leaned down, pulled her in tight towards him, and they kissed. As they kissed, Joseph let his hands slide down to Julia's bottom and he pulled her in even closer. Julia made no attempt to resist and stroked his back firmly with her hands. Joseph became aware of the sound of airplane engines in the distance, and as they became louder, he pulled away and looked up through the trees. Julia followed his gaze and they watched as a group of German planes flew directly overhead.

"I wonder where the RAF has got to?" Joseph mused to himself, still looking skyward.

"Come on," said Julia briskly, "there's no picnic for you until we get to the top."

They walked on for another twenty minutes before the path started to level out, and suddenly they were in full sunshine on open downland. They walked a bit further until they reached a chalk track that ran right along the spine of the hill. Looking back across the tops of the beech woods, they could see the Channel glistening in the distance. They stopped, side by side, looking out to sea, just like they had countless times before, with their parents, their families, their friends – and now as lovers.

"I know a good place," said Julia, "Over that way, down by the old yews." And with that, she left the track and headed off slightly downhill again, back towards the beech trees.

Joseph caught up with her as she reached the edge of the woods, and they walked beneath the giant boughs until they came to a group of seven yew trees. The middle one was the largest and had the widest open space around it. Its great gnarled roots spread out from its base like some ancient petrified octopus. In places between the roots, beech leaves had piled up, and in others a carpet of bright green moss grew. The marbled bark was flaking heavily on the old trunk and long dense branches spread out like a giant umbrella. Joseph and Julia walked slowly around the great tree, looking up through its canopy, shielding their eyes from the sun that was almost directly overhead. Bright red berries shone out from their hiding places amongst the deep green pine needles.

Julia picked the sunniest spot on the moss bed between the great roots, spread out her coat and sat down. Joseph dropped his coat alongside hers, gently placed the picnic basket down and sat next to her.

"Quite a spot," he said.

"Beautiful, isn't it?" she agreed.

Julia leaned over, opened the picnic basket, pulled out a small blue and white checked cotton table cloth and spread it out between them.

Joseph was used to picnics – he picnicked almost every day of his life on the farm – but they didn't call it picnic, they called it lunch. All the farmers and farm workers that he had worked with always stopped for their lunch at about half past nine in the morning. They would take shelter where they could and sit down; under some trees, by a hedge, in a barn or on or under a trailer, depending on the weather. Lunch tended not to vary much, especially in the last few years since the war started. It was nearly always bread and cheese, perhaps a piece of fruit cake, and often at this time of year, an apple. He watched in anticipation and hope as Julia started to take individual items from the basket and place them on the table cloth. There was no great quantity of anything. Food, like everything else, was scarce. Joseph's expectations weren't high, although he was hoping for a bit more than a ploughman's lunch. He smiled as Julia gently placed two large scotch eggs on a white plate in the middle of the blue table cloth. There was a jar of home-made pickles, a small wedge of cheese, two perfect bright red tomatoes and half a cottage loaf of white bread. Julia reached down and removed a lid of grease-proof paper from a small jar that held butter; such a rich yellow in colour that it appeared almost unreal.

Last from the basket, Julia took a bottle of ginger beer and two glasses. She looked up at Joseph and passed the bottle to him, holding the glasses ready to be filled. Joseph knelt up, flipped the hinged bottle top off with his right thumb and poured the fizzy liquid before quickly securing it again and gently laying it back in the basket. Julia handed one of the glasses to Joseph and as he took hold, she chinked her glass against his and said, "Here's to us."

Joseph leaned forward and they kissed gently. "I love you more than ever," he whispered. They kissed gently again and then drank their ginger beer. Joseph had never had champagne, but he didn't think that it could possibly taste as good as Julia's ginger beer.

Julia took a knife and cut the scotch eggs and tomatoes into quarters. Joseph broke a chunk of bread from the cottage loaf and spread some of the golden butter on it. They each took a little of everything onto their plates and smiled at each other as they tucked in.

"What a treat!" said Joseph, "You know the quickest way to a man's heart!"

Julia laughed at him, "You're easy to catch, aren't you?" she giggled.

"You can catch me anytime," Joseph grinned, and he leaned across and kissed the tip of her nose. As he looked down to see what he might eat next, he saw movement out of the corner of his eye. He stopped and looked past the yews to the beech trees.

Julia followed his gaze to where five young fallow deer bucks stood in the sunshine. They were all in perfect condition, standing proud with their heads up and the sunshine catching their near white antlers. They sniffed the air as they twitched their tails and slowly looked around. Joseph and Julia kept perfectly still, enjoying the moment. They were a hundred yards away and obviously hadn't spotted or sensed them yet.

With the gentle breeze, such as it was, blowing towards Joseph and Julia, they knew that the deer wouldn't be able to pick up their scent, and so keeping perfectly still, they watched, as very slowly, the young bucks relaxed and started to browse on the tips of some blackberry bushes that formed a low clump between the beech woods and the yew trees. Julia leaned in against Joseph's back, her arm around his waist, her chin on his shoulder, watching the stags every move. She felt wonderful.

They watched the deer for fully five minutes until they edged back into the woods.

"That was a real treat," said Joseph, as he turned back to look at Julia.

"It was," she agreed, "So beautiful".

They returned to their picnic, sitting in complete silence.

"Is there any more ginger beer?" Joseph asked.

"Yes – just a little." She took the bottle back out of the basket.

"Just one swig each," she said, as she raised the bottle to her lips and drank. "There," she said, "Just one mouthful left for you."

Joseph smiled, took the bottle from her and drank the last mouthful. He could taste her lips on the bottle.

He watched as Julia collected up the picnic things and packed them away. She lifted the basket out of the way, across and over one of the great yew tree roots, and then slowly, lay back on the blue and white table cloth with her arms stretched out behind her head.

"Just such a perfect day," she said softly as she turned her head slightly towards Joseph and closed her eyes.

Joseph looked down at her for a while studying her soft face – she was beautiful – perfect. As she breathed, her chest rose and fell gently. He slowly lowered himself so that he was close to her side, his lips close to her neck. She felt his breath on her and without opening her eyes she moved her head slightly, exposing her pale neck further. Joseph saw the shadows of the yew tree branches dancing on her face as he leaned in closer and kissed her. Her skin was soft to the touch of his lips and he kissed her neck like a butterfly kisses a flower; softly, gently, over and over again. Julia slowly brought her left arm forward and across, resting her hand on the back of his head. As he continued to kiss her neck, Julia pulled him in towards her; all the time with her head tilted away.

For a brief moment, she half opened her eyes and looked up through the dark green branches of the great yew tree that stood above them. The sun poured down through its branches, the air was still and warm, and Julia could feel her heart pounding as Joseph placed his hand on her breast as he shifted his weight and began to kiss her lips.

They kissed open mouthed; at first softly and then more passionately as Julia moved to her side, dropped her arm around Joseph's back and pulled him towards her. He was breathing quickly now, and he moved his hand down across Julia's back, across her bottom, down the backs of her legs and then on reaching the hem of her dress, moving his hand under it, gently stroking her soft warm thigh. Julia raised her left leg and laid it across Joseph's. He moved his hand further up inside her dress and touched her underwear. Julia moved her hand to Joseph's hip and started to pull at his shirt. After a few seconds, she pulled slightly away and reached down for his belt buckle. She undid the belt and the top catch on Joseph's trousers and then worked her way down, undoing the buttons.

As she did so, Joseph moved his hips slightly, pushing himself towards her, and at the same time he ran his hand again against the inside of her thigh. As Julia undid the last of his trouser buttons, she allowed the back of her hand to fall back against his body. She could feel his hard penis pushing against his underpants and for a few moments she very gently brushed her hand against it.

Joseph sighed as they broke away from kissing and they looked at each other, panting.

Julia gently pushed Joseph back, pulled further away and then, rising to her knees, started to undo her blouse. Joseph followed suit, undoing his shirt and quickly pulling it off. Looking around to check that no one was watching them, they stood up and held each other so that they didn't fall over as they struggled to be rid of the rest of their clothes and then stood naked under the yew tree, a short distance apart, staring into one another's eyes.

Joseph reached out and cupped Julia's breasts, and then, with the backs of his hands, gently stroked them. Julia looked down at his hands and then further, to his erection. Placing her hands briefly on his hips, she then slowly moved to touch him, running the tips of her fingers down the side of his penis. Joseph dropped his hands to her bottom and pulled her towards him. Sliding her arms around his neck, she kissed him as he moved his right hand down between her legs. She parted them slightly, and Joseph very gently rubbed his fingers against her. She could feel his penis pushing hard against her stomach, and a new feeling of excitement ran through her body. She widened her stance slightly more and began moving her hips so that Joseph's fingers rubbed more against her.

After a short while, Julia reached down, took hold of Joseph's arm and gently pulled it away from her body. She then, very slowly sank to the ground and lay on her back. She reached her right hand up towards him, and he dropped down on his knees, turned and lay down beside her. Caressing her breasts, he slowly moved his head down until he was able to kiss them, very gently – first one and then the other. Her nipples were firm and she lifted herself slightly as she ran her fingers through his hair, round his neck and across his back.

Eventually she pulled at his shoulder and opened her legs, moving her hips up and down as she did so. Joseph lifted himself over and gently lay on top of her. She opened her legs further, still moving her hips, and then lifted her legs to wrap them firmly around Joseph's. He stopped kissing her breasts and slid up to kiss her neck. As he did so, he reached down and guided himself gently just inside her, lifting himself slightly again so that their eyes met. Very gently, he dropped his weight down onto Julia's hips, allowing himself to enter her as far as he could. They both sighed and then, open mouthed again, they kissed, hard. Julia pulled him into her as hard as she could as they moved quickly together.

Joseph lifted his lips away from Julia's as he felt his orgasm coming, and grunted gently as he came. She reached up and kissed the tip of his nose and smiled at him as their rhythm began to quieten. A bead of sweat ran down his face and she gently wiped it away with the back of her hand. They smiled at each other as their movements slowed to a standstill. Joseph dropped his head beside Julia's and closed his eyes. She stared up through the beautiful branches of the great yew tree, listening to him panting in her ear.

After a few minutes, Julia gently slapped Joseph on his

bottom and said in a comic voice: "Too heavy!"

Joseph laughed, took his weight on his elbows and drew himself out from Julia. He then rolled over and lay on his back next to her. They both gazed up through the branches of the yew tree above them and lay perfectly still, eyes closed, listening to the comforting sounds of the woods around them.

After about twenty minutes, Julia opened her eyes, turned to Joseph and said, "I think I need to get dressed. I'm getting cold".

Joseph turned his head, leaned across and kissed her on her cheek. Slowly he got to his feet and reached down to help her up. They embraced for a while, kissed, and then separated and started to dress. After checking that they had packed everything away, Joseph picked up the picnic basket and then, holding hands, they walked slowly out from under the yew trees. The sun was still shining brightly as they walked out onto the open down land, but the temperature was dropping quickly.

"It's going to be cold tonight," said Julia.

"Yes," Joseph replied, "we might get an early frost".

Chapter Twelve

THE DROP

In the middle of November, Joseph received a message to meet in the woods at eight o'clock the following evening. The code passed on by the postman made it clear that he should be fully armed and ready to be out all night.

As usual, Joseph went to find his father, to explain that yet again, he would not be around to help with the milking or any of the rest of the day's work on Friday.

Charles knew what was coming as soon as he saw Joseph walking across the farm yard. Whenever Joseph went to tell his father that he would have to be away on active duty for a while, his body language was always the same; he walked more hesitatingly than usual, his hands were in his pockets and apart from the occasional glance up, his eyes were on the floor. Before his son had a chance to speak, Charles stopped stacking wooden apple crates against the side of the barn, stood up straight and said, "You look like you've got your tail between your legs mate. What's up?"

They both knew what was up, and for a few seconds,

they just looked at each other.

"Tomorrow night," said Joseph. "I'm needed tomorrow night. Should be back at first light, but probably not early enough for the milking; and I don't suppose I'll be much good for anything all day, having been out and about all night. Can you manage?"

This same conversation had played out so many times during the last six months that they both felt like they were in a play that repeated itself over and over again.

"Course we will," Charles muttered, "You'd better make sure you're home for breakfast though."

They smiled at each other and Joseph spoke again as he turned to go; "Wouldn't miss Mum's breakfast for the world."

The next evening, Joseph had an early supper with his mother. As they ate their stew and dumplings, they talked about the farm and people that they both knew from the village. Joseph even mentioned Julia a few times.

Mary was careful not to ask too much about Julia, she didn't want to interfere – but inside she was as pleased as punch that they were courting. Mary knew Julia's family; she knew that they were good people and that Julia was a lovely girl. They both went out of their way not to talk about the war.

After finishing their stew, Mary took Joseph's back-pack from the coat rack and the old thermos flask from the window sill above the sink.

"There's a nice bit of cheddar and some of Gran's cake," she said as she collected up and wrapped the various food items from around the kitchen. She held up the thermos: "Tea?"

"Yes, please Mum," he replied as he cleared the dirty plates to the sink. "I'll be back for breakfast."

Two minutes later, he swung the back-pack over his shoulder, and he and Mary hugged each other tight in the middle of the kitchen. A minute later he was outside in the dark, pushing his bike towards the old chicken shed to fetch his rifle.

By ten to eight, Joseph had left the road, ridden down a forest track and was hiding his bike in amongst a great mess of old ferns and brambles. Five minutes later he walked up to a spot known locally as Six-Ways, where six pathways met, and although it was dark, the full moon threw enough light down through the bare branches to be able to make things out without too much difficulty. As he approached the meeting place, Joseph could see a single figure on the path ahead of him. It was the unmistakeable figure of Commander Henry Clay.

"Good man," said Henry as they shook hands. "We'll wait here for the others to join us, and then we'll head off to the landing strip."

Joseph didn't know where tonight's landing strip would be, as Henry was the only one who would have been told the coordinates, but he knew what it was. It was a secret parachute dropping zone for weapons, ammunition, explosives and other supplies that the Resistance requested from time to time. The drops were always made at night by planes that usually came in from the north. Once, ten paratroopers had landed that way to carry out some special mission. They'd only been with them for about an hour, before marching off east into the night. They never saw them again.

After another twenty minutes, the rest of the men arrived. Henry spoke to two of them, giving them specific instructions as to exactly where he needed them to be with the truck in one hour's time. The men nodded to the others as they turned and headed off to collect the truck.

Henry and the rest of the men walked off in single file heading north. An hour later, they emerged from the beech woods into a large area of coppiced hazel and then came to some small meadows that ran along on the last of the relatively low land before it started to rise up to the Downs. They walked up to the edge of the first meadow and stopped, still standing under the cover of the overhanging hazel trees. Henry took a torch from his backpack, pointed it across the field, and gave three flashes.

Almost immediately, three flashes were returned from the other side.

"Good," Henry whispered, "They're ready with the truck and it's all clear". He checked his pocket watch. "About another twenty minutes to go."

Fifteen minutes later, Henry waved Joseph towards him. "Right," he said, leaning in close, "You know what to do don't you?"

"Yes." Joseph nodded.

The other men had already removed the staples from the chestnut fence posts immediately in front of them, and were holding the barbed-wire down to the ground with their boots. Joseph handed his rifle to Alex, stepped between the two men holding down the wire, and made his way slowly out into the open field. He walked in a dead straight line towards where the flashlights had come from and when he was about thirty yards from the far side of the field, he turned, took a flare from his bag, placed it firmly on the ground, lifted the fuse clear, pulled off the protective end cap, struck a match and held it to the fuse. It spluttered into life immediately, and Joseph started to retrace his steps. He had only gone a few paces before the flare burst in to full life, throwing a brilliant white light out into the dark night.

Joseph walked on, still counting his paces as he went and on the count of twenty he took another flare from his bag; the fuse caught first time, and he walked on again, counting another twenty. The fuse of the third flare took two attempts to catch, but it soon joined with the others in lighting up the middle of the field as Joseph made his way back to the waiting men.

"How long do they burn for?" Alex whispered as he passed Joseph's rifle back to him.

"About four minutes."

They all knew that this was the most dangerous time on these drops. If a German patrol just happened to be in the immediate area, or a German reconnaissance plane was to fly over, they would be in big trouble.

After what felt like an eternity, but was in fact only about two minutes, Alex whispered, "Hark, there's a plane coming!"

They all turned their heads and listened, and sure enough, there was the unmistakeable sound of an airplane approaching from the northwest. They all looked up to the sky as the noise of the engines became louder. Even when the noise of the engines was right overhead, they still couldn't make out the aeroplane, but as the noise moved away to the southeast, Joseph was the first to spot the three ghostly shapes in the sky.

Soon the men on both sides of the field could make out the parachutes, and as the flares died down, they stood out more, their pale shapes silhouetted like giant moths against the dark sky behind them. In the inky darkness, it was difficult to judge how high up they were, but although they were falling in the general direction of the field it was becoming clear that they were going to overshoot.

Before the parachutes landed, Joseph handed his rifle back to Alex and ran back into the field wielding his trenching spade. One by one, he lifted a large divot of turf from the field, knocked the still smouldering flare into the hole, dropped the divot back on top of the flare and then jumped up and down on it a few times to make sure that it was extinguished and out of sight. As he dealt with the last one, the first of the parachutes landed right on the edge of the field, only about fifty yards along the fence from where they had been standing. As he headed off towards it, he saw the second parachute sail on for what he guessed would be a further one or two hundred yards into the hazel coppice. He guessed that the third would land a similar distance further on again; probably in amongst the beech woods.

As Joseph reached the first parachute, Alex handed him back his rifle, and they took out their knives and started to cut through the strings so that they could gather in the great flailing canopy as quickly as possible. As they did so, they heard the sound of the truck engine start up, and watched as its dark figure came straight towards them.

As the truck reached them, they had the main canopy rolled up and had started to undo the ropes that held the heavy-duty netting that was wrapped around about a dozen wooden crates. As quickly as they could, the four men lifted the crates, the netting, and the parachute canopy onto the back of the truck and checked the field as best they could in the dark for debris. The driver jumped back into his seat and drove through the lowered barbed wire as Joseph and Alex held it down, and followed the track through the hazel coppice in the general direction of where they thought the next chute had landed. Joseph and Alex lifted the barbed wire back up and secured it by knocking the staples back into the chestnut fence posts.

"Good job," Alex said as they turned and headed off down the track after the truck.

Henry and the other men had easily found the second parachute and its load, and had already sorted it out by the time that the truck reached them. They managed to get the truck to within about twenty yards from where the second load of crates had come to rest in amongst the hazel coppice, and so didn't have to work too hard to get everything picked up and loaded. They checked the area as best they could to make sure that they hadn't left any evidence of the drop and set off in search of the third chute whilst the truck was driven slowly along the track behind them.

Sure enough, about two hundred and fifty yards further on, there was the third parachute, hanging precariously half way up a huge beech tree, with its load swinging in its net six feet off the ground. Three large wooden crates had escaped from the netting and some of their contents were spilled out onto the forest floor.

"Jesus," said Henry, as he walked up to the crates, "They're explosives!"

The men stopped in their tracks.

"It's OK," Henry assured them, "We just have to be careful. Now, let's pick these up gently and then we'll deal with the rest of the load. Alex, stop that net from swinging, whilst we clear this lot up."

Alex walked over to the swinging net, reached up and held it steady. The others very gingerly collected up the spilled explosives, placed them gently back in their original crates and carried them over to the truck.

Alex stood absolutely still, holding on tight to the netting, looking up every few seconds at the parachute trapped in the branches above him, then at the crates in front of his face and then across to his mates carrying the crates of explosives across to the truck. As they walked back towards him, the main parachute canopy, stuck up in the branches above Alex's head ripped, and the netted load slipped, swayed, and slipped again as Alex held on to stop the crates from spilling out from the net.

They eventually dropped hard onto the forest floor as Alex finally lost his balance, but still holding on to the net, slowly fell forwards across the top of the crates as the whole of the canopy descended from the branches above him with a great whooshing noise, covering him and the netted crates in a massive heap of white cloth. He let go of the netting, slipped down to his knees and crawled out from under the parachute just as Henry, Joseph and the other men reached him.

"Well done," said Henry casually, "I was wondering how we were going to get that down."

"Never mind that," Alex retorted, still rattled and breathing in short, laboured breaths, "What about the explosives?"

"What about them?" asked Joseph, as he walked away. "They're safely on the truck. Your crates are full of rifles!"

"You bastards!" Alex shouted as he stood up, freeing himself from the last of the parachute.

"Yes; good job though!" – Joseph broke into a broad smile.

Alex stared at the ground, and then, feeling his usual good humour returning, he looked at each of the men smiling at him, smiled back, wagged his finger at them and said, "You'd all better watch out, 'cos I'll get you back one day!"

Henry spoke again. "Come on lads, let's get this last lot loaded and get out of here".

Chapter Thirteen

BACK TO THE VILLAGE

Since the previous week's parachute drop, things had been relatively quiet. Joseph had been busy working, and apart from a few German planes flying over every now and then, there didn't appear to be much going on.

As the end of November was approaching, the days were getting very short and in between the clear, fresh, sunny days of late autumn, there had recently been a few days of strong winds and cold rain to remind everyone that winter was coming.

Granny Carter hated this time of year when the wind blew. No matter how quickly she stoked the kitchen range, or even if they kept open fires burning during the day, the old house never got warm. It was the wind that upset her the most; not the short days and dark evenings, not even the cold rain – but the wind.

"That damned wind upsets my mind," she often said to whichever member of the family happened to be nearby. "Doors bang, smoke blows back down the chimney into the house, the curtains billow and you can't sit comfortable anywhere without a draft whistling down your neck."

There was no doubt about it; "The damned wind" certainly did upset her mind. She was never more agitated than when the wind blew; and the whole family knew it.

Joseph felt much the same. He had never liked the wind either – it upset his mind too: he didn't trust it. He felt, like Gran, that it spoilt everything. If the wind got up when he was out hunting, he would always call it a day and go home early. He couldn't concentrate when it was blowing; it was too distracting, whistling through the trees and sending the branches thrashing about all over the place. It wasn't fair either. It wasn't fair on him as a hunter, nor on the animals that he was hunting.

How could his senses work properly when the wind was being so disruptive? He couldn't hear or feel properly when it blew, and he was pretty sure that the animals felt the same. He certainly didn't want to creep up on deer under the cover of the howling wind. Where would the sport or skill be in that? Joseph felt that, in nature and in life, there should always be a proper balance; and as far as he and his grandmother were concerned, the wind unbalanced everything, especially the mind.

This last few days, he had been feeling particularly unsettled, and as he cycled off towards Watersham at midday on Saturday, the wind was still blowing hard.

Great black clouds raced across in front of heavy grey skies, and every now and then a shower of ice cold rain fell to the ground, bounced on the shiny tarmac and then ran away to join the great puddles that had formed along the sides of the road. Joseph pedalled as hard as he could into a headwind, shoulders hunched and head down, hardly able to see where he was going through the pouring, stinging rain.

About halfway to the village, he decided that enough was enough and stopped under a large chestnut that overhung the road. There wasn't much shelter from the bare branches overhead, but by standing hard up against the trunk, he was able to protect himself from the worst of the wind and the rain. He stood, his back pressed hard up against the tree with his bike leaning against him, for nearly ten minutes, before the rain suddenly stopped and the wind eased.

His trousers were soaked through, his overcoat sodden and he could feel rain running down the back of his neck. He ran his fingers through his wet hair, shook his head and his hands to get rid of some of the water, and then wiped his face. He wondered about turning back for home, but, deciding to carry on, he wheeled his bike back out onto the road.

As he put his foot onto the pedal and was about to push off, he looked ahead, and there, only thirty yards further on down the road, parked up on the side, was a German truck. Sitting in the back were about a dozen or more soldiers. The three or four sitting nearest to the tailgate were looking straight at him.

"Shit," he murmured to himself, "There's definitely no turning back now."

He scooted forward with his left foot on the pedal until he was right up close to the truck, where he stopped and looked straight up at the soldiers. Then, slowly stretching his arms out to his sides, he shook his hands and his head and did his best impression of a half-drowned rat as he shouted, "I'm bloody soooaaaked!!"

The Germans didn't know what he was saying, but knew exactly what he meant, and they all laughed and pointed at him, as Joseph played to the gallery a bit more by frowning heavily and hunching his shoulders further. Then, very slowly, he walked on by, waving to the driver and passenger in the front of the vehicle as he shook first one leg and then the other in a comical fashion. He walked on for a bit further; then changed to scooting along for a short distance, before throwing his right leg over the saddle and pedalling off.

Ten minutes later, as he rode into the village, he noticed another German troop truck parked half on the pavement on Blacksmith's Corner; but this one was empty. As he came to the Red Lion pub, there was a third truck parked outside, with a Mercedes staff car parked a little further on.

Joseph slowed to almost a walking pace, as it dawned on him for the first time that, apart from a group of German soldiers up ahead of him there was nobody else in the street. A cold shiver ran up and down his already cold and wet back and he slowed to a complete stop, dismounted, and continued to walk towards the soldiers, his heart beating faster as he tried to behave normally.

Out of the corner of his eye he spotted movement in a narrow side street off to his right. He turned his head slightly to see a thick-set man, dressed in a heavy coat and wearing a large brown trilby hat, cycle to the junction, look both ways, and, without stopping, pedal off in the direction from which Joseph had just come.

Their eyes met for only a split second, but although they instantly recognised each other, neither man showed any outward sign that they knew each other. Commander Henry Clay cycled slowly away and Joseph carried on walking towards the Germans, his heart beating even faster now.

As Joseph came up to the soldiers, he could see that they were almost as wet as he was. They must have been out in the rain and the wind for some time. One of them stepped off the pavement and onto the road, the thumb of his left hand hooked under the leather strap of the rifle that was hanging on his shoulder, and held up his right hand. Joseph stopped immediately, just as a fresh gust of wind and rain blew down the street, forcing curses and swearing from the main group of soldiers. They were clearly fed up with the weather, and were becoming agitated. An image of Granny Carter flashed across Joseph's mind.

"Papers," the soldier demanded in a thick accent.

Joseph slipped his hand inside his jacket. He felt the papers there almost immediately and inside he breathed a sigh of relief; he was not too good with official papers and quite often forgot to carry them. He handed them to the soldier who quickly flicked over them, then looked back again at the front page, which held a photograph of Joseph. He looked backwards and forwards between the photograph and Joseph's face several times, and then, satisfied that the one belonged to the other, he handed the papers back to Joseph, stepped back onto the pavement and waved his arm, indicating that he could go on his way. Joseph tucked the papers back into his inside pocket, did his coat buttons back up again, offered a slightly hesitant, "Thank you" to the soldier, and walked on down the street with his bike.

The rain was starting to come down much heavier again, and seeing the bus shelter up ahead, he walked on quickly until he reached it and took cover. He looked back down the street just in time to see two men being taken away by the soldiers that he had just encountered. The men walked between the Germans in their shirts and waistcoats in the pouring rain, with their hands on their heads. Joseph couldn't make out who they were.

As the group walked further away towards the truck, a middle-aged woman appeared in a doorway near to where Joseph had been stopped, waving her arms, screaming and shouting. The wind and the rain were making so much noise that Joseph couldn't catch whose names she was calling. After a while, two other women appeared next to her, and as her shouts calmed, so the two women persuaded her back inside and the door closed behind them.

Joseph stood under the shelter for another twenty minutes as the rain lashed down, the wind every now and then picking up and sending a curtain of water down the street. Eventually the wind and the rain eased off a bit, and Joseph decided to carry on through the village to see if he might be able to spot

Julia in the café. As he rounded the slight bend in the road, he could see three German cars parked by the café up ahead. Standing on the pavement on both sides of the street, five or six paces apart, were a group of soldiers.

Joseph walked on slowly, and as he came up to the first car, he moved with his bike out in to the middle of the road. The German soldiers looked at him as he walked by, and as he did so, he glanced into the café. There was so much condensation running down the inside of the windows and so much rain on the outside that it was difficult to see – but what was clear to see in a glance was that the place was full of German officers.

As he walked on, the front door of the café opened and out came Arthur Williams. Joseph looked away, pretending not to notice him, and quickly pushed his bike from the pavement to the street. He knew that he wasn't going to get a chance to see Julia today. He remounted his bike and steadily peddled off down the street.

At the end of the main street there was yet another truck parked on the side of the road and German soldiers standing on the pavement. As he came near to the back of the truck he got a clear view of George Ashton sitting between two soldiers in the back of the truck. He glanced towards the terrace of houses where he knew the Ashton's lived, and seeing more soldiers standing by the front door, he looked away and pedalled on, at any moment expecting to hear a soldier cry Halt! But to his relief, no one called after him.

He looked straight ahead and pedalled at a steady speed as he reached the last house that marked the far end of the village. Two hundred yards further on was a narrow farm lane that led down to Lower Watersham Farm; and from there up into the woods.

Joseph looked back over his shoulder to check that the coast was clear and swung across the road and into the lane. He pedalled harder, determined to get away from the main road and the village as quickly as he could. The rain stopped and the wind dropped as he pushed on past Lower Watersham Farm and up the lane towards the woods. Once into the trees, he jumped off his bike, pushed it up a small earth bank and picked up a footpath that he knew well.

For over a mile he pushed on hard, his feet slipping and sliding on the muddy and leafy forest floor. His heart was racing again, he was worried, he was wet, and although he was sweating, he felt cold.

He stopped to catch his breath and leant against a beech tree that stood where three paths divided. He knew this spot well; he'd been here many, many times before. After a minute, he felt better and headed off down the middle path knowing that he was only two miles from home.

He emerged from the woods a few hundred yards to the south of the farm yard, lifted his bike over a barbed wire fence, ducked through the fence and cut straight across the field to a hedge that ran along the other side. He followed the hedge that led him to within twenty yards from the back of the main barn that ran along the southern side of the farm yard.

Stepping through a gap in the hedge he walked to a small door that was set in the centre of the back of the barn. He listened for a while, and then hearing nothing unusual, slowly opened the door and pushed his bike inside. He leaned it against a feed bin that was just inside the door and walked to the front of the barn. He listened again, and then carefully opened the side door next to the main double doors at the front of the barn. Seeing that there was no one around, he walked quickly across the yard, opened an empty stable door and went inside. He knew that he would get a good view of the lane and the front of the house from here, and so he picked up a handful of straw and wiped away the cobwebs and some of the dust from one of the window panes. Holding his breath, he peered out, quite expecting to see German soldiers and vehicles in the lane or by the house.

There was nothing.

He gave out a sigh of relief, opened the door of the stable, walked back out into the yard, turned, walked out through the main gateway to the yard, stopped, and looked up and down the lane. Still there was nothing. He walked on up to the house and made his way around to the back door.

As he stepped into the warm kitchen, Lily looked up from the kitchen table.

"Joe! I thought you'd gone to the village? Blimey, you look wet."

Joseph unbuttoned his coat. "Where is everyone?"

"In the front room, I think."

"Could you go and ask them all to come in here? I'm soaking wet."

As Lily went off to fetch the others, Joseph hung his coat over the back of a chair and bent down to untie the laces on his boots. As Charles walked into the kitchen, Joseph was sitting on a chair pulling his socks off. Charles walked straight over, picked up his son's sodden boots and took them outside, leaving them turned upside down on a pile of logs by the back door. The rest of the family walked into the kitchen.

"What is it?" asked Granny Carter. "What's up?"

As Joseph started to speak, his mother stood right in front of him, first feeling his soaked shirt, then holding his hand and touching his face.

"My God!" she cried, "You're soaked to the skin and half frozen to death! Now, before you say anything, get yourself upstairs, get out of these wet clothes and get yourself dry. What you have to tell us can wait a bit longer, I'm sure."

As she finished speaking, she and Lily were already pushing him towards the door. Mary went to the airing cupboard next to the kitchen range, took out two bath towels and handed them to Lily. "Here," she said, "Take these up to your brother."

Lily ran upstairs with the towels, knocked on the bedroom door, handed the towels to Joseph, and sat down on the top step of the stairs. As she waited, she could hear cups and saucers being placed on the kitchen table, and after a while, the soft, high pitched whistling noise of the big old black kettle coming to the boil, drifted up the stairs.

"That looks better," said Lily, as Joseph stepped out onto the landing.

He was wearing an old dressing gown over some dry clothes, his slippers and one of the bath towels around his neck. His hair was tousled, and as he walked back into the kitchen, Mary thought that he looked just like a little boy again. Granny poured the tea, as everyone settled in their places around the kitchen table. Joseph took a sip of tea and then started to tell them what he had seen during the afternoon. No one interrupted his story, and when he finished, there was total silence. After a while, Granny Carter pushed her chair back, stood up, and made her way back to the range to push the kettle back onto the hot plate, muttering under her breath as she went.

"That's the bloody wind for you," she said, "Always messing everything up." They sat for some time in silence as Catharine refilled the teapot and sat back down.

"I wonder how many they've taken away?" Charles said quietly.

Harold answered sombrely. "There's no way of knowing. We won't know until later, when news comes up from the village. And then of course, there's all the outlying farms... who knows?"

They looked around the table at each other and then sat in silence again. Suddenly there was a noise from outside. They all jumped and stared at the back door. A heavy shadow appeared through the glass and there was a knock. The door opened before anyone could get up to answer it, and in walked Commander Henry Clay. They all jumped up from their chairs as one and, in sheer relief, started to speak at the same time: "Come in!"

"Come in! Sit down... have a chair!"

"Come on... take mine!"

"Are you alright?"

"Is there any news?"

"Get those wet clothes off!"

"Come over by the range and get warm."

Eventually Charles raised his voice above the others and brought about some order. "Quiet! Quiet now! Give the man a chance".

Everyone calmed down as Henry took off his hat and coat. Charles offered him a seat as Catharine fetched another cup and saucer from the cupboard.

Henry looked across at Joseph. "Glad to see you made it back old son: I was worried about you".

"I was worried about you too," Joseph replied. "I couldn't believe it when I saw you riding through the village!"

For the next five minutes, the two men told each other what they had seen. Between them they reckoned that at least seven men had been taken away, but they had no idea if there were more. They would have to wait until tomorrow before they could find out. Henry quickly downed two cups of tea and Charles took him upstairs, gave him a towel and found him some of his spare clothes.

"You can use our bedroom" Charles said, pointing to the door. "Come down when you're ready and we'll have some supper."

"Thanks Charles," said Henry. "I appreciate it."

As they ate, they all tried hard to keep off the subject of what had happened during the afternoon. But it was impossible, and time and again one of them would reintroduce the subject. Whilst the table was cleared and they did the washing up, they continued to talk, and by the time nine o'clock came around, they were still discussing it.

Suddenly Charles said, "Who's on milking duty in the morning?"

"We are," Joseph and Lily replied in unison.

"Right then; time we were all off to bed in that case. Henry, do you need anything else?"

"No", said Henry. "Thanks, you've been very kind".

"There's a spare blanket in the cupboard in your room if you should need it," said Mary.

At a quarter past five the next morning, Joseph and Lily were sitting by the kitchen table drinking their tea when Henry came down the stairs.

"Morning," he said, "I've come to see if my clothes are dry".

He walked over to the chairs that had been turned with their backs to the range with his wet clothes hanging from them.

"Great", he said, "They are".

He collected the clothes up in his arms and went straight back upstairs. Five minutes later he was back down again and, after pulling on and lacing up his still damp boots, he stood, and with Joseph and Lily following closely behind, he made his way out through the back door.

"Right, I'll be off then. Thank your folks for me for last night's supper and the bed. I need to get back to make sure the wife's alright. She'll be worried sick. I'll get news to you about how things are in the village as soon as I can. In the meantime – keep your head down."

He turned and smiled at Lily as he added, "Goodbye young lady. You make sure you keep an eye on your brother for me, won't you?"

"Course I will Mr Clay," she said.

"One more thing Commander... before you go?" Joseph stuttered. He looked back at Lily, who immediately got the message and made her way back inside.

"I need to ask you about Arthur Williams."

"What about him?"

They walked a little further away from the house.

"I don't know. But he's beginning to worry me. Every time I turn around, he seems to be there, and he seems to be very comfortable in the company of some of the German officers. I don't know what he's up to, but I've got a bad feeling about him."

Henry placed a hand on Joseph's shoulder, looked him straight in the eye, and spoke slowly and quietly. "You're not the only one worried about Mr Williams. Several of us have noticed that just like a bad penny, he always seems to turn up. Don't worry about it though. It's being taken care of. Whatever you do, don't mention it to anyone else."

Joseph nodded. "Whatever you say Commander. I was just getting a bit concerned."

"Quite right Joseph. Now, I really must be heading back home."

The two men shook hands and Joseph watched as Henry rode off into the early morning gloom.

Joseph walked slowly back inside and went straight to the kitchen table where he found his cup. Taking a last gulp of tea, he looked across at Lily, who was standing with her back to the kitchen range. She smiled at him.

"Ready now soldier boy?"

"Come on then," replied Joseph. "Let's get on with it".

They took their coats from the rack, Joseph opened the kitchen door, and they walked back out into the early morning. As they set off down the lane towards the waiting cows by the dairy, Lily said, "Not a bad morning Joe."

"No," replied Joseph, "and no bloody wind, thank God."

Two days later, just before dark, Arthur Williams received an unannounced visit from Bert Stubbs, Alan Brenton, James Miles, John James and Albert Rose.

Arthur opened the door and seeing Bert and his men standing on his doorstep, he turned and walked slowly and silently back down the hall and into his tiny sitting room. The men followed him and James Miles, being the last man in, closed the door behind them and stayed standing in the hallway.

Arthur sat down on the armchair that was pulled up by the fire and looked nervously at the men crowding into his sitting room. A few dull red embers glowed in the grate, and a weak flame licked the sides of a half-burnt elm log in the fireplace. The heat and comfort emanating from the fire was negligible – the room smelt of a mixture of wood smoke and damp. Bert Stubbs sat in the second armchair on the other side of the fireplace and his men stayed standing, blocking out most of what little evening light there was coming through the cottage window.

Bert leaned forward in his chair, and even though the light was bad, it was good enough for him to see that most of the colour had drained from Arthur's face.

"So, you like to be friendly with the German soldiers?"

Arthur, his gaze having fallen to the floor as Bert asked his question, lifted his head slightly and stared at the backs of his hands as he answered hesitatingly.

"No. Not really. I mean; I just pass the time of day with them. I don't... I mean, I don't go out of my way to talk to them. I mean; well, I only talk to them if they talk to me and I..."

Bert leaned forward slightly further and raised his hand as he interrupted Arthur's faltering answer.

"But you do like to talk to them. Don't you Arthur?"

Arthur looked at the floor again and rubbed his hands up and down on his knees.

"No, no. I don't like talking to them. I only talk to them if they ask me questions."

"What sorts of questions do they ask you then Arthur?"

"Oh... nothing really. Just everyday, ordinary questions really. Nothing unusual, you know. Just the normal sort of questions. Just, well... nothing really... you know."

Bert raised his hand and interrupted Arthur again.

"Give me an example of the sorts of questions they asked you Arthur."

Arthur cleared his throat and stilled his hands by forcing them together and pushing them down between his legs. He started to rock himself, very gently, backwards and forwards.

"Well, as I say, they never really asked much about anything. They just wanted to know what I'd seen. You know. If I'd seen anybody or anything suspicious, like... well you know. Like things going on in the village.""

Like what going on in the village Arthur?"

"I'm not sure really. Just unusual things."

"So, you told them when you saw some of the villagers going off together somewhere did you?"

"No! I... I... I wouldn't have said anything about you Bert, or Henry Clay!"

Alan Brenton shifted his weight from one leg to the other and rested his hand on the top of Arthur's arm chair.

Bert looked up at Alan. "I didn't say anything about Henry Clay. Did you Alan?"

"No. I never mentioned him. In fact, I don't believe that anyone did."

Bert returned his gaze to Arthur. "None of us mentioned Henry Clay, Arthur. So why did you feel the need to mention him?"

Arthur stared at the floor again. "I don't know. I didn't mean him in particular. I just meant... as an example like. Yes. That was it. Just as an example."

"So, who else have you been talking to the Germans about, Arthur? Given that you didn't talk to them about me or Henry Clay?"

"No... look! It's not what you think! I didn't really talk to them about any of you! They just asked me to look out for men coming and going! I couldn't really tell them much, 'cos I didn't see much… just a car here and a van there… sometimes I saw some men moving about… Nothing much though."

"Did you like riding in the staff car, Arthur?"

"No. Now listen to me. I didn't want to go with them in their car. They said that I had to." Arthur was speaking much faster now and looked up into the faces of the other men. "I didn't have much choice. I didn't tell them anything though. What would I know about the big fire at Amersham? I mean – well, I mean… I wouldn't know who was missing from the village or the farms would I?"

"So; they asked you about what happened at Amersham did they?"

"I didn't tell them anything! I swear I didn't!"

"No; I'm sure you didn't, Arthur. After all, you didn't know anything, did you?"

"No! I couldn't help them! I mean "tell" them… tell them anything… I told them that I didn't know anything about it!"

"And then they asked you about the farms, didn't they Arthur? Did they ask you which of the men you saw coming in to the village from the farms? Did they ask you to keep an eye out, Arthur?"

"Well, yes, they did ask me about the farms. They did ask me to keep a bit of an eye out on who was coming and going. But I didn't tell them much. I only told them about who I saw moving around. I didn't tell them what they were up to though! Well, I didn't know what they were up to, did I?"

"And did you tell them about the men in Henry's van, Arthur? You know; when you were on your bike in the village – watching, and keeping an eye out?"

Arthur slowly lifted his head, and for the first time, looked straight into Bert's eyes.

"Bert: that's all I did. I just kept an eye out. I didn't give away no secrets. Well, I didn't know any, did I?"

"But, you told them who you saw, didn't you Arthur? And you told them who you saw coming into the village from the farms, didn't you?"

"Yes! But I only told them what I saw! It wasn't as though I was spying on anybody! I don't know who's in the Resistance and who isn't! And that's what I told them when they asked me! I told them that none of the other men in the village talk to me anyway... I told them I didn't really know anything... But they said that that was alright, if I could just keep an eye out and let them know who was moving around, that was all... that was all I did... that was all I told them."

"We don't like collaborators, Arthur."

"I'm not one of those! I'm not a collaborator! Don't say that! You can't say that! Bert! Please don't say that! It's not true!"

Arthur quickly looked around at the faces of the men in the room, but their expressions hadn't changed. They stared back at him, cold, and with no sign of compassion. Alan shifted his weight again and moved slightly further behind Arthur's chair allowing both of his hands to rest on its worn wings. Arthur turned his head slightly to look up and back at Alan.

"You believe me, don't you Alan? You know that I didn't mean any harm, don't you? I was just being a bit... well... I was just being a bit friendly with them. You see; they liked to talk to me. Not like most of the villagers. They never let me join in! They were always unkind to me... even at school they never let me join in! They were always picking on me..."

Slowly his gaze fell back to the floor again and he started to cry. He leaned forward and held his head in his hands and sobbed.

Bert watched Arthur for a while and then suddenly stood up.

"Stand up Arthur!" he shouted.

Arthur jumped and wiped his sleeves across his face and realised that Bert was now standing in front of him. He looked around at the other men and wiped his face again.

Bert spoke slightly softer this time. "Stand up Arthur."

With some difficulty, Arthur pushed himself up from his chair and stood facing Bert with less than a foot separating them.

"I've heard enough Arthur. I don't want to hear any more from you. Just listen to me."

Alan Brenton pulled the chair back a few inches. For a few seconds, the dragging noise of the chair on the bare wooden floor filled the room. Arthur began to shake, and he held his hands tight together in an attempt to control himself.

"I don't ever want to see you again Arthur. We don't want to see you again. The villagers don't want to see you again. We don't want you here, Arthur."

Arthur could hear what Bert was saying, but he was struggling to understand.

Did this mean that they weren't going to kill him?

"You don't belong to this village any more, Arthur. If you ever show your face around here again, I'll know about it – and that will be your last day in this village or any other."

Bert slowly stepped away from his chair and waved towards his men to leave. As one, they all turned and made their way out from the front room. James Miles opened the front door, stepped outside, and seeing that there was no one around, waved the others out. James quietly closed the door and followed the others off down the dark street.

Arthur Williams stood by his chair in the near dark sitting room, still trembling, for about five minutes. Eventually he pulled himself together, held onto the back of his chair for a while and then made his way up the narrow stairs to his bedroom, where he lifted down a large suitcase from the top of the wardrobe. For the next twenty minutes, he wandered from room to room collecting up essential items and packing them into the case. Then, still fully dressed, he climbed onto his bed, lay down on his back and closed his eyes. He couldn't sleep a wink – he spent most of the night replaying in his mind what had happened during the evening. It was cold. He pulled the bed blanket over himself and shivered in the dark. At six o'clock, he got up, picked up his suitcase, went downstairs and took his overcoat from the hook on the back of the front door and put it on. He turned up the collar on his coat, did the buttons up to the top, put on his old trilby hat and headed out into the dark, cold autumn morning.

He saw no one as he walked to the bus stop, where he waited for the twenty to seven that would take him away from the village forever.

Chapter Fourteen

HARVEST SUPPER

There had been a Harvest Festival in the village of Watersham for as long as anyone could remember. According to the parish and church records, some sort of celebration of the harvest had taken place every year back to when local records began. The Normans had been great bureaucrats and administrators and referred to the celebrations in their records of life in the eleventh century. English literature and the church referenced the festivities time and time again in writings, poems, songs and hymns.

For the last two years since war had broken out, the Harvest festival hadn't been quite so easy to organise. In that first autumn, there had been so much uncertainty, so much confusion, that the festival had almost been forgotten. It was only at the last minute that some of the older members of the village; especially those with a strong association to the church, organised a harvest supper to follow the church service on the first Sunday in October. Although called a harvest supper, because no doubt in times gone by the festivities were held on the big farms in the evenings; the majority of suppers were held at midday, directly following the morning service, and were in fact lunches.

Again, as far as anyone could remember, the lunches were now always held centrally, as a social event in the village hall, rather than on the farms. Most of the participants attended church first, even if they weren't regular churchgoers. That October, Mary and Catharine Carpenter had helped to decorate St Martin's with flowers and vegetables that had been harvested from local farms, allotments and gardens.

This year, everything was far more difficult. To start with, the Parish Council had felt obliged to notify the local German administrators about the festival; as, these days, they notified them about everything. To the surprise of the Council, a letter had been received from the administrators stating that the local German Commander and one of his assistants would be attending the lunch. The news went around the village like wildfire and went down like a lead balloon.

The first Sunday in October turned out to be a fine dry day. At a little before eleven, a large group of villagers stood chatting on the main Yorkshire Stone path that led to the front door of the church. The early autumn sunshine still had some strength in it, and people were pleased to be able to enjoy standing outside to chat. The main topic of conversation concerned their expected German guests.

"Surely," said Olive Tindall, "They won't come to the church service – will they?"

"Wouldn't think so," replied Granny Carpenter. "German soldiers don't go to church – do they?"

The general opinion seemed to be that they didn't and wouldn't.

The vicar, Timothy Simms, walked among his flock doing his best to reassure them. "Look," he said to the separate groups dotted along the path, "No matter what we think of them... If they come to the church, they'll be part of our congregation, and as such, we'll treat them just like any other members of the congregation. It won't hurt for us to share our church and our Harvest Festival with them for a few hours. In fact, it might help us all a bit."

Not one of the villagers could find the right words to reply to the vicar – their lack of response said it all. The Reverend knew exactly what they were thinking; in fact, deep down inside, he knew exactly what he was thinking as well.

By five to eleven the congregation had swollen to good numbers. With the sun's rays pouring through the stained-glass windows, there appeared to be a golden glow in the church. The shafts of light picked out millions of tiny specks of dust that slowly rose up and then disappeared against the background of the dark ceiling. The villagers, having found their places, stood in silence, looking up at the golden rays and admiring the harvest offerings that Mary and Catharine had expertly arranged around the church. There were flowers, vegetables and fruits of every description.

Even in these difficult times, the locals had made a special effort to provide produce for the Harvest Festival. Giant orange pumpkins sat surrounded by dark green cooking apples and blousy dahlias. Shiny red skinned onions, white skinned potatoes, some with soil still sticking to them, and bunches of bright orange carrots, their grass green tops hanging down, were mixed together in baskets, boxes and crates on every available flat surface. Pears, leeks and beetroot lay on the window sills with thick white candles amongst them; their tiny flames flickering gently.

At precisely eleven o'clock, Miss Estelle struck the first key on the organ and started off on a shortened rendition of Elgar's Organ Sonata No 1 in G. She had played the same piece at the harvest festival every year for the last twenty-seven years. She loved it and so did the congregation. It wouldn't be the same without Miss Estelle's Elgar at Harvest Festival. As she finished playing, the vicar prepared himself and took three short steps up to the lectern in readiness to speak to his congregation.

As the last of the echoing organ music ran off down the vaulted ceiling, there was the unmistakable clunking sound of the main door handle turning. The door opened, and in walked two German officers. The entire congregation turned their heads as one and watched as the two men, aware that all eyes were upon them, quickly found a pew at the rear of the church and sat down.

The eyes of the congregation returned to the vicar, who cleared his throat and began to speak.

"Tradition and our faith bring us together here today, in our beloved church, to give thanks to God for another successful harvest. We give special thanks to our hardworking farmers for growing and harvesting our crops and for caring for the farm animals. We thank Mary and Catharine especially for decorating our church so beautifully today. Let us stand together and sing hymn number 207: We Plough the Fields and Scatter."

Miss Estelle needed no further encouragement and played the introductory refrain with gusto, and allowing a slight hesitation after the first bar for those in the congregation to ready themselves, she set off with the villagers in full voice.

The German officers, having found the correct page in the hymn books in front of them, joined in as best they could.

Whilst the singing went on, every now and then, one of the members of the congregation would half turn to see how the Germans were getting along. After the second hymn, most had stopped worrying about the officers and were just pleased to be enjoying the service.

As Miss Estelle brought the hymn to an end, the Reverend walked back up to the lectern to deliver his special harvest festival sermon. Suddenly, he felt uncertain, uncomfortable and exposed. The church looked beautiful and was nearly full. Clearly everyone had enjoyed the singing and shortly they would all be going off to enjoy the Harvest Festival lunch.

As he had said to his congregation outside the church less than an hour ago, "We'll treat them just like any other members of the congregation..."

He stood at the lectern in total silence for about thirty seconds whilst contradictory thoughts ran around inside his head. Twice, he opened his mouth to speak, and twice no sound came out.

The congregation, slightly alarmed and uneasy now, stared up at their vicar with concern.

He looked out at the expectant faces before him and towards the two German officers seated at the back of the church. He looked across at Miss Estelle who had turned away from her organ to face him.

For a moment, she could see in his eyes that he didn't know what to do, and although she had no idea what he was thinking or what he was about to say, she knew, as he already knew, that there was no going back from here. She straightened her back, tightened the grip of her clasped hands on her lap and with the smallest of movements that only very few people noticed, she nodded her head.

The vicar saw her nod from the corner of his eye and he looked out again at his congregation, some of whom were now starting to shift uncomfortably in their seats, pushed back his shoulders and began to speak. He spoke so quietly and hesitantly to start with, that not many in the congregation could catch much of what he was saying.

"Our beloved England... the village... in the countryside... at this time of year... thinking of those who are no longer with us... the suffering goes on..." were the only parts of his speech that they managed to hear.

As he went on, so his voice gradually became stronger and clearer and the congregation, as one, suddenly realised what he was saying.

The German officers both had a pretty good understanding of the English language, but because they were at the back of the church and the vicar was at first hesitating so much, they had no idea what he was saying to begin with, but after a while his words reached them and every corner of the church very clearly.

For the next five minutes of his speech, he left no one in any doubt as to what he meant; everyone understood exactly what he was saying.

"Our village, like most other villages in the south of England, has been occupied by enemy forces. We did not invite them here. They are not our guests..."

Everyone sat very still and bolt upright, staring directly at the Reverend Simms. Some put their hands up to their mouths, some now closed their eyes and some held their breath, but as his words echoed around the church, they were all concentrating in a way that they had never concentrated before on one of his sermons and on the meaning of every word. "It's our duty to speak out. It's our duty to resist. It's your duty not to cooperate with the enemy. This is our village, not the enemy's..."

The longer that he went on, the clearer he became and although he was frightening himself and his congregation with what he was saying, he knew in his heart that he was doing the right thing. These people were his flock and he knew that today of all days that they would listen to him.

"Render unto Caesar the things which are Caesar's, and unto God the things that belong to God," he carried on "And when they take us away one by one, ten more shall take our place..."

Most of the congregation were looking at the floor now and some were quietly weeping and holding their heads in their hands – partly in prayer, partly in fear; but mostly in sheer sorrow at what had happened to them, to their families and friends and to their village, since the invaders had come.

As the vicar finished his sermon, he left no space or time for thought – and in one seamless move, he nodded to Miss Estelle to get ready, indicated the congregation to stand and said, "And now our favourite: hymn No. 282 – All Things Bright and Beautiful."

As he finished speaking, catching the urgency of the moment, Miss Estelle played the first bar of the hymn as loudly as she could, as the congregation got to their feet and prepared to sing like they had never sung before. People in the high street stopped what they were doing and looked up towards the church, surprised by the sound of the organ and the singing ringing out.

After the service, the German officers were the first to leave the church. They made their way down the high street towards the church hall, followed at some distance by a slow-moving line of villagers. Inside the church, a core of elders was talking quietly to the vicar. One by one, they shook his hand and patted his arm.

"Thank you," said Catharine. "Thank you. That was the best sermon that you've ever given. You've given us strength."

They all spoke to him and gave their thanks. Miss Estelle added hers and smiled at him.

"God help us all now," said the reverend Timothy Simms, "God help us all."

It took twenty minutes for the last of the villagers to enter the church hall. The German officers moved uneasily amongst them, making small talk about the weather, the harvest and how beautiful their church was. Cups of tea were eagerly taken up, drunk and replenished, and then Alf Thomas banged a ladle against the side of the tea urn and shouted, "Silence please – silence – silence please!"

The room went quiet and then Mrs Clay called out, "The pumpkin soup's ready; so, if you could form an orderly queue; we'll get you served as soon as we can. There's bread and butter, plates, knives and spoons on the tables – so if you could bring your bowls up .... and there's cheese, apples and pears on the other big table on the other side of the hall for afters, if you could just help yourselves."

They didn't need to be asked twice, and soon a long queue snaked around the hall. The Germans fell into line towards the back of the queue. Captain Muller turned, and noticing that the vicar was three or four spaces behind him, politely stepped aside, allowing those behind him to pass until he was standing next to the vicar.

"I do not think that we have met before. Allow me to introduce myself: my name is Captain Jan Muller."

The reverend Simms took his hand, looked directly into the Captain's eyes and replied, "I hope that you enjoyed our service. Do you hold Harvest Festivals in Germany?"

Both men were pleased with the question. It neatly avoided the issue of the sermon.

"Yes," the Captain replied, "The church in my village is very similar to yours. I expect my family are there today."

Chapter Fifteen

A LONG SHOT

For several days, there had been a rumour that large numbers of German reinforcements had arrived at some of the main Channel ports, and a further rumour that they were preparing for an attack on London. It was difficult for the local Resistance leaders to know what the truth was. Certainly, the German controlled radio station that had suddenly sprung into life a few days after the invasion regularly confirmed that German units were taking more and more control of everyday life along the South Coast, and constantly went out of its way, with news items, to reassure locals that they had nothing to be concerned about and that life would eventually be so much better under their administration.

On the other hand, the BBC broadcasts, now coming from some unknown place in the North of England, assured the population that recent setbacks were temporary and that soon, the invaders would be pushed back into the sea.

Getting good and accurate intelligence was more difficult for both the Resistance leaders and the villagers with each week that passed. Although they realised that much of what was being broadcast by both sides was just propaganda, never the less, most locals had faith in the optimistic broadcasts from the BBC. With such large German forces, so visible every day, however, it was difficult to maintain that optimism all the time. The news that German officers had even attended the Harvest Supper confirmed many villagers' worst fears. The German administration was becoming more entrenched with every day that went by.

When Commander Henry Clay received instructions to destroy the local German radio transmission station, he had very mixed feelings about the job. He knew from the very precise instructions that he had received that this was to be a combined operation right across southern England. The plan was to knock out every single German communications centre at exactly the same time, causing the maximum amount of disruption and confusion for the enemy.

Henry assumed that this also meant that a major counter attack by the British forces was about to happen. This was all good news, and Henry was delighted to receive it; they had been waiting for something like this for a long time. The bad news and the worrying bit was the specific target itself. He didn't know about German transmission stations and communications centres in other areas, but their local one was the most heavily fortified and defended base anywhere between Portsmouth and Brighton.

It was based right on the top of Burton Hill in the South Downs, about eight miles north of Watersham. Burton Hill was an ancient Neolithic camp and at about six hundred and fifty feet, it was the highest hill in the area. The top was one hundred acres of bare downland grass that for centuries had been grazed by Southdown sheep. The remains of the Neolithic fortifications could still be clearly seen. An earth mound with a dry ditch each side ran around the entire hilltop. Thousands of years ago, the local tribe would have used this place to defend themselves and their livestock from marauding animals and hostile tribes. In those days, there would have been heavy timber barricades and fences along the entire length of the ditches, and inside the defences, there would have been roundhouses for the people, and corrals for their beasts.

Now, in 1940, it was a modern military camp with two huge steel pylons carrying the Germans communications aerials. Beneath the great aerials there were generators, fuel tanks, a dozen trailer offices of various shapes and sizes, some wooden barracks, and a large collection of small buildings and sheds and enough army vehicles to run a major transport business.

The whole central area was fenced off with three separate meshed fences spaced about thirty yards apart, and in between sat four equally-spaced anti-aircraft guns mounted on fixed turntables. Further out from the centre there were sandbagged positions dotted over the hillside, where heavy machine guns were mounted.

Around the perimeter, following the lines of the Neolithic ditches, ran two heavy chain fences with rolled barbed wire running along the top.

Henry knew, from the regular intelligence reports that he received, that there were always at least fifty German soldiers based there, as well as the radio operators and technicians. Attacking and destroying the facility was going to be a nightmare. Henry knew that if he could call on the Royal Air Force for their help, life would be a lot easier – but he also knew that in the present circumstances, help from the RAF wasn't very likely. Never the less, he had already put in a request, through the normal channels to his unseen Commanders, with detailed coordinates and timings.

Having digested his instructions, Henry immediately sent out messages to his key lieutenants; and at seven o'clock that evening, ten men sat on up turned wooden crates inside the main barn at White Horse Farm, just outside of the village. A single paraffin lamp had been placed on the dirt floor in the middle of the barn, where its glow gave off enough light for the men to see each other well enough, and cast their long black shadows back across the stacks of straw to the sides of the barn.

Henry outlined the gist of the mission to his men and waited for a while for the sheer enormity of what he had just said to sink in. He was met with silence as most of the men stared at their boots. They were all thinking the same. Did they have enough men and resources to do it? Would they be able to knock out the radio station? How many men would they lose? After a while, Henry spoke again.

"It's going to be this coming Sunday. We're under strict instructions not to start the attack until three o'clock in the afternoon, and to be sure to have totally destroyed the radio station by seven in the evening."

Again, there was total silence as the men realised that the coming mission was even bigger and more important than they had first realised. Eventually, George Houseman spoke.

"Sounds like a long shot to me," he said. "Don't suppose we'll get any help, will we?"

"Don't bet on it George."

"Didn't think so," George mumbled.

Slowly the men got over their initial shock and started to talk amongst themselves about the nitty-gritty of what they needed to organise before next Sunday, and who they needed to call up. After an hour, they had sorted out most of the logistics and reckoned they could muster about seventy trained men between them. Once they had agreed a rendezvous point and time – in the beech woods just to the south of Burton Hill – Henry quickly ran through what he thought their tactics would be for the attack and then told them all to get off home.

"I'll get around to seeing many of you personally before the end of the week, to make sure we're all clear exactly what we're doing."

He stood up, lifted the oil lamp, and stood to one side as the men stacked the crates back against the side of the barn and trooped out into the dark November evening. Henry looked around to check that everything was in order, put out the lamp, walked across to the rear gate of the farmer's house and hung it on a nail on the gate post. He knew that the farmer would take it in before going to bed. He looked up at the sky. It was as clear as it could be, with stars twinkling right down to the horizon in the cold night air.

"Beautiful," he said to himself "just beautiful".

Over the next few days, Henry visited his key men and ran over his plans with them. At the same time, weapons, ammunition, explosives and other essential kit was made ready in scores of different hiding places, and more instructions were fed out to men further down the line.

At one o'clock on Sunday afternoon, 68 men assembled in the middle of the beech woods at the designated meeting place. They all knew these woods well enough, having trained in this area many times. During the previous hour or two, they had each made their way to this spot from their homes. They had collected everything that they needed as they made their way to the woods; avoiding the roads, keeping away from houses and farms, and always checking that they hadn't been spotted. Much of their training was based on this sort of activity – getting around the district without being seen – and so it was no surprise that they hadn't bumped into each other until they were about a quarter of a mile from the rendezvous. They acknowledged each other with nods and smiles as they met, but nothing was said. They stood in the middle of the woods in complete silence.

The Commander and his Lieutenants split up, and without fuss, the men fell in behind their allotted leader and they set off through the trees in their separate groups. The plan was very simple. Each one of the nine groups had a specific primary and secondary target to knock out, and in each group, there were two men carrying the main explosives that would hopefully be used to completely destroy the radio station. Henry watched as his men deployed to the edge of the woods, and then lost sight of most of them as they formed their positions in a horseshoe shape facing the station. He had stressed to his Lieutenants that they were not to completely encircle the compound, but to hold the horseshoe shape at all times.

"That way," he said, "We've half a chance of not shooting each other."

Once he was certain that everyone had had enough time to get themselves into their positions, Commander Clay raised his hand to indicate that they should move forward. The two groups either side of his relayed the message to the next, and within ten seconds, all groups were ready to move again. Although it was still only two o'clock, the November light was already fading under a heavy leaden sky and a light drizzle was falling. The air wasn't particularly cold, but the damp conditions made it feel much colder than it was.

Before breaking cover, lookouts in each team scanned the horizon with their binoculars to check for German guards patrolling the perimeter fence that ran along on the top of the outermost Neolithic bank. As far as they could see there was no activity, and so each team moved quietly out from under cover, and, half doubled over, made their way towards the bank.

As instructed, twenty yards from the outer ditch, they all got down on their knees, then edged their way forward on their bellies from there. The grass was very wet, and within minutes, they were all soaked to the skin.

It was raining more heavily now.

As each group reached the first ditch, they spread out,

and, still on their bellies, pushed themselves up to the top of the bank until their noses were almost up against the bottom of the mesh fence. There was still no sign of soldiers patrolling the perimeter, and there was no one moving about in the open. Through the rain, they could make out the internal fences, the anti-aircraft guns, the sandbagged defence positions and, in the middle, the two main aerials with all the offices, trucks and paraphernalia that went with them.

With no enemy in sight, two men in each team, still keeping as low as possible, set about cutting holes in the fence. The clicking of the wire cutters was muffled by the steady rain, and in very short order, it was finished and the mesh wire was folded back, leaving gaping holes. One by one the men crawled through and dropped down into the second ditch on the other side of the great bank.

Immediately they spread themselves out again, then crawled and wriggled their way up the other side of the ditch. They stopped to catch their breath, all the time checking around for movement.

Most of them were beginning to feel very uncomfortable – wet and cold as their clothes soaked up even more of the rain. They all knew that the next bit would be the most difficult. If they got caught out in the open, halfway between the ditch and the inner fence, they would be sitting ducks. They absolutely had to get to the sandbagged areas without being seen.

Henry lifted his binoculars again and slowly scanned the whole area from left to right, stopping at every key point to check for movement. He was pretty sure that no one was manning the anti-aircraft guns, and if there were soldiers behind the heavy machine gun posts, they were keeping their heads down and out of the rain. He wanted to get a better look at the buildings and vehicles in the centre, but his binoculars were now so misted up he lowered them, cursed under his breath, pulled a soggy handkerchief out from his trouser pocket and started to wipe the lenses. He cursed again as he saw the glass instantly smear. He'd forgotten that just before they set off, he'd used the handkerchief to wipe away some surplus gun oil from his machine gun. As he waved to Alex for him to hand over his binoculars, he suddenly became aware of a rumbling noise in the distance. He put his hand up flat, indicating to Alex to stop, and listened again. Although the noise of the rain was blotting out most background noises, there was no doubt in Henry's mind: he could hear an airplane engine, and it was coming straight towards them.

"Shit!" he whispered to Alex, "Get everyone in the ditch, quick! Quick! Take cover!"

Henry and Alex waved frantically; indicating that everyone should take cover. The message was quickly relayed along the horseshoe line and each man, without hesitation, turned and slid back into the ditch. They could all hear it now, and so could the German soldiers. Peering over the top of the ditch, Joseph and his men watched as a number of doors opened and armed men ran out, pulling on helmets and coats as they headed towards the anti-aircraft guns. As the German soldiers reached the gates that led through to the space between the two inner fences, where the main gun placements were, a twin-engine Mosquito suddenly dropped below the base of the cloud and appeared to be coming in no higher than the height of the aerials themselves.

Within seconds, the plane was on them, machine guns blazing, engines roaring, flying at more than 350 miles an hour as it released a bomb from its belly. Almost instantly, two of the trailer offices were enveloped in a great ball of fire that shot into the air from the exploding fuel tanks next to them. The noise was deafening.

With his hands held tight over his ears, Joseph looked up, just in time to see a second Mosquito coming in on the same line and trajectory. He dived for cover again as the machine guns strafed the main compound and another bomb fell and exploded, sending one of the anti-aircraft guns, sandbags and men spinning up into the air.

Henry watched the two planes as they flew on and started to bank to make a return run as his men peered back over the top of the ditch to see what damage had been done.

German soldiers were now running all over the place, desperately trying to extinguish the fires and attend to the injured. Three or four soldiers had picked themselves up and were stumbling towards the remaining anti-aircraft guns and the sandbagged areas.

The noise of the Mosquitos coming back in was suddenly very loud again, and Henry's men all threw themselves back into the bottom of the earth ditch.

The sound of the first Mosquito's machine guns was frightening as bullets ripped through the trailers and vehicles parked near to the aerials. As the second plane approached, one of the anti-aircraft guns opened up in defiance, as more bullets raked across the grassland and into the buildings and vehicles. One of the trucks exploded as the stored munitions on board were hit. The planes flew away undamaged as the lone anti-aircraft gunner fired after them.

Henry knew from experience that the Mosquitos would not return for a third run, and that they would have to strike now, whilst the enemy was still in shock. He waved at his men and the signal again went around the horseshoe.

The rain fell even heavier now, the air stank of burning fuel and tyres, and thick black smoke rose up ahead of them as they advanced, half crouched, half running towards the sandbagged oasis ahead of them.

The anti-aircraft gunner was the first to see them coming and he stood up, shouting a warning to his colleagues. Several shots rang out and he fell backwards from the turntable to the wet grass and mud below. Other soldiers looked up, dived for cover and returned fire. One managed to get to his heavy machine gun position before they reached the cover of the sandbags, and with one burst, he took out three of Henry's men before Henry himself dived against the bags, pulled himself up, reached up and over with his machine gun and fired a short burst. Instantly, the heavy machine gun fell silent.

Henry's men advanced without further loss and reached cover behind the sandbagged, heavy machine gun areas.

The German soldiers and technicians were trying to work their way away from the burning trailers and vehicles near to the main aerials. They had managed to start up some of the vehicles, and were busy driving them to safety towards the main gates on the far side of the hill.

Some of Henry's men tried to fire at the trucks, but without much success – every time they showed themselves from behind the sandbags, they were met with very accurate fire from the Germans still holed up in the centre. Another of Henry's men fell dead, hit in the head as he peered around the corner of a stack of sand bags.

Henry couldn't see very well through the smoke and the rain, but he guessed that the Germans would soon have the main gates open and would try to get as many as possible of their vehicles away. He looked across to the next wall of sandbags to see Alexander taking cover. Henry waved his arms to get his attention and eventually, Alexander saw him. He turned, took a deep breath, and ran as fast and as low as he could to join Henry. A burst of bullets, from a German machine-gun, splattered into the mud behind him.

"Alex! I need you to take some lads from the right flank and work yourselves over to a position nearer to the main gates! Take a heavy machine gun with you and give everything you can to those trucks that are trying to get out! We need to block the gateway. Quick as you can now – go on!"

Alexander gave his Commander the thumbs up, turned on his heels and ran fast and low back to where he had come from. More machine-gun bullets followed him. He took three or four more deep breaths, wiped the rain from his face and took off again towards the safety of the next pile of sandbags.

There was plenty of noise from guns of every description being fired by both sides, but for the moment none of the bullets were coming his way. He ran on to the next group of bags, where he found three of his men taking cover. Phillip Green was rearranging some of the bags in order to set up the heavy machine gun that he was in charge of.

"Never mind that!" Alex shouted, pointing at the heavy gun. "I need you to follow me further round with your gun," and then directing himself to the other two men, "Give us some covering fire as we set off!"

Behind the next set of sandbags, they found Jack Ferguson.

"Right Jack, follow us two!" said Alex, and with that he headed off towards the last group of bags. Phillip and Jack dived in behind him as more bullets whistled overhead and some thudded into the other side of the sandbags. Alex started rearranging the bags as he spoke to his men.

"Get the heavy gun set up here as quickly as you can. We need to stop those trucks!"

Within half a minute Phillip was all set up and ready to go. He took aim at a truck seventy yards away that was just about to go through the gates, and fired a short salvo that ripped through the passenger door of the cab and out through the windscreen, across and through the bonnet into the engine compartment, back down to the front wheels and finally, like stitching, back along the full length of the underside of the truck, ending with the rear wheels. Diesel sprayed out from the fuel tank, the bonnet sprung open, and clouds of smoke shot into the air from the engine. The truck lurched to the right, smashed into the main steel gate post and ground to a halt; stuck tight in the gateway.

Phillip then swung his gun to the left and opened up on the next truck that was heading towards the gate. Jack lifted the lid on the metal magazine cases that he had lugged along with them, reached inside and pulled the end of a string of bullets out, then stood half-bent next to Phillip, ready to pass it across as soon as the first string was exhausted. Whilst Philip was firing, Alexander ran back to the previous sandbags, to give him more room and to allow him a better view of what was going on. Back to his left he could see men were slowly but surely moving forward, and ahead, more smoke rose from the mess that was once the centre of communications. There were muffled explosions coming from the sheds, trucks and caravans as fuel tanks, gas cylinders and ammunition exploded.

Henry ran low and dived in behind one of the anti-aircraft gun emplacements. He landed right next to another of his men who was lying face down in the mud, arms outstretched. The man's rifle had fallen some three or four yards in front of him, the front of its barrel stuck in the ground like a spear, with the stock eighteen inches off the ground.

Henry looked across at his fallen friend to see if he could recognise him, but he couldn't; he reached across, intending to turn the man's head. As he did so, a torrent of bullets lashed the air above his head, and without thinking, he pushed himself hard into the muddy earth. After a few seconds of silence, Henry looked across again at the dead comrade lying next to him, reached out, touched him on his shoulder and said under his breath, "Good man – good man – you're a good man."

Slowly but surely, the German soldiers fell back until a white flag could be seen waving from the side of one of the only trucks that was still more or less intact.

After a few seconds, the shooting stopped. Henry waited for a while, and then very cautiously, he stood up. He took a deep breath, and then very slowly, walked towards the white flag. As he made his way, his men came out from behind their cover and followed him. As he approached the truck, twenty German soldiers stepped out from their hiding places, laid down their weapons and put their hands in the air.

Henry stopped ten paces from the truck, as his men, spaced well out, worked their way up behind him. Captain Joseph Kepler stepped forward, marched up to Henry, saluted and bowed his head slightly in his direction. Henry returned the salute and reached out his hand to Captain Kepler. They shook hands firmly, each staring into the others eyes.

"Captain," said Henry, "Do you speak English?"

"Just a little," the Captain replied.

"Collect up your men, your wounded and your dead. You have just thirty minutes. Then you can go. Take one of the trucks, if you can find a good one, and head off down the track. You and your men are free to go. I don't have the resources or facilities to hold prisoners, so you had better get on your way".

Captain Kepler didn't understand every word, but he understood enough to get the message, and he turned to his men and gave a succinct translation. Facing Henry again, he came to attention and saluted him again. Henry returned the salute and they both turned away to get on with their work.

Well before the half an hour was up, and having managed to drag the damaged vehicles out of the way, Captain Kepler and his men went through the main gates in one of the few remaining serviceable trucks – one of its shredded rear tyres bumping and scraping as they made their way slowly down the chalk track.

Henry checked with his Lieutenants. There were seven dead, three with serious injuries and four or five with minor injuries. They managed to load their dead and the wounded onto the last of the trucks and with several able-bodied men running alongside; they also set off down the track.

Henry, Joseph and Alexander walked back up towards the aerials, taking care to keep as far away as possible from the smouldering buildings, vehicles and equipment that lay all around. Every now and then there was a loud bang or cracking as something else exploded amongst the devastation.

As they reached the base of the first aerial, they could see that Alan Benton and his men were already busy securing explosives to the main steel girders that supported the aerials. Off to the sides, in the buildings and equipment trailers that were relatively undamaged, other men were setting yet more explosives and running out wires.

"Four minutes!!" Henry shouted, as loud as he could.

Alan Benton looked across to Henry and waited for his signal. Having secured the explosives and finished running out the cables, Alan, Henry, Alex and Joseph were the only men left on top of the hill, taking cover in the great earth ditch just to the side of the main gate. The others had already started to make their way back down the chalk track. Alan's hands rested on the plunger on top of the detonator box. Henry turned his head slightly towards him and nodded.

About twenty charges went off almost at once, with just a split second between each.

The sound of the explosions reverberated around the old encampment, and the flat white and orange fire-flash spread out and reflected off the underside of the heavy leaden clouds that were still threatening to engulf the top of the hill.

The four men raised their heads and looked towards where the communications centre had been. There was a great tangled mess of steel where the aerials had once stood; just two ragged stumps sticking up from the ground. All around the remaining vehicles, buildings, trailers and various pieces of equipment were burning and smouldering, great palls of dense black smoke ballooned up to meet the dark clouds rolling overhead. The four men stood and looked on for some time, studying their handy work, until Henry broke the silence.

"It's stopped raining," he said.

Chapter Sixteen

UNDER THE YEW TREE

This November morning had started well. There had been a hard frost overnight and at first light Joseph and Lily stood in the doorway of the barn looking out across the fields that spread in cold white silence beyond the dairy. Steam rose from the backs of the cows that milled around them, anxious and pushing to be let through the gate that led back to their fields. The smell of early morning milking hung in the barn, and although the air was cold, there was warmth to the smell.

The cows themselves smelt of a strange mixture of grass, dung, warm hides and fermenting gases; and as always, there was the overriding smell of warm milk and dusty hay. The steam coming from the animals rose steadily around them and drifted off to mix with the clear blue sky that was now starting to show its true colour as the first of the sun's rays broke across the farm.

Joseph wondered how many others saw such beauty in their everyday lives; the beauty of first light in the countryside.

He wondered about the friends that he had lost. How many mornings, how many moments like this had they been able to enjoy in their lives? What about the German soldiers? Surely, many of them must be from farms, just like him. Surely, they must have witnessed the same as him? So where was the sense in it all? Why were they killing each other?

He kicked at the ground and then walked slowly over to the main gate, unhooked the top loop and pushed it open. The cows pushed and shoved their way through the gate and ambled off down the frosty track towards the meadows. Lily watched them go and then looked over to Joseph who was closing the gate.

"Must be breakfast time!" she shouted.

Joseph didn't answer; he was miles away, thinking about the German soldier who had waved to him and Julia from the back of the truck that day that they had gone for their picnic.

"Surely he must have seen the beauty?" he thought.

Lily shouted again – "Breakfast?!"

Joseph looked towards her, waved, and walked back into the barn to collect his things. Lily watched her brother as he unhooked their coats from a wooden peg, and as she took her coat from him, she asked, "Penny for them?"

Joseph smiled, let out a deep sigh, looked across at Lily, smiled again and then took her hand as they started to walk slowly back towards the farm house.

After breakfast, Joseph went to his room to change and to collect some things that he needed for today's exercises in the woods. He had received his instructions in the usual way via the postman the previous morning. He returned to the kitchen at just before nine o'clock, and as it was Sunday, the whole family were still seated at the breakfast table. Mary got up from the table and put her arms out. Joseph walked slowly over to his mother and folded his arms around her.

"What's this all about?" he said.

"Oh," she said, "You know what us mums are like. We

need to cuddle our children every now and then."

As she spoke, she could feel a tear running down her cheek, and she buried her face in Joseph's shoulder and held him more tightly. Charles looked up and instantly caught the significance of the moment. Nothing more needed to be said or done.

Charles looked away, pushed his chair back, stood up and walked over to the kitchen sink, where he leaned on the draining board and looked out through the kitchen window. The white frost still lay on the grass, and the wintry sun was filling the garden with welcome light.

"It's certainly a fine morning," he muttered.

Lily smiled as she watched Mum and her brother still holding each other, eyes closed and now swaying gently in the middle of the kitchen, as if dancing. She looked across at Harold and Catherine. They were absolutely still, staring straight ahead at Joseph and his mother, their hands clasped tight together on the kitchen table.

After what seemed like an age, Joseph and Mary separated; he kissed her on her forehead and said softly, "Don't worry Mum; I'll be alright – don't upset yourself. I'll be back tonight."

Charles turned from the window, leaned with his back to the sink for a few seconds, then pushed himself away, marched to the door, opened it quickly, stepped outside and walked out across the frosty grass, taking in great gulps of cold air as he walked. He stopped in the middle of the lawn in his shirt sleeves, his hands thrust deep into his trouser pockets, staring up at the powder blue morning sky, the sun's rays catching his steamy breath.

Joseph took his coat and hat from the rack by the back door and bent down to pick up his backpack from the floor. He then walked back to the table, behind where his grandparents were sitting, placed his hands on their shoulders, bent down and kissed them on their heads.

"I'll be back tonight. Don't wait up for me though."

Then he kissed them again, patted them on their shoulders and walked back round to Lily's side of the table. Lily stood up and threw her arms around her big brother.

"Stay safe," she said, "I'll see you in the morning."

"You bet. I don't want you milking those cows on your own and making a complete mess of it!" He pulled away quickly as Lily aimed a playful slap at his arm.

Mary walked towards the door with him and stopped just outside to give him another hug and a kiss and a pat on the back. She held on to the door post and watched as Joseph made his way across to his father who was still standing in the middle of the lawn looking at the sky.

"Take it easy old son," he said, as he reached out to Joseph and patted him gently on his arm. "Promise you'll come back safely to us, won't you?"

"Of course, I will Dad. Don't I always?"

They held each other tight and in silence for longer than they had since Joseph was a little boy. Eventually they released each other and Joseph walked back towards the house where he had left his bike propped up against the log pile that was covered by an old tarpaulin. He lifted it, stiff from the frost, slid his bike out from under the cover, turned it, threw his leg over the saddle, pushed off, waved and pedalled off down the garden path.

As he cycled away from the house he shouted, "See you later tonight or early tomorrow morning!" and headed towards the old chicken sheds to collect his rifle.

He cycled down the farm track and stopped at the junction with the main road to listen for vehicles. As he had his rifle wrapped in sacking and strapped to his cross bar, he couldn't afford the risk of being stopped and checked, but knew that if he could get a clear run for about a quarter of a mile, he could take the old drovers track up into the woods without being seen.

After listening for a few seconds, he satisfied himself that there was nothing coming, and he set off as quickly as he could down the road. Two hundred yards from where he intended to turn off, he heard the unmistakeable noise of a large truck approaching from behind, and as it got closer, he knew from its sound that it was a Mercedes engine. Within fifty yards of the turning, the truck driver gave three long blasts on the horn as he overtook him, so close that Joseph nearly lost his balance and crashed, as the bright red brake lights at the rear of the truck came on.

For the briefest of moments, as the truck slowed, Joseph looked up to see that it was full of German troops, several of whom were looking straight at him. As the truck slowed further and then came to a standstill, Joseph stood up on his pedals and pedalled as hard as he could, straight passed the truck; turning sharp left from the road onto the woodland track.

As the tyres of his bike hit the loose chalk and flints that made up the track, he nearly lost control of the bike. He was travelling at twice the speed that he would normally ride on a track like this, and it took all of his strength and skill to stay upright.

All the time, he listened out for the tell-tale signs behind him. He had already heard the sound of the tail-board dropping as it bounced and clattered on its hinges, and he was pretty sure that he'd heard the sound of men shouting. He steeled himself as he slipped and slid along the track, expecting at any moment to hear the cracking of shots being fired in his direction. No such sounds reached him as he pedalled on as hard as he could, knowing that with every second that went by, he was just that bit further away from his pursuers.

Five Germans made their way along the track behind him as the truck moved off for another two hundred yards down the road, where it stopped to let off five more soldiers who pushed their way straight through the roadside hedge and set off in to the woods. The truck then moved on again, stopping three more times, until all 25 soldiers were deployed in the woods.

The third group made quick headway; as luck had it, they had been dropped in an open area of the woods that was dry under foot and the going was easy. After a few minutes of fast walking, one of the soldiers pointed towards a large oak tree slightly off to their right. Leaning against the tree was a bicycle. The soldiers spread out, slowed down, and half raised their rifles, releasing their safety catches as they did so.

On the other side of the tree, totally oblivious to what was going on around him; Tim Washbrook was having a pee. He was not quite eighteen years old and had only been training with the resistance for the last four months, but as yet, they hadn't let him join in with any active missions. He was hoping that he would soon see some action. He was looking down doing up the buttons on his fly as he walked back to the other side of the tree. The German soldiers spotted him immediately, stopped walking and raised their rifles. Tim looked up at exactly the same time as one of the soldiers fired. The bullet hit him in the middle of his chest, killing him instantly, and knocking him hard back against his bike and against the oak tree. For a moment, he seemed to pivot on the bike, as if he were going to sit on the cross bar, but then in slow motion, he slipped down on to the ground and toppled sideways.

"Shit!" shouted Sergeant Halle as he glared at the soldier who had fired, "What the hell did you fire for? You could see that he wasn't armed!"

"Sorry Sergeant!" the shocked soldier replied "I didn't mean to fire! It just went off! I didn't mean to! I mean... it just went... well... you know... I'm sorry..."

Sergeant Halle shook his head and started to walk towards Tim's body. "Fucking imbecile!" he murmured under his breath.

The moment that Joseph heard the rifle shot, he steered his bike off the rough track and in behind some holly bushes. He laid his bike down, undid the ties that held his sacking wrapped rifle, laid the rifle carefully to one side and did his best to scoop up twigs and leaves to cover his bike. There wasn't enough material to do a great job, but after a while, most of the bike was covered under a carpet of leaves, with only one of the handle bars and one pedal sticking up in the air. Even so, someone would have to be pretty close before realising that a bike lay beneath the winter leaves.

Joseph then sat perfectly still for a few seconds, his senses fully alert, his rifle lying across his crossed legs.

He took long deep breaths, and almost immediately he could feel his heart rate coming back down to something like its normal level. He wondered at whom or at what the rifle shot had been aimed. He wondered how many German soldiers were now in the woods and why they were there. Were they just after him or was there something much bigger going on? Had they been betrayed? Did they know about today's exercise? What he was certain of was that he couldn't stay where he was. He was too exposed. As he stood to move off, he heard voices behind him. He stayed low as he made his way at a fast walking speed deeper into the woods.

After about five minutes he stopped again to listen. He was breathing very heavily again and beads of sweat were breaking out across his forehead and trickling down his face. He tried hard to calm himself so that he could hear properly. Half doubled; he leaned against the shiny trunk of an old ash tree, taking in great gulps of air. It had been slightly uphill for the last few hundred yards and the climb had taken its toll.

After a while, Joseph felt calmer and his senses cleared. He could still hear voices in the distance, but worryingly, he was certain that he could hear more now than he could five minutes earlier. As he listened, he suddenly realised that the sounds were coming from a much wider front than before; in fact, he was fairly sure that he could hear three separate and distinct groups spread out behind him. As he listened more, he could also make out, for the first time, the unmistakable sound of dogs barking.

"Bugger!" he exclaimed, and set off again deeper into the woods.

A half a mile ahead of Joseph, right in the middle of the woods, Henry and the first of the men who had arrived at the allotted meeting point were on full alert. They had all heard the earlier rifle shot and the first of the arrivals had reported on the unusually high numbers of German troop trucks and the general increase in German activity in the area. Men were arriving all the time; each with his story of how he had had to dodge the Germans to get there.

Henry, concerned that they had been betrayed, gave the order to disperse. Knowing that all the activity at the moment was to the south, they spread out as quickly as they could and headed north. As they left the area, others arrived, and finding three pieces of timber lashed together in the form of a small pyramid, they immediately understood and without hesitation, also headed off in a northerly direction as quickly as they could.

Joseph made good progress through the woods, every now and then stopping for a few seconds to check on his pursuers. The sounds of the men calling and the dogs barking seemed to be about the same each time that he stopped to listen and he was worried that he didn't seem to be putting much distance between himself and the soldiers.

He decided that he would have to change direction. The last thing that he wanted to do was to lead his pursuers to the rendezvous point. For all that he knew; there were scores of them, easily outnumbering Henry and his men.

He set off again, but now, although still going uphill, he was heading off more to the west. A few hundred yards after changing direction, he came across a large dell that he had never come across before. For some reason that he regretted almost immediately, he decided to go straight through the middle. The dell was ancient and had remained basically undisturbed for thousands of years. The most activity that it had seen in recent times was when the foresters had come through here on a couple of occasions planting beech trees; the last time being during the Napoleonic wars, when prisoners of war had been seconded to do the planting. Centuries before that, men had cleared the old yew forests to expand their farms, and thousands of years before that, Neolithic men had dug here to find flints to make stone-age tools.

As Joseph slipped and slid his way down the side of the dell, he wondered about the enormous amount of work that his ancestors had put in to dig such a huge hole. On reaching the bottom; he started to scrabble his way up the other side and immediately realised that he had made a big mistake. He was in trouble. There was so much loose debris on the surface that it was impossible to get a good grip. Small pieces of chalk and flint lay on top of thin topsoil, and as he climbed up the side of the dell he slid all over the place, sliding back two steps for every three that he went forwards.

The only things growing on the steep chalky slope were a few struggling hazel trees. He grabbed at their spindly branches in an attempt to propel himself forward faster, but with little effect. Sweat was pouring down his face and his legs felt like jelly as he finally reached the top of the far side of the dell.

He grabbed hold of the bare roots of a great beech tree that was growing right on the edge of the lip of the dell, and with all his might, pulled himself up and over the ridge. As he gave a final kick, a small avalanche of chalk and flint set off down the side behind him, as he fell flat on his face, panting amongst the exposed roots of the great tree.

Joseph lay for several seconds waiting to get his breath

back. In the distance, somewhat closer now, he could very clearly hear the sound of voices and dogs barking. He cursed himself for being so stupid. Crossing the dell had cost him a lot of time and energy. He could have been at least a hundred yards further on by now and that much nearer to safety. By the clear sounds reaching him he knew that they were a lot closer.

Having recovered slightly, he pulled himself up by the side of the tree and looked back across the dell; fully expecting to see a German soldier or a dog on the other side; but to his surprise there was no one. Quickly, he turned and started to run towards the next stand of trees, about forty yards further on.

Just as he reached cover, he heard the crack of a rifle being fired, and at the same time he felt the most excruciating sharp pain in his right thigh. He completed two full forward rolls before falling flat on his face, with his backpack around his ears and his rifle some five yards ahead. The pain in his leg totally overwhelmed him, and it took him some time before he came to his senses enough to realise that he had been shot.

His natural survival instinct kicked in. He knew that he had to get behind the safety of the trees, but the pain was making it difficult for him to think straight. He took long deep breaths, pulled his backpack away from his head to his shoulders, focussed on his rifle and crawled forwards.

As he grabbed the rifle, another shot rang out, and chalk dust spat into the air just ahead of him. He struggled forward on his hands and knees and then pressed himself hard to the ground, took another deep breath, and as a third shot whistled a few inches over his head, rolled over three times until he was pretty sure that he was safely behind the trunk of the first tree that he came to.

He sat up and looked back over his shoulder to check that he was out of the line of fire. Slowly he eased himself up and leaned hard against the silver trunk of the tree. Ignoring the pain in his leg, he released the safety catch on his rifle, raised it and peered out back across the clearing. He quickly located the single German soldier who had fired at him from the other side of the dell, took one more deep breath, took aim, squeezed the trigger and watched as the impact of the bullet knocked the soldier back three paces. As the sound of the shot reverberated through the woods, a dog suddenly appeared from behind the fallen soldier, running fast towards Joseph. He took another deep breath, took careful aim and fired. The dog somersaulted forwards and crashed in a dusty heap.

Joseph ran his right hand down the back of his leg. He could feel an open wound in his thigh and his trouser leg was soaked in blood. He knew that he needed to get a tourniquet above the wound to slow the bleeding, but there wasn't time now; he had to get away. As he turned to move on, he heard a loud squelching sound as his right foot moved inside his blood-filled boot.

He hobbled away as best as he could to the next tree and turned to see if he was being followed. He couldn't see any soldiers or dogs, but to encourage them to keep their heads down he fired three rapid shots back across the top of the dell, turned again and headed off deeper into the woods.

The pain wasn't quite so bad now; in fact, he could hardly feel his leg at all. There was a ringing noise in his head, his mouth was dry and he felt sick. On reaching the next tree, he repeated the exercise, firing three times back towards the dell. This time a dog barked, but there were no other sounds, other than his shots echoing back through the trees.

Whilst leaning against the tree and keeping a look out for movement back towards the dell, Joseph managed to get his jacket off. Pulling his knife out from the sheath on his belt, he stuck the tip of the blade into his shirt, high up by his shoulder. He quickly cut half way round the sleeve and then, pushing the knife back into its sheath, he reached up with his right hand and with one pull, ripped the whole sleeve away from the body of the shirt and slipped it down his arm. He ran the sleeve around the top of his right thigh, high up by his crotch, and tied it off as tightly as he could. The bleeding slowed almost immediately. He straightened himself, checked back towards the dell and satisfying himself that the coast was clear, he hobbled on to the next tree. He wondered how long it would be before the German soldiers regrouped and started to spread themselves out into the woods. They knew that their quarry was wounded and probably wouldn't be able to move very fast.

As he looked back, he saw movement twenty yards to the right of the dell, and although he couldn't see a clear target, he fired off two more rounds without hesitation. The soldiers near to the dell all dived for cover. Behind them, the remainder of the unit had now arrived, and Sergeant Halle waved directions at them, indicating that they should spread out and move forwards.

Now about a mile away, Henry and his men had split up and were all heading further north. Eventually, under the cover of darkness, they would turn back towards the village and make their circuitous ways back home. Those that had never made it to the rendezvous point in the first place had long since cut their losses and made off in other directions away from the centre of the woods. They knew that there were a lot of German soldiers up in the woods, but who was doing all the shooting and who was being shot at; they had no idea.

As Joseph set off for the cover of the next tree, a cold shiver ran right through his body. He swayed slightly as he turned to look back and nearly lost his balance. There appeared to be a reddish mist in the distance, just above the ground, but when he closed his eyes for a second and looked again, he saw that it had gone. He raised the back of his hand to wipe the sweat from his brow, but realised that there was nothing to wipe; his forehead felt cold and clammy. Slowly he turned again and staggered on deeper into the woods. At this spot the trees had not been thinned as much, and although there were no leaves left on the trees, it was much darker here. Joseph noted the change in light and walked on without stopping. He weaved in amongst the trees, managing to keep up a reasonable pace.

Every now and then he looked back over his shoulder, dragging his leg as he went. He could hear dogs barking again; one lot immediately behind and another off to his left. With such a trail of blood, he knew that the dogs would follow him easily, and that whatever he did, he could not get away from them. He was pretty certain that by now his friends would have dispersed, and unless by some freakish coincidence he ran slap bang into a group of them, he knew that they couldn't help him.

For the first time, it occurred to him that they probably didn't even know that it was him that was being hunted; after all, he hadn't bumped into any of them this morning on his way to the rendezvous, so how could they know who was being chased?

He was sure that the dogs barking to his left were now slightly ahead of him, and for the first time, he realised that they were trying to overtake him – to cut him off. Automatically, he started to veer slightly more to the right. He glanced back over his shoulder again – still he couldn't see anyone behind him, but there was no doubt that they weren't far away. The barking of the dogs was slightly louder now.

As he rounded a group of ash saplings he tripped over the root of a beech tree that ran across the path and landed face first on a small pile of earth, flints and chalk where a rabbit had been scraping. For a moment, he was winded and it took him a while to lift himself up on to all fours; as he did so, blood dripped from his nose onto the dry grey and white soil beneath him. As he leaned on his rifle and struggled to his feet, a sharp pain returned to his damaged leg. He ran his hand down the limb and felt fresh warm blood soaking through his trousers. The tourniquet had loosened. He quickly undid the knot, pulled it up as tight as he could, and tied it off again. Blood continued to drip from his nose and he felt sick again. He looked back.

This time he saw movement immediately; at least three soldiers and two dogs were only about a hundred and fifty yards back through the trees. He set off again, swinging even further to the right and looking out for a good spot to make a stand. He knew that he couldn't keep going at this pace for much longer. At this rate, they would soon run him down.

Three or four hundred yards further on he came to a small group of yew trees. One of them had tipped over many years ago, but it had somehow managed to survive, and the branches that found themselves pointing into the air when it fell, had, over the last few decades, turned themselves into new growing points for the tree. Four or five branches now stood upright, growing out from the horizontal trunk like miniature trees themselves.

Joseph dragged himself as fast as he could over the last thirty yards, threw himself to the ground behind the fallen yew, ripped his backpack from around his neck, checked for spare ammunition, laid his rifle gently across the yew trunk, adjusted the sights, flicked off the safety catch, wiped another bloody drip from his nose with the back of his hand, took three deep breaths and then stared hard back through the beech trees. He was ready for them.

He kept perfectly still, taking long, slow deep breaths as he concentrated all his senses on his surroundings: watching, listening and feeling everything that he could.

There was no bird song, no sound of deer running through the woods and no breeze playing through the tops of the trees.

He could still hear the other group of soldiers, with their dogs, quite some way ahead – and he could now hear those coming straight towards him very clearly. He counted seven soldiers, two of them with Alsatians pulling hard on long leashes. He knew that he had to wait. Even though he was in a good position, he knew that the chances of dropping all the men before one or more of them shot him again were remote. The closer they came, the more certain he could be of not wasting any shots.

He decided that he would work them from left to right and lined up his sights on the soldier on the far left; he wasn't at all sure in what order he would deal with the dogs.

When they were within forty yards of his position, he opened fire.

The first man fell to the ground like a sack of potatoes falling from the back of a cart; the second man went down in a similar fashion, leaving his dog pulling even harder on its leash that was still secured to his outstretched arm. Sergeant Halle, being the third in line, had started to duck down and raise his rifle as Joseph's next bullet hit him in the right side of his chest, spinning him round like a top and throwing him against the trunk of a tree, where he slid down gently into a pile of leaves that had collected between its roots that ran out across the ground.

As Joseph took aim at the fourth soldier, the fifth one released the leash on his dog and dived behind the nearest tree.

The fourth man dropped to his knees and fell sideways.

The sixth soldier started firing in Joseph's general direction as he ran forward. Joseph held steady as bullets flew over his head. He fired twice at the soldier, who crashed to the woodland floor and lay spread eagled only twenty yards from him. Out of the corner of his eye, Joseph saw the seventh man raise his machine gun just as the freed Alsatian sprung to jump over the fallen yew tree.

Joseph swung his rifle back towards the dog and fired at its belly at point blank range. The dog fell across the trunk of the yew tree with a dull thud as the seventh soldier fired a short burst from his machine gun towards him before diving for cover. One of the bullets grazed Joseph's face, scoring a neat line across the top of his left cheek; another went right through the middle of the palm of his left hand. He dropped down behind the trunk of the yew, felt his damaged cheek with his right hand and stared at his bloody left.

His hand was completely numb, he couldn't move his fingers and blood trickled down and dripped onto the yellow and orange beech leaves by his knees. He reached into his trouser pocket, pulled out his handkerchief, stuffed it into the palm of his left hand and held it in place with his thumb; the only digit that still seemed to work. He turned the hand over to look at the damage where the bullet had exited. It was a mess. Bits of flesh, bone and cartilage stuck out from his hand and more blood trickled down the backs of his fingers. The whole mess needed strapping up, but there wasn't time; he had to move.

He collected up his backpack and rifle and crawled along behind the trunk of the yew until he was near its end. As he changed the clip on his rifle, three or four rapid rifle shots thumped into the tree trunk near to where he had first been crouched, and a few seconds later, a short burst of machine gun fire kicked up pieces of bark in the same place.

Joseph struggled to his feet, being careful to stay tight behind the great branch that grew up from the trunk. He swung his rifle up and slowly pushed it through the smaller branches, leaning most of his weight against the main branch. Blood trickled down the side of his face, his left hand was beginning to throb with new pain, and he still couldn't feel his right leg properly.

He stared at the beech trees ahead of him. He just needed

the soldiers to show themselves. The remaining dog had stopped barking and pulling at its leash and now sat looking lost and bewildered in the middle of the clearing, his head tilted slightly to one side, staring directly at the yew branches behind which Joseph was standing.

The machine gunner started to move from behind the tree where he had taken cover. First the gun appeared; then his right arm and the right side of his head. As he moved out slightly further to peer around the trunk, Joseph fired and the soldier fell hard back behind the tree. The dog jumped up and began to bark again. In the distance, but closer now, two or three other dogs answered him. Joseph fired again and the dog fell silent. The remaining soldier stood shaking behind his tree. Joseph was willing him to step out from his cover, but the man was too frightened to move. Joseph knew that he didn't have much more time; if he waited much longer, the next group of soldiers would be on him. He would have to force the issue.

Slowly he stepped out from behind the yew and, with his rifle trained on the soldier's position, he worked his way out further and further, dragging his damaged leg, until he could see part of the man's uniform. As he moved further round, the German turned his head slightly and their eyes met. The soldier was shaking like a leaf, and as he stared at Joseph, he dropped his rifle. Joseph lowered his own gun and with his damaged hand, waved at him to go. The soldier half waved back to show that he understood the signal and started to walk back through the woods.

Joseph moved back to the yew tree as quickly as he could, retrieved his back pack and reached inside and pulled out a bottle of cold tea. He was desperately thirsty and gulped down half of its contents in a few seconds, then slapped the top back on, pushed the bottle back into his back pack, swung it across his shoulder, checked all around to be sure that it was safe to move, and set off again. The German soldier kept walking away at a steady pace, not daring to look back.

Joseph didn't know exactly what the time was, but judging from the fading light, he guessed that darkness would fall within the hour. He knew that darkness was now his best hope. He thought that if he could keep moving, stay out of trouble and make it to nightfall he would have a fair chance of pulling through. As he walked, he ran his hand down the back of his trouser leg, now caked in half dried blood and dirt. Near the wound, his trousers felt wet and warm; he was still losing a lot of blood.

He stopped, leaned his rifle against a tree trunk and loosened the knot on the tourniquet. As he did so, he felt more blood running down his leg and he immediately retied the knot as tightly as he could. His left hand was so badly damaged that it was difficult to retie the knot and he decided then and there that he couldn't risk undoing it again. If it needed more attention, he would have to stuff something under the tourniquet to make it tighter. He looked at his hand.

Blood was still trickling down his fingers and he knew that once it was dark he would have to make a better job of bandaging it up. As he reached for his rifle, his leg gave way and he fell onto his knees and toppled sideways. He felt sick and thought that he was going to pass out. He closed his eyes for a few seconds, took some deep breaths, reached out for his rifle and slowly lifted himself back up to a standing position.

Steadily, he set off again, fully aware that he was now walking much more slowly. Every now and then he caught the sound of men shouting and dogs barking in the distance. He worried that some of the soldiers may have managed to get ahead of him, but as yet, all the sounds were still coming from behind him and off to his left.

He made steady progress for the next twenty minutes or so until he came to a rutted track. He recognised it immediately as one of the paths that led up to the top of the

Downs, and without hesitation he turned and started to move uphill.

After a few hundred yards, he stopped to catch his breath. He looked around and then up at the sky. It was nearly dark now, and a half moon was beginning to rise just above the horizon. For the first time since being shot, he thought of Julia.

"You wouldn't want to see me now my love," he muttered to himself.

As he reached the top of the track, he could only manage twenty paces at a time before having to stop to catch his breath. For a while, he stood looking out from the woods, across the open grassland at the top of the hill and he wondered again about the soldiers. He hadn't heard any men shouting or dogs barking for some time now, and for a few minutes he allowed himself the luxury of standing still and listening to the countryside.

He could hear tawny owls hooting in the distance and a long way off to the south a fox was calling. Just as he was about to set off again, he spotted movement about a hundred yards ahead of him near to the crest of the hill. He lowered himself to his knees and stared into the gloom ahead. The light changed from dull to bright as small clouds scudded across in front of the moon, the long shadows of the trees around him being cast across the downland beyond. A lone fallow deer stag strode slowly across the open space, making his way from one side of the hill to the other, his head held high, his great antlers catching the moon's rays. Joseph smiled as he watched the beautiful creature make his way.

He followed the edge of the woods east, keeping well under the tree canopy, heading the same way as the deer. Suddenly, he felt cold again and he stopped and fumbled with the buttons on his jacket and pulled up his collar.

As he set off, he lost his balance again and fell, dropping his rifle. His damaged right leg was bent underneath him and a stabbing pain shot up through his thigh. He rolled over and managed to straighten his legs and lay there for some time until the throbbing calmed. It dawned on him that he would have to find somewhere to stop so that he could get some rest. He couldn't go on like this. He turned over on to all fours and using his rifle as a prop, he staggered to his feet. He felt sick and dizzy again and he reached inside his back pack again for the bottle of tea. He struggled to get the top off this time, and noticed that he had pins and needles in his good right hand. He took three or four short swigs, relishing the taste of sugar in his mouth as he struggled to get the top back on and the bottle back into his back pack.

He moved off slowly and walked unsteadily for about fifty yards, stopping abruptly as he heard a cracking noise in the woods off to his right. Standing absolutely still for thirty seconds, he listened carefully to the tell-tale sounds coming from deeper inside the woods.

He smiled as he realised that it was the sound of a deer walking, every now and then cracking dry twigs with its feet, as it made its way through the woods. It was probably the same one that he had seen only twenty minutes earlier. He listened for a little longer, checking that there was nothing else, and then hobbled on, stopping by a large beech tree. Feeling light headed again, he leaned against the trunk and looked around as the moon lit up the trees around him. Suddenly, he realised where he was. He pushed himself away from the tree and looked around again.

"This is where I came with Julia on our picnic. Just through there is where the yew trees are."

If he could have run to the yews he would have done, but dragging his leg and supporting himself with his rifle, he set off as best he could towards them.

He had to stop three more times over the short distance to the yews, but eventually, with his leg completely numb and his whole body, aching, he found the picnic tree. He leaned his rifle against its trunk, pulled the backpack from his shoulder, turned slowly around and, with his back pressed firmly against the tree, slid down to the mossy ground below. He was completely exhausted, his breathing was shallow now, and he sat with his legs stretched out, his arms folded and his head tipped forward onto his chest. He closed his eyes.

His leg was throbbing more than ever and he shifted his weight slightly to try to ease the pain. It didn't seem to make much difference what he did, the pain was constant now. He wondered for the hundredth time how much blood he had lost and then thought about his hand. He remembered that he needed to do something with it and opened his eyes.

Slowly he unfolded his arms and held his left hand out to the moonlight. He was shocked to see the amount of blood that was still trickling down his fingers; his scrunched- up handkerchief just a wet mess in his palm.

With his good hand, he reached down for his belt buckle and with a great deal of difficulty, managed to undo it and, leaning forward slightly, he pulled it out from its loops. He sat back panting for a long time and then leaned forward again and lifted his right knee so that his thigh was raised slightly off the ground. He reached down and touched his damaged leg. It was still bleeding, and because his leg was raised, he could now feel warm blood running back to his crotch. He dared not undo the tourniquet, but reached down and pulled the belt under and around his leg. Satisfied that it was in the right position, he pulled the belt through the buckle as far as he could and, holding the pin upright with his left thumb, managed to locate a hole and let go of the end of the belt.

He fell back against the yew tree gasping for air, his leg throbbing with more pain than ever. He thought about his hand again and wondered if he could get his jacket off to get to his other shirt sleeve, but decided against it. He was already cold and thought that the effort of getting his jacket off and back on again would be too much. He reached out and felt around on the ground for his sheath knife, which had fallen off when he removed his belt. Finding it, he pulled his shirt front out from his trousers, undid some of the buttons and cut the folded seam by the buttons and at the bottom. He slid the knife back into its sheath and slipped it into his jacket pocket. Then, pressing the shirt as firmly as he could to his chest with his damaged left hand, he tore a long strip of material away.

He sat panting again for a minute until he had recovered enough to wrap the bandage around his hand; leaving the blood-soaked handkerchief in place. He took the knife out again and split the two ends of the cloth to make it easier to tie. Putting the knife away, he tied the knot off as best he could; using his teeth to hold one end whilst pulling the knot tight with his right hand. He did his jacket back up, pulled his collar up again and leaned back against the tree. He looked across at the moon and then closed his eyes.

He didn't know how much time had gone by, but when he opened his eyes, the moon was right overhead, the clouds had gone and the air was crystal clear.

Joseph was shivering and he felt sick like he had once when he had pneumonia as a child, but all of his aches and pains seemed to have gone. He felt puzzled and confused and thought of reaching out to touch his leg, but he couldn't find the strength to lift his arm. He closed his eyes again and realised that, never mind the pain, he couldn't even feel his leg or his hand. He was desperate for a drink and it felt like his tongue was stuck to the roof of his mouth.

He opened his eyes again and stared at his right hand. He concentrated all his mental powers on his good hand and after a while he managed to wriggle his fingers. Slowly he raised his arm as a dull feeling of pins and needles ran through his nerve ends. He touched his face with his finger tips and as they ran across the rough surface of caked blood on his cheek, below his nose and down his chin to his neck; he remembered the fall that had smashed his nose and the bullet that had creased his face. His hand dropped back to his lap, and now yesterday's memories came flooding back.

Tears ran down his face, cutting fresh channels through the caked blood and dirt stuck to his skin. He sniffed and could taste blood in his mouth and remembered again that he was thirsty. He couldn't get his left hand to move at all, but managed to turn his body enough so that he could reach across with his right arm towards the backpack.

After several attempts, he managed to drag the bag up on to his lap and pull the tea bottle out. It took him what felt like an age to get the top off, but eventually he managed to lift it to his lips and gulp the bottle dry. He tried to put the top back on, but decided that the effort was too much and pushed the bottle back into the bag, the top swinging from its wire hinge and clinking on the glass neck as he did so.

As he touched the side of the backpack, he felt the smooth hard surface of the willow picnic basket against the back of his hand and he heard the clink of the ginger beer bottle as it slid back inside.

As the moon shone even brighter now, he looked down by his side to see the blue and white cotton table cloth, as clear as day in the midday sunshine. His right hand slid from his lap to the cloth and he ran his fingers across its surface. He looked across to his left, and there was Julia, where he knew she would be, laying on her back, her right arm raised up and above her head, eyes closed, head tilted slightly to one side with a broad smile on her lips.

Joseph looked at her sweet soft face and with all the effort that he could muster, he moved his broken hand across the blue and white checks to touch her hair.

"Thank God you found me," he said. "I thought that I might die all alone here. I was frightened." He knew that she couldn't answer him, but that was alright, as long as she was with him.

He closed his eyes again and he could smell the warm milky smell of the dairy. Lily was sitting on a hay bale and looked up at him, saying something about breakfast, but he couldn't quite hear what she was saying as the cows were making too much noise as they jostled to be let back out to the meadow.

Then the picture changed again and they were all sitting around the kitchen table. Granny and Grandad were talking about the horses, Mum and Dad were talking about the war, and he and Lily sat drinking their cups of tea, smiling at each other like brothers and sisters often do.

As he stood next to his mother looking west through the landing window, she said "They're bombing Portsmouth again" – and the next thing that he knew, he was walking with his father through the woods; it was nearly dark and snow was beginning to fall.

As he left the woods he could see Commander Henry Clay waving at him from behind a flint wall in the middle of the village, and he ran with his rifle to join him. The Commander spoke to him, patted him on his shoulder, wished him luck and walked slowly off into the distance. Joseph waved at him, thinking that they would probably never see each other again, and then he turned his gaze to look down the street.

As he did so, he realised that his parents were standing next to him by the flint wall, and as he turned to look at them, his father pointed behind him.

There, standing in the garden, were the rest of his family, his friends, the villagers and farmers and his friends from the Resistance. His mother and father moved in closer and put their arms around him, and Lily ran forward to join them. The four of them stood there looking down the street into the village and Joseph felt safe.

Gradually the pictures in his head started to fade as he

drifted in and out of consciousness. He wasn't cold anymore; he wasn't frightened. He opened his eyes one more time and stared up through the branches of the yew tree to look at the moon. As he stroked her hair, the last few pictures of deer running through the beech woods flickered through his mind; and as he closed his eyes, his last thought was of Julia.

For more information on John Charles Hall

Website: www.johncharleshall.co.uk

Facebook: @authorjohnhall

Twitter: #authorjohnhall

Made in the USA
Columbia, SC
03 January 2018